Fleur McDonald has lived and worked on farms for much of her life. After growing up in the small town of Orroroo in South Australia, she went jillarooing, eventually co-owning an 8000-acre property in regional Western Australia.

Fleur likes to write about strong women overcoming adversity, drawing inspiration from her own experiences in rural Australia. She has two children and an energetic kelpie.

Website: www.fleurmcdonald.com
Facebook: FleurMcDonaldAuthor
Instagram: fleurmcdonald
TikTok: Fleur McDonald (Author)

FLEUR McDONALD

VOICES
in the DARK

ALLEN&UNWIN
SYDNEY•MELBOURNE•AUCKLAND•LONDON

First published in 2023

Allen & Unwin
Cammeraygal Country
83 Alexander Street
Crows Nest NSW 2065
Australia
Phone: (61 2) 8425 0100
Email: info@allenandunwin.com
Web: www.allenandunwin.com

Allen & Unwin acknowledges the Traditional Owners of the Country on which we live and work. We pay our respects to all Aboriginal and Torres Strait Islander Elders, past and present.

 A catalogue record for this book is available from the National Library of Australia

ISBN 978 1 76106 648 1

Set in 12.4/18.2 pt Sabon LT Pro by Bookhouse, Sydney
Printed and bound in Australia by the Opus Group

10 9 8 7 6 5 4 3 2 1

To my Great-Aunty Dinkie, I hope you would have had a laugh at the mention of Dinkie Downs and the story behind the name. You knew it well! I miss our chats and visits, your wisdom and love.

And

To my true north.

AUTHOR'S NOTE

Detective Dave Burrows appeared in my first novel, *Red Dust*. Since then Dave has appeared as a secondary character in sixteen contemporary novels, including *Voices in the Dark*, and six novels set in the early 2000s in which he stars in the lead role. These six novels are *Fool's Gold*, *Without a Doubt*, *Red Dirt Country*, *Something to Hide*, *Rising Dust* and *Into the Night*.

In the earlier novels, Dave is at the beginning of his career. His first marriage to Melinda has ended due to issues balancing their careers and family life. No spoilers here because if you've read my contemporary rural novels you'll know that Dave is currently very happily married to his second wife, Kim.

I had no idea Dave was going to become such a much-loved character and it's reader enthusiasm that keeps me writing about him. Dave is one of my favourite characters and I hope he will become one of yours, too.

CHAPTER 1

'You need to come now. Don't wait.'

The words felt like they were bouncing off her skull. *You need to come now.*

'Yes, I know,' Sassi muttered.

Don't wait, the memory repeated. *Don't wait.*

'I heard you, I heard you.' Her voice broke as she told the windscreen she was trying her best to get there.

Sassi pushed her foot down harder, clenching the steering wheel. Uncle Abe always said that driving at this time in the morning before the sun has started to rise, and the beautiful pinks and oranges spread out across the sky, is the most dangerous time to drive.

Kangaroos, wombats, even camels seemed to come out at this time of the day. And, inevitably, their feeding grounds would be across the road from their burrow or tree. The table drains beside the roads also held the sweetest grasses and water, especially when the flats were dry.

Her foot hovered above the brake pedal in anticipation of movement. It would only take one second—a small lapse in concentration—and there could be some serious damage to the ute. Not to mention to her and Jarrah, who was curled up in the passenger's footwell.

The black hazes of midges hung near the trees that lined the road, and kamikaze bugs hurled themselves at her windscreen. Bush shadows stretched out across the black strip of road but, thankfully, so far, not one of those shadows had morphed into a kangaroo or another animal she might hit.

The temperature gauge on the dash told her it was already twenty-seven degrees outside, and Sassi pressed her fingers to the window to check. The glass was warm to touch yet the sun hadn't risen above the horizon. She reached forward and turned the air-conditioner up a notch as Jarrah started to pant.

The dog's eyes closed in bliss at the coolness.

I should stop, she thought. *Give Jarrah a drink and stretch my legs.* The heaviness of her eyelids were a bit of a giveaway that she was tired after six hours of driving.

The phone call had come several hours before as she had put the kettle on for her nightly cup of tea.

She'd been throwing a tea bag into her mug, leaning her hip against the bench. Jarrah was at her feet, tail thumping against the floor as she looked up, waiting for any crumbs that might fall. It took all of the six-month-old pup's self-control not to move, while Sassi had her hand held in a stop sign. Jarrah's little body was quivering in readiness at the first sign she could move.

When her ringtone, Kaylee Bell's 'Keith', had ripped through the kitchen, causing her to jump, Sassi knew there was something amiss. No one called so late at night.

The photo that had been taken last Christmas of her and Abe flashed onto the screen and her first thought had been: *Which one is it? Which grandparent?*

'It's bad, Sassi,' her uncle told her when she answered.

Her hands shaking, she'd slid down next to Jarrah and buried her fingers in the kelpie's caramel fur.

'What's happened?'

'Not sure. Dad managed to raise the alarm but . . .' His voice had trailed off and Sassi realised her kettle was screaming a high-pitched whistle above her. Sticking a finger in her ear and ignoring the sound, she stayed where she was.

'The ambo couldn't say much, but he suggested we get everyone together as quickly as we can. I've rung your mother.'

Sassi snorted. 'She won't be much use.'

'Sassi.' As always, Abe's calm and conciliatory tone didn't change. Sassi was angry and he was the peacemaker. 'She's going to be on the first plane that she can get out of South Africa.'

'She'd probably prefer the borders were still shut so she didn't have to come back.'

Abe had ignored her comments. 'You need to come now,' he said. 'Don't wait.'

Kaylee Bell blared from the stereo in her ute now. The opening piano and lyrics for 'Who I Am' sent goosebumps shooting across her skin. Sassi was sure the writers of that song had peered into her past and found the words which suited her most. Kaylee sang about it being seven years since she'd left her home town. For Sassi, it had been longer.

She'd visited over those years, staying only long enough to get to know her cousins, hug her granny and sit quietly with her pa. Watch them communicate with each other through looks, nods and winks. Her grandfather was still mostly abled in his body, but not with his words. A stroke, some years before, had seen to that.

Still, Granny had always been able to understand him. What would Pa do without her?

When Sassi had finished Year Twelve, eleven years ago, Granny had suggested she take a year off before heading to uni, even though her results had got her into the ag science degree she was keen to enrol in.

Granny, smelling of lavender soap and shortbread biscuits, had sat down with her and held her hand. 'A year off will help clear your mind, love. So you can make sure that ag science is what you want to do.'

Abe was going to marry Renee and, in time, they'd have kids and then there'd be no room for her on the family's five-thousand-hectare property. She wasn't the son or daughter of the family farmer, she was the granddaughter.

Pa hadn't said a word. Only sat in the rocking chair and sipped his bourbon as he always did. Sometimes his eyes had darted her way, but more often than not, they'd stayed fixed on the TV or the *Farming Journal*.

The handwritten cashbook had been on his lap, and he'd licked the end of the pencil as he wrote figures and products into the columns. When he finished he'd looked over at her and squinted as if trying to work out who she was. Sassi was close to her grandmother, but her grandfather hadn't allowed her, or anyone, to get close to him.

Granny had squeezed her hand again and got up, leaving Sassi to her thoughts.

That had been when both of her grandparents had still been fit and able to live on the farm.

Neither of them were any of those things now.

'That might have been the best bit of advice she ever gave me, Jarrah,' Sassi said softly, reaching over to touch the dog's silky ears, which had flopped near the gear stick, while her chin rested on the console, causing her to have her nose in the air like Lady Muck.

Sassi returned her eyes to the windy stretch of bitumen and readjusted her grip on the steering wheel. Moments later, the sun rose from behind the ranges and rays of gold and red reflected off the clouds that had gathered above. Maybe there would be thunderstorms later in the day.

Only another fifty kilometres to go. That worked out to about the whole of the Kaylee Bell Essential playlist, so she reached forward and hit start again then focused back on the road.

You need to come now. Don't wait.

'Hang on until I get there, Granny,' Sassi said softly. 'Please.'

CHAPTER 2

The weather in Barker that morning reminded Mia Worth of her childhood. Hot, a strong northerly wind whipping up dust devils in the paddocks and on the dry footy oval.

Tightening her belt and making sure her handcuffs, taser, baton and everything else she had to lug around in the sleepy town of Barker were in the right place, she stepped out of her house only to be engulfed by a furnace. She could feel the grit on her teeth when she closed her mouth.

'Crap,' she muttered, sweat already breaking out on her forehead.

The northerly was forcing trees to bend over, nearly touching the ground, while leaves tumbled along the street and branches scraped the path.

Mia hoped all the volunteer fire-fighters were in town, really close to the shed that housed the truck. The day was shaping up to be the kind that would make controlling a blaze incredibly difficult. A catastrophic fire rating for sure.

Even though it was only a five-minute walk to the police station, she thought about going back and getting her car. Running from the air-conditioning of the vehicle to the air-conditioned office and then, if they had to do anything on the road, to another cool vehicle, held some appeal.

'Don't be weak,' she told herself. Those were the words her nan would have used. 'Take the easy way out and you'll be feeble before your time.'

'True enough, Nan,' Mia murmured, and ducked back inside for her water bottle, before legging it towards the police station on the main street of Barker.

Her heart ached at the echoes of her nan's voice. Only a month ago, they'd gathered alongside the grave in Barker to lower her coffin into the chocolate-red earth that Clara had loved so much. A fall, a broken hip and then pneumonia had taken a toll on her elderly body.

Mia had learnt that the sting of tears could turn up at any moment and memories of Nan hit her when she least expected them. She missed her grandmother like she'd never missed anyone before. Clara had raised her and loved her fiercely, and now there was just an empty hole in Mia's life.

The word 'orphan' reverberated around her head. No mother or father and now no grandmother. Clara had been Mia's reason to stay in Barker and now she was gone.

Still, Barker was her home town and the streets held memories of Nan, especially the shop on the main street that her family owned. It was no longer a cluttered haberdashery store but a busy cafe, one that supplied her with free coffee every time she visited.

Mia refocused her thoughts and waved at a young boy who lived a few houses down from her. He was always in the driveway of his house on his skateboard, no matter the temperature or time of day.

'Aren't you hot, Charlie?' she called out to him as he stood the skateboard on its back wheels and pirouetted. The wind almost whipped her words away, but he answered with a grin.

'Nah. Don't notice it,' he called back.

A true local. Or kid. Nan always said that she noticed the heat more and more as she got older.

Maybe twenty-five is the new old, Mia thought. A little rivulet of sweat ran down the side of her face and she swiped at it before giving Charlie another wave.

At the next house an unsurprising yapping noise reached her above the wind. Mia ignored the little Jack Russell who ran along the wire mesh fence, barking at her ankles. He sounded as if he'd tear an intruder limb from limb if they ever dared come inside his yard, but Mia knew it was a front. Whenever she'd reached over to pat him, the little dog had stood on his hind legs, tongue lolling, and accepted every caress and kind word she'd offered.

Yet, six months in, she still hadn't convinced him she wasn't a threat every time she pounded the pavement at the front of his home.

Rounding the corner onto the main street, she noticed the normal scattering of cars parked in front of the shops as the early birds came to collect their milk or mail before the heat increased in the middle of the day.

To her surprise, Dave was pulling up in the patrol car nearly an hour earlier than usual.

'Hey,' she called out, when he slammed the door behind him, pocketing the keys. Mia broke into a slow jog to catch him before he went inside. 'You're here early.'

'Morning,' Dave said, giving her a smile. 'How was your night?'

Mia shrugged. 'Pretty quiet. Night tennis is starting up again next week, but until then, it's me, dinner and a book. God, this wind is awful, isn't it?' Mia waited while he unlocked the front door of the station, and let her in. 'Have you been on a call-out?'

'Yeah. Quilby needed a hand. We're so damn short of volunteer ambos around here, and he couldn't lift Mrs Stapleton by himself, so he rang me.

'She was found by her husband, at about nine pm. We tried to stabilise her but, unfortunately, Mrs Stapleton died before we could transfer her to the hospital.'

'I don't think I know the family.'

'You probably haven't come across them yet. Elderly couple in Barker, living on their own. The husband has trouble communicating and can be a bit wonky on his feet, but they've been able to continue to live alone since they moved in from the farm.' He shut the door behind Mia, before getting a hankie out of his pocket and dabbing his brow. 'They've got a son, Abe. He's married to Renee with twin boys and took over the family farm a while back.'

'It's nice their family is close by to support the husband left behind,' Mia said, keeping her voice steady. To try to dull the ache in her chest, she reached for the air-conditioner remote and switched it on.

'There's a daughter I've never met. Quilby told me he wasn't sure Mrs Stapleton would last the night and, because the doc had to get over from Broad River, and every moment counts in cases like this we suggested that Abe ring all the family. Apparently, she's trying to get on the first flight out of South Africa. The granddaughter, Sassi, is on her way here now. Abe told me Sassi used to live with Mr and Mrs Stapleton until she left school. Funny, though,' he crinkled his brow, 'I don't remember her, and I would have been living here by then. Only just, mind you. Obviously, she never got into any trouble.'

'Well, that's got to be a good thing. The no trouble, I mean.' Mia turned on the computer, hearing the whirring above the noise of the branches scraping across the roof of the station.

'Yeah, but the not so good thing is that, even with Mrs Stapleton's medical history, the doc isn't prepared to issue a death certificate. And she didn't die in the hospital and the last one to see her alive was her incapacitated husband, yada, yada, yada.' Dave gave a grimace. 'So you know what that means.'

'We'll be preparing a report for the coroner.' Mia returned the screwed-up facial expression. 'What was the story with the granddaughter's parents? How come the grandparents raised her?'

'Not sure, Abe didn't say anything. There was no mention of her father last night. Kim might have some information, though. I'll ask her tonight when I get home.'

Mia absorbed what Dave said. 'Has Mrs Stapleton been ID'd?'

'Yeah. Son did that. We gave him all her property before we took her body to the morgue hospital.' Dave held out a piece of paper to Mia. 'One gold wedding band, one diamond and sapphire engagement ring and a gold watch. And I've dropped her clothes off on the way back here, which consisted of a nightdress and a pair of underpants. Abe's signed for them all.'

Mia nodded. 'That part was easy, then.'

'There is going to be a bit of running around because the husband is upset and can't be relied on. He's mostly all there, but he finds it hard to convey what he wants to say. We'll need to talk to him and try to find out exactly how he found her.'

'Dementia?' Mia felt as if the word was going to choke her. Her nan had been teetering between stages three and four of that bloody disease when she'd died. Many a conversation had taken place that didn't make sense and many that had. The confusion Clara had so obviously felt, and had realised she was experiencing, was another reason Mia didn't think her heart was ever going to mend. But on her good days, when she wasn't sad and feeling empty, Mia wondered if Clara's death hadn't been a blessing. She'd still been able to eat and speak and walk with her hand tucked into Mia's arm in the garden of the nursing home in Broad River.

'No,' Dave was saying, 'he had a stroke a few years ago and it seems to have affected every part of him, especially speaking.' Dave caught Mia's eye. 'How are you feeling?'

She gave a shrug. 'Still hits me sometimes. Apparently that's normal with grief. Everyone tells me that.'

'I'm always here. So is Kim.'

'I know,' Mia said softly. 'But you've done so much already.'

'And the problem with that is?' Dave asked gently. This time it was his turn to hit the on switch for his computer. He pulled out his chair without looking at her.

Mia would never forget the day she'd found out she was being stationed at Barker permanently. Her first posting had been at the Broad River Police Station, only an hour's drive away. Her nan had been in a nursing home there so that's where Mia had wanted to be stationed.

Mia's time there, less than a week, had been a disaster, before Dave had intervened and seconded her to Barker to replace his constable, Jack Higgins.

The day she'd arrived at Barker had been the day she'd landed on her feet. Dave and Joan, the receptionist, had welcomed her warmly. Unlike her experience at the misogynistic Broad River Police Station, neither Joan nor Dave had cared that Mia was a newly graduated constable with little experience.

Or that she was a woman. Or that she drove back to Broad River every second night to see her nan. Kim, Dave's wife, had befriended her from day one, too. There had been extra servings of all Kim's food. Mia often went home and found plates of lamb casserole or chicken salad in her fridge.

There had been jokes that Kim was not only trying to add a little weight to Mia's very thin frame, but she also was trying to get her to grow. Five foot nothing made for a very short police officer, Kim had told her once.

'You think?' Mia had laughed.

Kim had sat with Mia in the hospital room when Nan had first been admitted. The gurgling sound coming from Clara's chest, her sunken eyes and confused expression still haunted her granddaughter.

Kim's thoughtfulness meant she'd brought moisturiser for Mia to rub into Clara's dry hands and made sure she had been there to help soothe the frightened old lady if Mia had been out of the room.

Kim had also been the one to hold Mia when the gurgling had finally become silent and her nan's body still.

The debt Mia felt she owed Kim was too big for her to even know how to start showing her thanks. But Kim didn't seem to want thanks or payment, or returned favours. She'd been happy just to be there for her friend.

That's what they were now. Firm friends.

Mia cleared her throat. 'I can start writing up the report if you want. Is there anything else I need to know about for today?'

'Nah, it's looking pretty quiet.' Dave glanced towards the window as an extra strong gust sent the leaves slapping against the tin roof. 'Let's hope that bloody wind drops, though, and there aren't any idiots who feel like playing with matches or cigarette butts today.' He pulled out his mobile phone. 'I'm going to check in with the fire control officer and see if we have enough volunteers on standby. Thank goodness we have a few more of them than we do ambos.'

'Sure.' Mia picked up a pen and stuck it behind her ear as she turned her attention to the handwritten report on Mrs Stapleton's belongings that Abe had signed for.

Her watch vibrated just as Joan blew through the door.

'Gosh, blast and damnation, and any other rude word there is,' Joan said, trying to push her hair back into some kind of tidiness, and at the same time make sure the door was shut. 'That is a revolting day out there.'

Mia opened her mouth to answer but instead the door was flung open again, nearly hitting Joan.

'Oh.' The receptionist stumbled backwards as a tall man, who Mia didn't know, strode inside, dark hair tousled from the wind.

His hand flew out to catch Joan before she fell. 'Sorry, sorry.'

'I'm okay, Abe. Don't worry,' Joan said, still patting her hair into place. She eyed Abe. 'Are you all right?'

'I need help,' he said to no one in particular. 'My niece hasn't shown up and she should have been here by now.' He shoved his hands in the pockets of his shorts, then took them out again and ran them through his hair.

'I'll get—' But Joan was interrupted by the opening of the door from behind the counter.

'Abe,' Dave came around the desk. 'Sassi hasn't turned up yet?'

'Nah, and she's not answering her phone.' He paced across the room and stood beneath the air-conditioner. 'Her phone's connected to bluetooth, so she should be able to, even if she's still on the road. By my timing, she's late by a few hours.' He jiggled up and down in one spot.

'When did you hear from her last?' Dave was checking his watch as Joan looked to Mia, needing an explanation.

'She texted me from Broken Hill and that was before midnight. I rang her when you told me to, to tell her she needed to come right away and she left an hour later. Have you had any reports of an accident?'

'Did you ring Sassi to let her know that Mrs Stapleton had died?' Dave asked, ignoring the question.

'No. I didn't want her driving upset.' Abe bounced on his toes. 'Any accidents?' he repeated.

'No.' Dave was emphatic as Mia whispered to Joan what had happened during the night. 'How long would it have taken her from Broken Hill?'

'Only another six or seven hours, depending on how many times she stopped. Knowing her, she probably didn't have a break at all. Something must have happened.'

'It's eight thirty now,' Dave said. Then he snapped up a gear, pulling his phone from his belt and dialling a number. 'Abe, if you head home, we'll get looking.'

'I'll check on the system,' Mia said quickly and disappeared back into the office.

'I'm not going anywhere,' Abe said. 'My niece could be upended in a gutter somewhere.'

'What sort of car does she drive?' Dave asked.

'D-MAX. Isuzu.'

'Numberplate?' The words snapped out from Dave.

'Don't know.'

'Have you got a photo of her? Of the ute?'

A phone rang behind the desk and Joan snatched it up.

'Barker Police Stat—Oh. One moment.' She held out the phone to Dave.

CHAPTER 3

An annoying *tick, tick, tick* woke Sassi. That and the intense heat that was streaming through the window.

Her face was covered in sweat and she reached up to wipe the moisture away from her eyes so she could open them.

Her arm wouldn't move.

Frowning, she tried to kick the covers off and roll over. Where was she? This wasn't a familiar bed.

She flicked her eyes open. It wasn't the ceiling of a house she saw, but the roof of her car. Inches from the end of her nose.

Panic flared and hit her stomach at the same time her bladder gave a sharp contraction to let her know it had been neglected.

'What?' Confusion coursed through her.

Then the black and white shaking movie-framed memories before her eyes.

The kangaroo.

Out of nowhere.

Against everything she'd been taught, her foot had found its way to the brake and she'd turned the steering wheel. The front wheel had hit gravel on the side of the road and she'd tried to correct her mistake, but the tyres didn't follow the command of the steering wheel. Then all she'd heard had been a high-pitched yelp of surprise from Jarrah and a crumpling of steel.

'Jarrah?' Her voice was croaky, her lips stiff with something. Blood maybe? 'Jarrah? Girl, are you okay?'

Why couldn't she move? Sassi tried to turn to where Jarrah had been sleeping in the passenger's seat footwell, but her face was trapped between the seatbelt and the roof, while her left upper arm seemed to be pinned to her side.

Wriggling her fingers, she tried to stretch out towards where Jarrah should be, but there was nothing but air.

Terror now. And then the claustrophobia closed in. Everything was too close, she couldn't breathe. She had to push the roof further away from her face. Or yank the seatbelt so her head would turn into open space.

Her right arm was trapped between her body and the door, which was smashed in.

Breaths came quick and fast until her vision swam in front of her and there was a welcome blackness.

A high-pitched squeal reached her ears. Was it Jarrah? Had the dog been thrown from the car and was lying hurt somewhere?

The noise didn't sound like it belonged to a dog.

Sassi tried to put her hands over her ears and block out the sound. She wanted to rip at everything that was imprisoning her. To get free. To move.

'Stop it,' she implored. But the words didn't come out. They were only in her mind. Then she realised all the fear and panic—the uncontrollable mewling—was coming from her.

'Help me, please,' she finally whimpered as all the fight left her body.

Sassi kept her eyes firmly shut. Surely if she couldn't see everything so close to her face, there was nothing to be frightened of. The blackness was just like being asleep. She'd be able to get her breath.

'Deep breaths,' she whispered to herself, recalling what Uncle Abe had told her as a child whenever someone had upset her and she had started to cry. 'Deep breaths.'

Her senses started to come to life as she tried to calm herself.

She realised her jeans were damp and she could smell coffee. That's right. They'd stopped at Broad River. Her thermos had still been hot, so she'd poured a coffee and given Jarrah a drink. Walked around the parking bay.

The pup had bounced around, pleased to be free of the confines of the car. They'd only stopped for ten minutes and then hopped back in the car, headed towards Barker. Towards her grandmother.

She could hear breathing. Hers? Jarrah's?

Something wet against her hand.

'Jarrah?' She breathed the word out as she realised the dog was licking her hand. Sassi wasn't alone. 'Jarrah!' This time the word was a sob.

Deep breath, deep breath.

A rumbling noise reached her ears and Jarrah gave a small bark. The whoosh of tyres and then the noise retreated.

The car had passed before Sassi could even open her mouth to call out. Why hadn't it stopped? Surely, they'd seen her?

Unlikely, she realised. The ute had rolled down a steep embankment. The driver probably hadn't even seen the wreck.

Hot tears seeped out from beneath her lashes. 'Jarrah?' She waved her fingers around, trying to attract her pup's attention.

Where was her phone? This time, still keeping her eyes closed, she tried to move her arm to find it. Her fingers inched down towards the console but stopped short of where the phone had sat last.

She heard a snuffling sound and a sensation ran down her cheek. The noise was her; this time she was crying. 'Get a grip.' Sassi took another deep breath, pushing away the frustration of not being able to find her phone. 'Jarrah?' Her voice shook. 'Jarrah, are you okay?'

Another living, breathing being in the car with her was comforting, but she had to get out. Her bladder was going to burst and the heat was stifling.

Don't think about it. Oh, but what she wouldn't give for a drink of water!

She tried to lick away the sweat trickling down near the corner of her mouth. All the while, her mind raced. How was she going to attract attention?

The car rocked slightly as Jarrah tried to nuzzle her nose into Sassi's hand. A pungent smell hit her nose and Sassi gagged.

'God, Jarrah, don't.' Raising her voice, she screamed. 'Help me! Help me.' She needed to get out. Now.

Fear kept stabbing at her.

Jarrah whined, sensing her distress.

Sassi's head was throbbing. From the heat or stress or . . . Maybe she'd banged her head. The roof of the car was so close to her face, she must have. Was she bleeding? Her forehead did feel tight.

The sound of an approaching vehicle caught her attention.

'Please, please help!' She needed to bang on the roof, that would attract attention. Her arms were still pinned.

She was helpless. Alone.

Except for Jarrah, her brain prompted her.

But she's trapped, too.

The noise disappeared into the distance and Sassi sagged.

Her thoughts went to her grandmother. Granny would be so upset when she heard this had happened. Especially since Sassi was trying to get home to see her.

'Now, dear, it's always better to arrive alive,' her grandmother had told her when Sassi had moved to New South Wales. 'The excitement of coming home for a holiday will make you want to drive faster, or stay on the road longer, but you can't be tired when you're behind the wheel.'

Granny's advice had always been matter-of-fact. It didn't matter what it was about. Anything from what Sassi should be wearing to affairs of the heart.

'If someone says something mean, walk away. Their opinion doesn't matter,' she'd told Sassi when one of the girls at school had been teasing her.

'But what they say hurts.'

'Don't let it. The only thoughts that matter are yours. Emotions are there to be felt, but not to rule you. You'll never survive this ugly world if any small word or action makes you angry or sad.'

'How do you not let it upset you?' Sassi had been sitting at the kitchen table. Her tears had been in her eyes, but they hadn't fallen. She'd taken deep breaths, and listened to Granny.

Granny had left the bread dough she was kneading and joined Sassi at the kitchen table, her floury hands taking Sassi's own. 'Darling, at times, your heart will hurt. Your body will hurt, and you'll think you can't go on. Maybe someone you love will devastate you, maybe a friend will die. Maybe a boss will speak badly about you in public. People who don't even know you will have an opinion. Something to say about you or how you dress, the way you speak. All this is piffle. Minor things. Thoughts to be ignored.

'Now the bigger ones, the heartbreak, the moments when you think your body is going to break in two because every part of you is hurting, that's when you use your hands. You use them to bake, to garden, to do something practical. Physical.

'Hard work dulls pain, and the normality of that task will filter through your body. Then you take a breath and put one foot forward. Suddenly one day will have passed. Then another, then a week, then a month and in time, my darling, you'll wake up and find that the hurt is still there but it's not as debilitating and piercing as it was.'

Sassi had tried hard to keep up with those words, to take them in, but she hadn't really understood.

Not until Ewin had left her.

Then she'd worked. Worked and worked until she couldn't feel, couldn't think, couldn't smell or taste him in her memory. Except in the early hours of the mornings when no one knew she was aching from loneliness and sobbing into her pillow. No one except Jarrah.

Her hands had shown that work. The broken nails, soil inground into her skin, cracks where everything was dry and callused. Her arm had a long, thin scar from where fencing wire had scraped her. All signs that she had followed Granny's advice.

Granny. The whole reason she was here. Upside-down in her ruined ute.

Was Granny still alive? She had to be. There was still advice to give; Granny would have a lot to say about Ewin.

Sassi's heart began to ache. Surely Uncle Abe would have told someone she hadn't arrived yet? Why weren't they looking for her?

And she was so hot. Was it really tears that were sliding down her face, or sweat?

A crow cawed from outside and then she heard the scratchy noise of claws on the car.

Peck, peck, peck. The long, cruel beak tapped at the steel, investigating what this new, shiny thing was.

Panic arrived again with a punch. Could the crow get into the car? What if it tried to get to her eyes, as she'd seen happen time and again to sheep who were dying or dead? The merciless bird jabbing its beak at any part of the ewe. How would she stop it pecking at her eyes with her hands trapped?

'Jarrah? I'm scared,' she whispered.

There was no answer. Silence stretched out until all Sassi could hear was the sound of her own heart and blood pumping in her head. With all the windows in the car still up, the temperature rose higher and higher, and Jarrah puffed harder.

The dog whined. Stopped. Whined again.

Puff, puff, puff.

Sassi was sleepy. So sleepy.

The crow lost interest.

A noise filtered through her muddled brain. Her mouth moved in time to part of a song. Song? No, a ringtone. A mobile phone. Guitar riffs that made the song, 'Keith'. Her mobile phone.

Sassi scrambled to reach it, forgetting she was trapped, and let out a cry of frustration when it stopped.

It rang again, then a third time.

'Hello?'

Sassi was confused. She hadn't answered the phone. How . . .

'Hello? You okay down there?'

A man's voice.

'Yeah, Dave, we've got a single vehicle roll-over.'

The sentence didn't make sense. How was the sound coming through her phone? And her name wasn't Dave.

'Hello?' she whispered. Her mouth was too dry to let the word come with any type of volume. 'Help.'

Her eyes flicked open and she stared straight at the roof. This time she saw the rusty iron colour of blood.

Hers? Jarrah's?

A scattering of stones and the voice was close to her now. Near her ear.

'Single woman in vehicle. Ambulance and jaws of life required.'

Relief surged through Sassi as her bladder let go, but she didn't care. There was a man who had seen her car. A man who had stopped!

Summoning all her strength she screamed as loudly as her dry throat would let her.

'Help!'

'She's alive. Talking. Get here as soon as you can. It's too bloody hot for her to stay in the ute for long.'

'I'm here, I'm here!' Could he hear her? Please let him hear her!

'Hello there.'

Now his voice was so close, she imagined she could feel his breath on her face. A sob erupted from Sassi just as Jarrah gave a bark. The car rocked as Jarrah tried to move.

'Help,' she said again. 'Can you help us?'

'It's all right. I've called for an ambulance. We'll get you out in no time. What's your name?'

'Oh my god.' Her words were stuck and there were only tears of relief, and still fear.

'It's okay,' the man said. 'Can you tell me your name?'

'Sassi.' It came out in a rush. 'I'm Sassi and Jarrah, my dog, she's on the passenger side.'

'Okay, Sassi. I'm an ambulance officer. Michael Quilby. I'm going to stay with you until help arrives, okay?'

'Water? Have you got any? I need a drink.'

'Sure. Now I need to smash the window because the door is too damaged to open. Okay? I need to do this so I can get to you. Close your eyes.'

Squeezing them shut, Sassi felt the shards of glass hit her body then bounce towards the floor. Fresh air followed, although it was still of a furnace-like heat. It didn't matter, Sassi gulped deeply.

'Don't move yet, I'm just going to clear the glass away from around the frame. Keep those eyes closed.'

Another lot of glass.

'Okay, now we're right. Here, this will spill a little.'

Then she smelt Old Spice aftershave and felt the water bottle pressed to her lips. Dribbles of water ran down her chin, but she didn't care. The cool, sweet moisture wet her mouth. It was the sweetest drink she had ever tasted.

Then it was gone.

'More?'

'That's enough for the moment. Little bits regularly, okay?'

Sassi didn't answer. The car was moving again as Jarrah tried to shift from her position.

'Jarrah,' she said now. 'My dog.'

'I'll check.'

The man moved away. What was his name again. Something strange? Something like that sport that was played in the Harry Potter books.

Quit . . . Quich?

Her brain was addled.

Then he was back again.

'Jarrah is fine, but I can't get her out either. We're just going to have to wait until the emergency services get here. They're not far away now. Can you tell me when this happened?'

Sassi licked her lips. They were so dry. What she wouldn't give for some lip balm. There was some in the console of the ute. Maybe they'd give it to her once she was out of here.

'Early this morning. I'm going to Barker to see my grand-mother. She's sick.'

'You're a local?' There was surprise in his voice. 'I don't recognise you.'

'Grew up there. My granny is a Stapleton.'

'Ah, of course. Yeah, I know Abe quite well.'

Sassi felt her eyes begin to close again. It was hot, so hot, and the effort it was taking to keep them open was too much now there was someone here to help.

'Keep your eyes open, Sassi,' the ambulance officer said. 'Keep them open for me, okay? Tell me about your family. Abe is your uncle?'

'Umm.' Her brain felt as if there were letters floating through her mind, not in order. How did she make the letters become words and then say them aloud again?

'Sassi?'

Her body shook a little. It was cold. Had the sun gone down again? Maybe night had arrived without her realising. The darkness seemed to have come back. Perhaps a whole day had gone by.

Granny. A whole day? Oh no.

'Sassi, hang in there. You need to stay with me. Open your eyes.'

In the distance she heard sirens. Were they coming for her?

'Sassi!'

The word penetrated the fuzziness that was surrounding her and she pushed open her eyelids and looked at the man peering in through the window. His face swam in front of her eyes. Greying hair, blue eyes. He seemed kind.

'Hello,' she said. 'Are you going to help me?'

'I'm going to do my best, Sassi. Keep your eyes open.'

He seemed to say that a lot but Sassi really didn't want to keep them open when she was so tired.

'What's your ETA?' he asked.

Her mouth was dry again. So very dry and she didn't understand his question.

'E? What?'

The man said nothing this time, only rubbed her shoulder. She could feel his hands on her skin.

'It's hot. You'd better get a move on,' he said.

'I know,' Sassi mumbled. 'Really hot. Summer. Always hot.' Did her sentence make sense? 'I'm cold though.'

'Here, Sassi, have another sip.'

The cool water against her lips was heaven.

Was that the sound of sirens?

Sirens. They would bring help. And then she'd be able to get to Granny. Because Granny was why she was going back to Barker after all this time.

Granny, who was sick.

Granny who she needed to get to. Because Abe had said, 'You'd better come now.'

CHAPTER 4

'Is it Sassi?' Abe's voice was tense, and his face had drained of colour as he took a step towards Dave, who was holding the phone to his ear.

A prickle of adrenalin flowed through Mia. She needed to move. Get on the road. Go and look for this missing girl.

Dave held up his hand and left the room with the phone, walking quickly to his office and shutting the door.

'He's got to tell me.' Abe lurched forward, trying to follow Dave, but Joan stepped in front of him.

'Come through to the lounge,' she said gently. 'We can wait to see if there's any news in there. It might be nothing.'

'Like hell! I'm staying right here!' Abe looked like he wanted to jump over the counter.

Mia moved on the spot, her phone in her hand, feeling the weight of the police belt around her hips. The heaviness reminded her of the care and duty she had been trained to deliver.

Moving now towards Abe, she spoke in what she hoped was a gentle voice. One that conveyed care and compassion to someone in need.

'Abe? I know Dave will come and talk to you the moment he's finished.' She indicated the barren room that held a threadbare couch and a scratched coffee table. 'It's a lot more comfortable in here. Do you want to sit?'

'I'm not moving.' Abe folded his arms and planted his feet apart. His gaze never left the closed door of Dave's office. 'I'll wait right here.'

Mia drew in a sharp breath. What was she supposed to do here? Insist? Leave him where he was? What if it was bad news?

She tried once more. 'What about a cup of tea?'

This time, Abe didn't even answer her, he just tapped his foot quickly.

Mia had to do something, so she left the room, dialling the hospital as she went.

'Hi, Lisa,' she said when the hospital receptionist answered. 'This is Mia from the police station. Can I speak to the clinical nurse manager? Who's on duty today?'

'I'll put you through to Hamish,' Lisa told her and Mia listened to the automated voice tell her that visiting hours were from ten am until twelve noon and then from four pm until seven pm only.

Then the scrabble of the phone being picked up and Hamish's rich baritone voice saying her name.

'Mia, it's Hamish Carter. How can I help you?'

'Hamish, are there any volunteers available to drive the ambulance? I think we've got a car accident. I'm waiting for more details but we're probably going to need it.'

There was a pause, and she heard the scratch of a pen running down paper. 'Nope, we're fresh out. We had Quilby yesterday, but all the ambos, all three of them, have pulled out to be on call for fire brigades today.'

'Right.' Though her tone was cool and professional, her stomach was turning.

'Where's the accident?'

'Waiting to be briefed. Just wanted to get a handle on where we were at. I'll call you back. Sounds like I might have to drive.'

'I can come with you if needed. Simone is on call.' All of the five nursing staff available in Barker were on a constant rotation.

'Great, thanks. I'll let you know.' She hit the end button and looked out the window. The heat radiated through the glass and outside was deserted. Small country towns ran on volunteers, and Barker was horribly short. Three ambo officers weren't going to cut it if there was a multi-vehicle accident, gas explosion or any type of major incident. Five volunteer firies? Barker would be left wanting if a fire got going on a day like today.

She peeked into the other room where Abe was slumped forward on a seat, his hand over his eyes, while Joan was talking to him.

'Come on, let's get a cup of tea,' she was saying to the

distressed man in a no-nonsense but gentle tone. 'We'll work out what's happening when Dave is off the phone.'

Abe ignored her and continued to stare at the ground, his knee jiggling now. So much fear and worry. Mia wasn't sure quite what to do to help.

Joan backtracked to the kitchen and switched on the kettle. 'Cup of tea always helps any situation,' she said to anyone who was listening.

Mia let herself into the office where Dave was standing looking at the map of the shire, his finger on a spot about twenty kilometres from Barker.

'Right, we'll be there ASAP. Thanks for calling it in.' He put down the phone and turned.

Mia's body was buzzing now. 'Problem?'

'Car accident.'

'I've spoken to the hospital, and if we need the ambulance, I'll have to drive, but Hamish can crew.'

'You're up then,' Dave told her. 'Text Hamish and give him the heads-up. He knows the drill. I'll head out in the patrol car and organise Mucka from Broad River to mobilise the emergency services. Quilby reckons we're going to need the jaws of life.'

Mia winced. Must be a bad one. Her thoughts flew to her friend, Chris. They'd graduated from the academy at the same time. On his first day on the job he'd been involved with helping at a double fatality road accident. 'The first one never leaves you,' he'd told Mia. Well, this would be her first.

Taking a deep breath, Mia refocused. Dave was still speaking.

'. . . and send a tow truck over. You good?'

Mia nodded, the thrill of responsibility and adrenalin running through her. 'I'm good,' she said as she tapped out the text to Hamish. 'What do we know?'

'Roll-over, run off the road going through Jumbuck Creek and gone down the embankment. Single, female occupant. Condition unknown although she was conscious and talking.' Dave was gathering his phone and hat. 'Quilby said it looks nasty from the outside. The heat won't be helping whoever is in that vehicle.'

'Okay.' She broke off as her phone beeped. 'Hamish is bringing the ambulance here. ETA seven minutes.'

'Right. I'll speak to Abe. Tell him what's happened.' He glanced at her as he hurried towards the door. 'You should come and listen. Good learning experience for you. None of this is any fun.'

Mia didn't get a chance to answer because Dave disappeared towards the reception area. The last time Mia had ever seen Dave move so quickly was when Tahlia Chellow had been found. The little girl had been missing for hours before Mia had found her at the top of a haystack in a shed.

She hurried after him and saw that Abe hadn't changed position. Dave had a hand on the man's shoulder.

'There has been an accident, Abe,' Dave said softly.

Abe let out a groan and his head flopped backwards.

'We can't confirm that the driver is Sassi, but the occupant is female. There's no one else in the car—'

34

'Is she all right?'

'The driver is conscious, yes, but Abe, I repeat, we cannot confirm it's Sassi.'

'I'm coming with you.'

'No, you're no good to me when you're in the state you're in,' Dave said firmly. 'Stay with Joan or go home to your family, and I'll ring you as soon as I know something.'

'Like hell! She's my niece! I've got my first aid certificate. I can help.'

'We don't know—'

'Well, who else is it going to be?' Abe exploded. 'A single person in a vehicle.'

'Look, you're not a volunteer, Abe. And you haven't got the right insurance or anything to help. I'm sorry. We've got the ambulance coming and Mia and I are going out there now.'

'She was bringing her dog. I don't know what breed but she asked if she could . . .' Abe's voice trailed off. He looked around as if he was unsure what to do. 'If it's her, then she'll have a dog.'

'Right, we'll keep an eye out. Now, I need you to go back to your family. Joan will run you home.' Mia saw Dave look at Joan who nodded swiftly. 'Or you can stay here. The moment I have any news, I'll call you. Okay?'

'*Okay?* Are you serious? What the hell type of question is that?' Anger erupted from Abe.

'I'm sorry, Abe,' Dave said, simply. 'I promise, the moment I know something, I'll ring. I won't leave you hanging, but Mia and I need to go now and do our job.'

A horn blared from the street and Mia realised Hamish had arrived. Joan was already moving purposefully towards the upset man.

'Come on, Abe. Let's get you back to your family. Easier if I take you, so you're not driving upset.'

Dave didn't wait to hear what Abe said, but moved quickly towards the door, checking just once with Mia. 'Good to go?'

She nodded and grabbed the laminated note that had been stuck to the inside of the station door and changed it to the outside as she left.

The station is unattended. Please call Detective Dave Burrows' mobile for assistance. The number was listed below in large black lettering.

The ambulance was parked with the lights flashing, but without the siren. Mia noticed a few of the store owners were standing on the street, arms crossed, solemn faces. Everyone in a country town was invested when there was an accident, because more often than not, the victim was well known.

Hamish was strapping on the seatbelt in the passenger's seat as Mia ran around to the driver's side, the wind at her back, the heat encompassing her. What would it be like to be trapped in a car in the height of summer? Even if the windows had smashed open during the accident, the victim would be out in the elements. If the glass hadn't broken, the temperature could be twice as high inside as out.

The temperature gauge on the dash was nudging forty-two. A quick glance at her watch told her it wasn't yet nine in the morning.

She had barely said hello to Hamish before she flicked on the blinker and pulled out onto the road. Driving an ambulance hadn't been part of her academy training, but it had been part of her country cop, Dave-training, which differed quite considerably from what her city counterparts would learn. They had access to all services, whenever they needed them.

'Out here,' Dave had said, 'you are the service and when it comes to the ambulance, if none of the volunteers is available, your job will be to drive.'

'Why's that?'

'Because the nurse will be caring for the patient.'

'How long before the heat can kill someone?' Mia now asked Hamish, her words coming out as swiftly as her heart was beating.

Hamish shook his head. 'Too quickly. But on the upside, it's still early morning and, even though it's bloody hot, it hasn't been that way for long.' He took a breath as Mia hit the sirens.

'Quilby says it doesn't look pretty,' Mia said as she kept her eyes on the road, the steering wheel vibrating under her hands.

Cars came towards her, pulling towards the edge of the road as she passed. She could see the curious looks in drivers' eyes as the ambulance sped past.

'They never look pretty,' Hamish answered. 'Any ID?'

'No. But we suspect it might be Sassi Stapleton. Abe just came in to tell us she hadn't arrived as expected.'

Hamish screwed up his nose. 'Serious? Some families have all the luck.' The last word was heavy with irony.

'Yeah.'

They lapsed into silence, both lost in their own thoughts, wondering what they would find when they arrived.

In the rear-view mirror, something caught Mia's eye. Coloured, strobe-like lights. Dave was behind the ambulance but wouldn't be for long. Within moments he had gained enough speed and the blinker flashed as he pulled out to pass, then disappeared just as quickly into the distance.

'This your first accident since you've been in Barker?' Hamish asked.

'First accident ever, actually,' Mia said, holding the ambulance steady. She really hoped her nervousness didn't show.

Hamish looked over at her and she stiffened. This would be good. What would be going through his mind?

Working with a rookie.

How will she hold up?

Hope she doesn't make any mistakes.

He surprised her when he said, 'Don't worry. This is what you train for. You'll know what to do. And we're all here.'

For a moment, Mia wasn't sure how to respond, then she flashed a grateful smile.

'There's always a first time for everything,' Hamish continued. 'You'll be fine. Trust me, we've all been there.

I can still remember the first accident I attended.' He looked at the road ahead. 'Looks like this is it. Damn, those last twenty ks are the most dangerous of a long drive. You know you're almost there and start to relax. Not pay as much attention as you should.'

Mia saw Quilby's old white Holden ute was pulled up on the side of the road. Next to it, Dave's patrol car's lights were still flashing a warning to motorists coming from either direction to slow down. She lifted her foot from the accelerator, all the while taking deep breaths. Hamish was right, this is what she had trained for.

'You can get the stretcher out,' Hamish said, 'and I'll assess the patient.'

Mia nodded, pulling up to a stop and silencing the sirens, but leaving the lights on.

Pulling open her door, she jumped down, landing on the bitumen and feeling the warmth emanating from the black tar. With a glance around, she saw the skid tracks heading towards an embankment, crushed bushes and broken branches where the car had gone over the edge.

The heat created mirages that glimmered in the distance and the land was strangely silent. Every living being must be taking shelter in the shade. There wasn't even a galah in the sky.

Dave appeared at the top of the rise, wiping his brow as he pulled himself up.

'What have we got?' Hamish asked as he opened the rear doors and reached in for medications and bandages.

'The victim is Sassi Stapleton and Quilby is right, she's trapped. Emergency services from Broad River are en route. ETA—' he glanced at his watch '—maybe ten minutes.'

'And the patient?'

'In and out of consciousness. Quilby's with her.'

'Right. I'll check her out.'

'What do you want me to do after I get the stretcher?' Mia asked.

'I'm going to ring Abe and let him know, then wait for the guys from Broad River. You can start setting up the blocks to slow any other cars down.'

As he spoke a silver Toyota LandCruiser pulled up alongside them and a young woman rolled down the window.

'Are you all okay here?' she asked. 'Do you need any help?'

'No thanks, ma'am,' Dave said. 'You continue on.' He waved in the direction that she was already headed and gave her a smile.

'If you're sure?'

'We're sure, thank you.'

A moment later, the car pulled away and Dave pushed back his hat. 'Need to keep the traffic moving. Don't let anyone stop, just wave them on.'

'No worries.' Mia grabbed some witches hats out of the patrol car and started to close one lane of the road. 'Want me to let the media know about the road disruption?'

'Call it in to HQ. They can do that,' Dave said as he headed over the embankment again, phone to his ear.

'Abe?' Mia heard him say. 'Sassi has been involved in an accident . . .' His voice faded.

Mia worked steadily, feeling sweat run in between her shoulder blades while she carefully placed the cones on the circumference of the scene, including where the vehicles were parked. Flies buzzed around her head and the bitumen was sticky under her feet.

The last cone in place, Mia went to the crest of the embankment and sneaked a peek over the edge.

The car looked to be about eight metres below the road, on its wheels, its nose firmly embedded in the ground. The roof was caved in to about halfway down the window and the rear window was shattered but not broken. Other car parts were strewn across the embankment. A side mirror was caught in a bush and shards of glass glinted in the sunlight.

Quilby was leaning in towards the passenger's window, one arm inside and the other holding a bottle of water, while Dave was setting up a tent to shade the car from the sun.

Wasn't there supposed to be a dog somewhere? Hamish was at the driver's window, holding a bag in the air. He was setting up a drip to keep Sassi hydrated.

Shuddering, Mia took in the damage to the vehicle. Sassi wouldn't be able to walk away from such carnage uninjured, would she?

It only took a split second to change a life.

CHAPTER 5

'Okay, we're just about there,' a male voice said. 'A last bit of noise.'

He was standing at the front of the vehicle dressed in bright orange overalls, holding a large piece of machinery. It cut the struts holding the windshield in place, then two men started to peel the roof back.

The sound of screeching and shattering glass tore through Sassi's ears, but she didn't care. These men, these wonderful emergency workers, were here, helping her. Helping her to get to Granny.

Seconds later, the white of the shade that had been erected came into view, then the smiling face of the man with red hair and freckles, and Sassi felt like she could breathe again.

'That's better, isn't it? Get that roof away from your face. Can you squeeze my hand, Sassi?' The nurse was holding her right hand. Sassi couldn't remember his name. She squeezed hard and watched as a smile broke out across his face.

'Steady there, you'll break my fingers. Now what about your left?' He reached across and took her other hand.

She squeezed hard again.

'Good. Now I want you to wiggle your toes for me. Can you do that?'

'I can do that.'

'Great. I'm going to put this collar around your neck now and, once I've done a few more checks, we'll shift you onto the stretcher. You might feel some pain when we start to move you, so you can suck on this.' He handed her a green tube. 'It's a strong painkiller. Trust me, the green whistle—that's what we call it in the trade—will be your new best friend.'

It felt like such a freedom to be able to reach out and accept what the nurse was handing over. Sassi wanted to close her eyes and cheer. 'Thank you,' she murmured.

A bit more noise and shuffling as the stiff collar was placed around her neck making Sassi want to pull it off. Instead, she inhaled on the puffer, and tried to think of something nice. Nana's shortbread biscuits. Jarrah's soft ears. Ewin's hands in her hair.

Swallowing, Sassi tried to push Ewin aside. He had no place being in her thoughts.

Soon hands and arms were lifting her and moving her to the stretcher.

'Now I'm going to attach the blood pressure monitor.'

The ripping of the cuff, then Sassi felt the building pressure around her upper arm.

'How are you feeling, Sassi?' This man made her feel safe.

The terror that had been weaving its way through her veins, threatening to overwhelm her, was slowly disappearing as he stood alongside her, promising that he wasn't going to leave.

'Okay, I think,' she said. 'Where's Jarrah?'

The man grinned and jerked his head towards another tall man with grey hair in a police uniform. He was walking towards the foot of the stretcher, holding a lead, Jarrah on the end.

'I think Jarrah is asking the same question about you,' the ginger-haired man said. 'Dave's got her.'

Suddenly there were paws on the stretcher and warm breath in her ear. Tears pricked Sassi's eyes as she tried to move her arm to pat her friend.

'Jarrah. Oh my god, Jarrah. Is she okay?' Her voice was pleading. 'Let me look at you.'

'Well, I'm not a vet,' the policeman said, 'but she looks just fine to me. Just needed a drink and a potty stop and then she was keen to get back in the car with you.'

'Sassi? I'm Mia, another police officer.' A woman appeared in view. 'Dave and I will make sure Jarrah is looked after, okay? You don't need to worry about her, just get back on your feet.'

The fluids in Sassi had made her feel much better. She had a bit of a headache and her face felt tight, but other than that, her body felt normal. Although she wouldn't mind getting out of the sun.

'You should have smelt the farts she did while we were waiting to be found,' she said. 'You're the world's best farter, aren't you, girl?'

Everyone laughed as the three men and Mia moved the stretcher from the bottom of the embankment to the back of the ambulance. Sassi felt the bump as it was placed on the guides and locked into place.

'You're in great hands,' Mia told Sassi, with a smile. 'I'll be driving you back to Barker.'

The ginger-haired guy took his place next to her and once again checked her blood pressure and then her IV.

'Going okay?' he asked.

'Yeah, thank you.' She dropped her eyes, so she didn't have to look at him. Sassi was acutely embarrassed at her stupidity, at creating so much work for these people, these *kind* people. 'I actually feel fine. Do you even need to take me to the hospital?'

'We're getting you checked out by a doc, so the answer is yes. Tell me how you're feeling in the rest of your body. Anything overly sore, or places you can't feel?'

Sassi's eyes snapped back to him, running a mental check across her limbs. 'Um . . .' Concentrating, she focused on her toes, ankles, legs and moved up until she was at her head. 'I think everything is okay. I've got a bit of a headache.'

A smile broke out across his face. 'You took a real whack on the head, but from my examination, the biggest problem you have is dehydration from the heat.

'We're taking you to Barker, where the doc is doing his rounds, because I think your wounds are only superficial and we can look after you there instead of taking you to Broad River. Although heat exhaustion can still be dangerous.' He looked down at her, a half smile on his lips. 'I have to tell you, Sassi, you are one lucky lady.'

At the mention of Barker, tears appeared in Sassi's eyes. God! What was wrong with her? She'd not cried for a while; not since Ewin had packed his bags and held her hand for one last time. Told her he was sorry. Not that it made any difference; he'd left anyway.

And now, here she was blubbering like a baby at nothing. She pushed her ex-boyfriend's memory aside.

'My granny,' she hiccupped. 'Do you know if she's okay?'

'Your granny?' he replied slowly.

'Yeah. Cora Stapleton. She was taken to hospital last night.'

He opened the back door and motioned to someone. Then he turned back to her, leaving the door ajar.

'That's why I was driving at stupid o'clock,' she continued. 'What's your name again?' She'd tried and tried to remember, but it hadn't come back to her.

'Hamish,' Ginger told her, with a grin. 'I'm the Clinical Nurse Manager at the Barker hospital.'

'A man?' The words escaped from her before she could stop them, then she giggled. 'Sorry, this green thing, full of good painkillers, you said—' She waved the long thin tube around. 'It must be making me talk rubbish!'

'Yep, the green whistle,' Hamish answered, laughter in his voice. 'It does loosen you up a little. But yeah, in answer to your question, I'm a male nurse in a very small country town, which was cause for a few raised eyebrows when I first started. And I had plenty of people ask me if I was gay, which I'm not, in case you were wondering, because everyone else seems to.

'I've been here a few months now and everyone is really welcoming and accepting. There's something about Barker, it gets into your blood or does crazy things to a bloke, because I've even started to think of it as home.'

'Granny and Pa have lived there all their lives,' Sassi said. 'Well, out on the farm. They only moved to town when Abe got married. You must know something about Granny, she was at the hospital last night.'

'I wasn't on shift last night, Sassi,' Hamish said quietly.

There was something about the nurse's demeanour that made Sassi think he wasn't telling her the truth.

Before she could answer, the door opened fully and the sunlight streamed in, making Sassi squint from the brightness.

Hamish stood up and moved out of the ambulance as he talked. 'Sassi, this is Dave Burrows, your local dog whisperer. He's a police officer at Barker. Dave, Sassi is asking about her grandmother.'

The two men exchanged glances and then Dave climbed into the ambulance.

Sassi stared at the man with the kind blue eyes.

Her mouth was dry and she brought the green whistle to her lips and sucked hard, as if the gas inside could cancel out what Dave was going to tell her.

'Your uncle was worried about you and came in to report you missing earlier today. Almost the same time as the phone call came in, reporting the accident,' Dave began. 'I'm sure you know Abe had been at your grandparents' house while we were there last night.'

The lump in Sassi's throat was so large, she couldn't speak. Instead, she nodded.

'We've let your family know that you're okay and Abe's going to meet us at the hospital.'

'And Granny?'

Dave paused. 'How about we talk about that when you get to the hospital and you've been checked out by the doc. He's at Barker visiting his patients as we speak.'

'I didn't make it in time, did I?' Her voice broke as grief washed over her.

Granny, the woman who had held her hand, loved her, read to her, guided her, been her inspiration in so many ways—gone.

'I'm sorry,' Dave said quietly, but she almost couldn't hear him for the rushing in her head. 'She passed away early this morning.'

Sassi covered her mouth with her hand, tears rolling down her cheeks now. She tried to not make any noise, or to let her body give away the fact she was crying. Instead, with her eyes closed, she pictured Granny at the kitchen bench, a floury rolling pin in her hand as she rolled out pastry for a quiche. Or showing Sassi how to make envelope corners on her bed. Or helping Pa out of his chair and walking beside him, gently guiding him to the sunroom, or to the table or to bed.

Her beautiful, selfless granny.

A thought struck her. 'What time?'

'Sorry?'

'What time did she die?'

'I'm not sure of the exact time of death.' He paused and looked at her. 'What time was your accident?'

'Not sure. Maybe it happened at the same time.'

'Funnier things have happened, Sassi.' He gave her hand a squeeze.

Sassi knew exactly what Dave meant. She'd heard stories of people who had died and, at the exact time of their passing, they'd appeared to loved ones who were too far away to be there with them when it happened.

Had Granny been with her as she'd been driving? She tried to remember every moment. When she'd been frightened, or when she'd cried. Could she remember a calming hand on her shoulder or arm? Maybe she could. Or, Sassi's brain teased her, are you just recalling it that way because that's what you want to remember?

'Let's get you to the hospital and properly checked out,' Dave said. 'I'm sorry I didn't have better news for you.'

Sassi felt the ambulance move from side to side as Mia got in and the engine started. Seconds later, Hamish was back alongside her, his warm hand feeling for her pulse and checking her vitals.

'I'm so sorry, Sassi,' she thought she heard him say, but the rocking motion of the ambulance, coupled with her exhaustion, grief and trauma, lulled her into the safety of sleep.

CHAPTER 6

'Geez, Sass, you gave us a scare.'

Sassi turned from the hospital window that looked out over the familiar ground of browned lawn and trees.

'Abe.' She tried to move quickly, but her whole body ached, and her scalp pulled where the doctor had inserted four stitches. Bruises criss-crossed her body, but as Hamish had told her earlier, it seemed that all her injuries were superficial.

'No point in keeping you in here when you need to be with your family,' he'd told her. 'But if you get any symptoms like dizziness or vomiting, you must come back straightaway.'

He'd looked at her so sternly, she'd said, 'I promise!'

Abe now enveloped her in his arms and Sassi breathed in her uncle's familiar smell.

'She's gone?' Her voice broke as she muttered into his chest.

'I'm sorry, Sass. Yeah. She didn't wake up.'

'Why?' God, she felt like a three-year-old, asking questions to which the answers didn't matter because Granny was dead and there wasn't any changing that.

Abe took a step back and gathered her face in his hands, smoothing back her hair as he did. 'Her heart gave out. It was time. She'd been tired for a while now. But how are you? The doc says you're okay, that all your injuries are minor.'

She nodded and watched his eyes search her face, before giving a rueful smile. 'You'd be very disappointed in me, Abe. I used the brake when I shouldn't have. Reflex reaction.'

He pulled her to him again. 'I'm just glad you're going to heal quick sticks.'

'What about Pa? Where's he?'

'Still in the house, but we're going to have to organise care as quickly as we can, otherwise he's going to need to go into a home.'

Sassi heard running feet and laughing, then two little boys tumbled into the room. Two little much-longed-for humans, who had taken too many rounds of IVF to appear.

'Sassi!' one called and threw his arms around her legs. The other stood back a little and waited for his turn.

'Ah, look at you,' Sassi said, falling to her knees and pulling the first one in close, ignoring the soreness in her body. 'Harry, I swear you've grown so tall since I saw you last! How old are you now?'

'I'm four and so's he.' Harry pointed at his brother.

'That's because you're twins!' Sassi said, laughing. 'Jimmy, where's my hug?'

Another little warm body pressed into hers and she hugged her cousins tightly. She couldn't believe how normal she was acting, when inside she felt as if she'd cried thousands of tears since she'd heard Granny was gone.

She dropped kisses on both the little boys' foreheads and hugged them again.

'You're squishing me,' Harry said, twisting away.

'Sorry.' Sassi let them both go. 'Where's your mummy?'

'Right here.'

In the doorway a tall, blonde woman smiled at them all. Sassi had always marvelled how Renee had kept her shape after giving birth to twins.

'Renee.' Sassi stood now and hugged her aunt by marriage.

Both Abe and Renee were close to her age—only five years older—and so often they felt more like her brother and sister than aunt and uncle, which is why they'd told her to drop the aunt and uncle titles many years ago.

'Don't ever do that again, Sassi,' Renee said, her voice sounding as if her throat had closed over. 'Don't frighten us . . .' Her voice trailed off as she squeezed Sassi's hand and looked into her eyes.

Sassi looked from Renee to Abe, then down to the little boys who were now wrestling each other in the corner, her heart swelling. 'I'll try not to,' she answered, pushing her emotions down. How good it was to be home and enveloped by love. Not having to battle on her own in another town, on another farm, by herself.

'Are you ready to go?' Abe asked. 'We're going to see Dad.' His face dropped for a second. 'We've got to organise the funeral.'

At those words Sassi wanted to let out a guttural cry. To throw herself on the bed and sob unchecked until she didn't have any more tears left inside her, but she couldn't. Not with the twins in the room.

Fanny Lumsden's song 'Grown Ups' flashed into her mind. Fanny sang of how the people they'd always thought of as the adults, the people in charge, were passing on and now the ones left behind were the grown-ups.

I'm not ready for this, Sassi thought. *I'm not ready to be the adult. Granny should still be here to look after us.*

That wasn't how life worked though. The child became the adult, while the adult became the elderly and the elderly had to die. That was the way it went.

Forcing a smile, she faced her family. 'Yeah, I'm ready.' She reached for the bag of medication that Hamish had left on the bed when he'd signed the discharge papers after the doctor had given her the all-clear.

'Jimmy, Harry, can you please carry Sassi's bag between you?' Abe indicated to the duffle bag someone had extracted from the ute and brought with them in the ambulance.

'I love Jarrah,' Harry said, putting his hand into Sassi's, leaving Jimmy to pick up the bag.

'Do you? I bet she's loving being with you.' Sassi gave a look of mock alarm. 'But I hope you haven't let her inside? She can be very messy.'

'Nah, dogs can't be messy,' Jimmy said as he took her other hand with his spare one. 'Can they?' Uncertainty filtered through his words.

Looking down at the serious blue eyes staring up at her, Sassi wanted to cry again. Her grandmother wouldn't see these two precious little people grow to become men. How Granny had loved these two. Baking for them, playing cards with them, taking them for walks when they'd come to town.

'Well, she drops a lot of fur because her coat is thick. And that means lots of sweeping and vacuuming. Are either of you good at that type of housework? You'll need to be so you can help Mum out.'

Renee gave a little laugh. 'I think the boys are excellent at bringing dirt into the house and then pushing it around with their tractors and bulldozers rather than helping. Aren't you, boys?' she said, lugging the duffle bag.

In the hallway now, they walked towards the nurses' station.

'Hey, Dad!' Harry yelled and took off down the hallway. 'Look at this!' His legs stopped and he let his feet slide along the polished floor for an incredibly long time before he overbalanced and landed on his hip.

'Shh, stop it, Harry. You're not on the farm now.' Abe hurried along and scooped his son up in his arms before the boy could utter another word. 'You need to be quiet in a hospital. There are sick people here.'

'But it's so slippery!'

'Yeah, and you should have shoes on, not just socks.'

'Too hot for shoes,' Harry informed the whole hospital.

'If it's too hot for shoes, then surely it's too hot for socks,' Abe said.

'Shh!' Renee tried, but now Jimmy had dropped Sassi's hand, pulled off his shoes and copied Harry's slide. 'Oh my god.' Renee put her hand to her forehead. 'I'm going to have to take these two home, Abe,' she said. 'I can't have them in your father's house like this. He won't cope with the noise.' Glancing over at Sassi, she shook her head. 'Bring on school. Two days a week at kindy is nowhere near enough!'

It was only then that Sassi noticed the tiredness that seemed to have seeped into Renee's face and settled there. Her smile was still as bright and her face as welcoming and happy, but her eyes were bloodshot with dark rings underneath.

Abe grabbed Jimmy's collar and hoisted him to his feet. 'Behave,' he growled and put Harry on the floor. 'Another word out of either of you and there'll be trouble.'

Sassi caught a sidelong glance from Harry to Jimmy, trying to get his attention to cause more mischief. Jimmy averted his gaze on purpose.

Nice to see he listened to his parents, even if Harry didn't! The family had been told that when Abe and Renee went through the IVF treatment, a multiple birth could be a possibility. Abe had joked that having twins must be like having a mini school yard—some classes only had two kids in them in the country.

The twins' antics now made Sassi agree with Abe's words, back before they had known how chaotic life would become.

'You haven't told me if you've taken Jarrah inside,' Sassi said, trying to distract them both. She could almost see their active minds churning at what type of mischief was up next.

Before they answered, Hamish appeared and smiled at them all. 'Ah, so you're ready to go?' he asked, nodding to Abe and Renee.

The two little boys looked up at Hamish, eyes wide. No wonder, Sassi thought, because he was very tall and with his shock of red hair and skin that was covered in freckles he would stand out on the street in Barker. Especially in his nurse's uniform.

'Yep, everyone is here to take me home,' she said. 'Do you know my uncle and aunt, Abe and Renee?'

Hamish held out his hand to both. 'I haven't yet had the pleasure. But that's a good thing because it means you're all healthy. And,' he paused, 'I'm sorry to hear about your mother's passing, Abe.'

'Yeah, thanks. It was a bit of a shock, but at the same time it wasn't.'

Hamish nodded his understanding. 'And who are these two tearaways?' He bent down, his hand in his pocket.

Harry stood tall in front of Hamish. 'I'm Harry and he's Jimmy.'

'G'day there, Harry and Jimmy.' Hamish pulled out two lollipops. 'Do you like lollipops?'

'Cor, yeah,' the twins answered together, hands outstretched. They began trying to pull the wrappers off and silence descended on the hospital once more.

Hamish stood and assessed Sassi. 'You understand how to use all the medication and that if you get dizzy or any pain you haven't felt before, you need to come back?'

'Yeah, I will.'

He put his hand on her shoulder. 'Make sure you're kind to yourself. You've had a couple of big shocks, so you're sure to feel a bit wonky for a little while.'

'Are you her boyfriend?' Harry asked from around the lollipop he'd finally managed to get the wrapping off.

Sassi let out a gasp, while Abe put his hand to his eyes and shook his head.

Hamish just grinned. 'No, I'm a nurse in charge of the hospital here and your—' He looked at Sassi for help.

'Cousin,' Renee said.

'Cousin,' Hamish continued, ignoring everyone's embarrassment, 'has been in the wars.'

'Who with?' This time it was Jimmy asking the questions. He turned his face to Sassi. 'Who did you fight? Dad says it's bad to fight.'

'A kangaroo,' Sassi told him.

The boys looked at her as if she were joking. 'You can't fight a kangaroo,' Jimmy told her scornfully. 'They rip ya guts open and all your insides—'

'Oh my god,' Renee muttered under her breath. She spoke in a no-nonsense tone. 'That's enough, Jimmy. Let's get to the car. Now.' She turned to Hamish. 'Thank you, and sorry. And so you know, I am a good parent, it's just that sometimes they like to shock. Nice to meet you. What do you say, boys?'

Both Harry and Jimmy seemed to know they were beaten. 'Thanks for the lollipop,' the boys chorused together. They followed their mother out of the hospital, Harry pausing at the door and turning back. 'All your insides fall out on the ground,' he said.

Renee grabbed his arm and pulled him through the door.

Hamish chuckled. 'I'll remember that,' he called back.

Sassi snorted and Abe looked mortified.

Only eight months had passed since she'd last seen her cousins and they seemed to have grown not only in size, but in personality and cheekiness. No wonder Renee looked tired.

'Sorry about that,' Abe said. 'They're terrors. Both of them.'

'Not at all,' Hamish said. 'Good fun, I'd say.' He turned his attention back to Sassi. 'Now, since you know what it's like to have a fight with a kangaroo, my professional advice is to try to avoid that again. Okay?'

This time, Sassi laughed, and the action felt foreign to her. When was the last time she'd done more than just smile? Well before she and Ewin had broken up, she was sure. Life had seemed to take them over and they'd forgotten to laugh and talk for a long time.

'I promise not to fight with another roo if I can help it,' she said. 'And thank you for everything.'

'You were lucky you weren't killed, Sassi,' Abe said.

'And even more lucky to come out with so few injuries,' Hamish added.

'I know.'

'Right-oh. Well, I hope I don't have to see you again,' Hamish said. 'If you get my meaning.'

They said their goodbyes and Abe ushered her out of the hospital, towards his ute.

Sassi squinted in the sunlight. 'Well, that was a homecoming if ever there was one,' she said, glancing around. Then the reality of Granny's death and the rolling wave of grief hit her again.

They would be at her grandparents' house in about seven minutes and her grandmother wasn't going to be there. She turned to look back at the hospital, guessing that's where her body was, in the cold morgue. Waiting.

Swallowing, she walked alongside Abe, listening as he talked.

'Dave called the tow truck and I've organised for your ute to go to the wreckers in Port Augusta, because it's totalled. The insurance company will write it off for sure.

'Anyhow, there's a spare ute at the farm you can use, or maybe you can use Mum and Dad's car. Dad's not going to be using it and Mum—' Abe cleared his throat. He didn't continue.

Sassi gave a little shudder at the thought of being behind the wheel again. The shattering of glass and crunching of steel kept echoing every time she let her guard down. It felt like a heavy cloak was smothering her, just as the roof had, every time she shut her eyes.

As if reading her mind, Abe tossed her the keys. 'You can drive. Get straight back on the horse.'

CHAPTER 7

Kim put the lid on the last alfoil container and pressed it shut.

Even with the air-conditioner on, it was hot and there was sweat running beneath her long, curly blonde hair, which she'd pulled under the hair net she wore.

Her kitchen smelt of roast lamb, lamb stew and corned beef. The leftover roast lamb she'd sliced and left to cool, so later she could make up plates of cold meat and salad.

Taking off her apron and washing her hands in the sink, Kim counted the containers. Five of roast lamb and three of stew. Four corned beef. She needed a trip to Port Augusta to get some chicken so she could mix the meals up a bit. Her freezer was a bit low on meat.

The front door opened, the heat rushing down the passageway into the kitchen.

'God, what a horrible day,' Dave said as the door banged shut, sending the photos on the walls swinging. 'That bloody wind! Geez, it's been hot.'

Coming around to the other side of the bench, Kim gave her husband a kiss and handed him a cold drink from the fridge. 'You okay, honey? What a day for there to be an accident.'

His tiredness after working for hours in the heat didn't take away his good looks. Dave was still, well, hot. That was the only word for him. Even with his hair turning grey and silver-framed glasses on his nose, Dave turned heads. He had a magnetism that not many people possessed.

'Revolting day, and thank god that car didn't spark a fire. Who knows what would have happened if it had. All the emergency services were there, pulling their weight, but we didn't have a fire truck.

'Sassi is a very lucky girl. How she didn't have her neck broken—' He shook his head. 'Bloody kangaroos.'

'Is she out of hospital?'

'Yep. She was incredibly dehydrated, but some deep bruising and a gash on her head were her only injuries. Doc told her she could go the minute he'd finished checking her over.'

He focused on her. 'You're a sight for sore eyes.'

Kim smiled again and ran her finger down his arm. 'So sexy . . .'

Dave pulled her into a hug. 'You shouldn't talk about yourself like that. I might get all sorts of ideas.'

She swatted him. 'You need a shower.'

'You're not wrong there.'

'And I have to run these meals across to Mr Stapleton. His daughter-in-law rang me today and asked if I'd make up a few days' worth of meals for him. Just until they can get some help from outside. You have a shower and I'll be back.'

Dave dropped a kiss on her head and then went to the fridge to pour another glass of cordial. 'Didn't they have help already?'

'They might have had someone pop in once a week and do the bigger chores, like hanging out the sheets and so on, but they've been carrying much of the load by themselves.

'Amber has been living in South Africa for years now. Married a guy from over there. Not sure when she was home last.'

'Yeah, Abe said something about that. She's the daughter, right?'

'Abe's sister.' Kim started to stack the containers into an esky. Next, she reached into the fridge and grabbed some tomatoes, slicing them and adding onion, which was already chopped. A few shakes of salt and pepper and a splash of vinegar, the salad was done. Another container into the esky.

'I haven't seen you make that salad for ages,' Dave commented as he started to unbutton his shirt.

'The older generation love it when I make the old-style meals like corned beef. You know I like to try to cook what they like to eat, otherwise, what's the point of Catering

Angels?' she said. 'We need to give them food they love. That way, even if they don't feel hungry they at least pick at their dinner.'

Dave patted her bum on the way past. 'Should be called Cooked With Love,' he said as he headed for the bathroom.

'Great name! Where were you when I was trying to think of one.'

'Do you know if the family has got anyone in mind to look after Mr Stapleton?' Dave called from the shower.

Kim added a green salad and container of white sauce to her stack, then followed him through, leaning against the door, watching the steam fill the bathroom.

'I don't think so. There's a home-care company that come over once a week from Port Augusta who clean houses, and collect washing, but there aren't any full-time care options that I know about. Unless he goes into the hospital, but that's not ideal either. Sometimes the oldies just need their familiar surrounds, and if they don't require full-time care, why should they have to go into a sterile environment that runs on shifts and times, like a hospital?'

'Does he need that amount of care?'

Kim could hear the soap suds hitting the tiles as Dave washed his face and hair. On the mirror, she drew a love heart.

I love you.

'Not sure. I can find out. Why are you asking? Have you got an idea?'

Dave stuck his soapy face out from behind the curtain. 'Well, I just might. Joan's been mentioning a lady who arrived in town a few weeks ago and is looking for work. She might be suited to a job like this.'

'Do tell.' Kim flicked away the soap from near his eyes and leaned in to touch his lips.

'Careful, I might have to drag you in here,' he said, his blue eyes sparkling with mischief.

'In my clothes?' Kim sounded horrified at the thought. They both knew she didn't mean it.

'Come on,' he tugged at her hand gently. 'Come in here with me.'

Kim gave him a slow, suggestive smile and reached behind to unclip her bra.

~

'What can you tell me about the Stapletons?' Dave asked. He took a sip of beer and ran a hand through his damp hair. 'Here, I'll take that.'

'Thanks.' Kim handed him the esky and picked up a plate filled with roast lamb and veggies, for tonight's meal. 'I don't know that there's much to tell. Farmers, the parents moved to town not long after Abe and Renee got married. Not sure how long ago that was, but the twins are four or five I suppose.

'They're a bundle of trouble those two,' she said with affection. 'They sometimes come into the roadhouse when I'm there, pestering their mother for a bucket of chips or an ice cream. They love iced chocolate drinks and green snakes.

'I remember both Abe and Renee were going to Adelaide a lot before they were born and there were some rumours they were having IVF.'

Kim led the way down the hall to their garage as she talked. 'Amber, the daughter, left to go to boarding school in Year Eight. Like so many kids here do. Then she got pregnant and came back to finish her pregnancy at the farm.

'Sassi was born here and, to be very honest, I couldn't tell you whether Amber finished her schooling after Sassi was born, or not. Mr Stapleton is very old-fashioned and the talk of the town was he was upset his daughter had a child when she wasn't married.'

Dave grunted as he set down the esky. 'Bit ironic if the IVF story has any truth to it.'

'Huh, very true. Hadn't thought about it like that. But we really didn't see Amber much once Sassi was born. They were living out on the farm, and one day we realised no one had seen her for ages. Then Abe told his teachers that she'd gone. Left Sassi and gone away. Sassi was quite small. Maybe four or five. I remember because there was a bit of gossip around town as to where Amber had gone. Some said she'd left to get away from her parents, others thought Sassi's father had come back and picked up Amber.' Kim tucked her hair behind her ears. 'No one knew for sure and the gossip never bothered Mrs Stapleton. She just carried on, loving Sassi and ignoring everyone else. As she liked to do.' Pausing, Kim tapped her finger to the roof of the car. 'There was a lot of conjecture over who the father was, and again, whether he was local or not. I'm sure that question has never been answered. Or, if it has, I don't know the answer.'

Kim opened the driver's door and popped the boot for Dave to put the esky in. 'Why don't you come over and see for yourself? And you can carry that esky for me.' She winked as Dave looked around the edge of the car.

'Your wish is my command,' he quipped. 'Don't know what you've got in here, but it's as heavy as a tank.'

Letting out a giggle, Kim climbed into the driver's seat and hit the button to raise the garage door.

'How did Mia go today? Was the road accident the first she'd attended?' Kim asked when Dave settled himself next to her.

He clipped in his seatbelt. 'All things considered, she did well. It's not easy being out in that sort of heat, let alone dealing with a highly emotional situation. Driving the ambulance was new to her, too, but she seemed to handle it. Glad we did some of that training a few months ago.' He gave a sigh. 'I'm going to have to try to rustle up some more volunteers from somewhere. We're so short.'

'Every town needs more volunteers,' Kim said. 'No one seems to want to put their hand up for anything anymore. Kids' sports clubs, sports clubs in general. The Rotary Club in Broad River is going to fold, I heard. Not enough people committing to help out. It's really sad. Our towns are built on volunteers and community spirit.'

'It's a huge worry when we have accidents or fires. I know we need all the other kind of volunteers as well, but the ones we need for Barker will save lives.'

They were silent for a moment, then Kim said, 'I left some dinner in the fridge for Mia. Thought she'd be buggered like you.' Kim paused. 'Neither Chris nor Josie have been back since her grandmother's funeral . . .' She left the sentence hanging. 'I'm a bit worried she hasn't made too many friends here yet.'

Chris had been through the academy with Mia, and Josie was her best friend. Both had spent time in Barker on and off and Kim liked them very much.

'I wish Chris would get up the courage to ask Mia to be something more than a friend. It's so obvious that he's in love with her.' Kim flicked on the blinker to turn onto the main street and waved at a couple of young kids riding their bikes on the footpath.

'Hard being a country cop, as you know,' Dave murmured thoughtfully, then he seemed to snap to. He shot her a glance. 'Don't you go interfering.'

'As if I would,' Kim said demurely.

'That's exactly what you'd do.'

'And it worked for Jack and Zara.' Her tone was smug. 'Zara rang today actually. She's going to be up around here in the next couple of weeks, to interview some farmers, so she asked if she could come and stay a night or two.'

'Your ex-partner,' she said, referring to Jack, 'has only got another two weeks of detective training and he's done. Apparently, he's loving it.'

'Yeah, I spoke to him a couple of days ago. He's hoping to go into Major Crime when he's finished. Jack would like that sort of investigation, but every adrenalin junky wants to get into Major Crime, so he's going to have to stand out. He's more of a plodder. Methodical. Which is in fact why Major Crime would be great for him.'

Kim turned the car into a narrow driveway on a hill overlooking the plains that surrounded the town.

'Neat little cottage, isn't it?'

The fence facing the road was lined with roses, while the eastern side had lavender blooms and the west geraniums. A thin path ran to the front door, and on either side there was lawn that was still green, but looked like it needed a good water.

A ute was parked on the footpath and, despite the cheery garden, a heaviness hung over the house.

Before Dave and Kim could get out of the car, the front door swung open and Abe was gesturing them to come inside.

'Hi,' he called. 'Dad's nearly ready for dinner. Come on in.'

Kim collected the dinner plate and waited until Dave had the esky before walking up the path. She paused next to Abe and put her hand on his arm. 'I'm sorry to hear about your mum, Abe.'

'Yeah, thanks.' Abe nodded and Kim continued down the hallway inside.

In the kitchen she put the plate down and looked around. The room was worn, but clean and cared for. A vase of roses was in the middle of the table.

Kim felt a sting of melancholy as she remembered that the woman who picked these, probably only a couple of days ago, was no longer with them. Their petals hadn't fallen, and yet she was gone.

A thud came from another room and Kim peered into a doorway to see an elderly man sitting in a rocking chair with a cane close by. His mouth opened and closed in concentration as he tried to get up.

'Can I help you, Mr Stapleton?' Going into the room, Kim realised the seat was too low for him. She took his arm, and he grunted his thanks.

'Where would you like to go?'

'Out.' The word was muffled as if a rag had been placed in the old man's mouth. Kim had to think for a moment, trying to work out exactly what he meant.

'Outside? Or to the kitchen?' she asked.

Mr Stapleton seemed to ignore her. He put his cane purposely in front of him and shifted one leg in a dragging motion, while the other moved easily.

'Careful, Dad.' Abe came in and took his arm.

'Oomph.' The elderly man snapped, pulling away.

He teetered for a moment and Kim held her breath, wondering if he was going to fall, but somehow he got his balance and continued shuffling towards the kitchen.

Abe closed his eyes, just as the back door banged. 'I don't know how Mum did it,' he said. 'I can't always work out what he's saying.'

'I think I've found what you wanted, Pa,' a female voice said. 'Is this it?'

A young lady with two black eyes, bruising on her arms and stitches on her scalp walked in holding a photo album.

Kim smiled. 'Hello, you must be Sassi.'

'Here.' Mr Stapleton held out his hand.

'Yes, I am, hello. Oh, hello.' She sounded surprised at seeing Dave in the house, then her gaze cut across to the man who was swaying slightly. 'Come and sit here, Pa,' she said, putting the album on the kitchen table.

His shaky hand reached for the table, but he didn't sit. Instead, he flipped open the cover and gazed at the inside.

Over his shoulder, Kim saw black-and-white wedding photos. One with Mrs Stapleton by herself, holding a bunch of roses. Then another one with Mr Stapleton, tall, strong and dressed in a suit.

'How are you feeling, Sassi? I heard you had a nasty accident,' Kim asked as Mr Stapleton started to pull out a chair and sink down.

'Considering where I was at six this morning, I'm one thousand per cent better, thank you.' She paused. 'I'm sorry, I'm not sure I . . .'

'This is my wife, Kim,' Dave said. 'And you are looking one thousand per cent better than you did this morning. In fact, I can't believe you're out of hospital. Don't you have even a headache?'

'A little bit of one, but I didn't bang my head. The only reason I had stitches was because the rear-view mirror glass cut me. Pretty lucky, huh?'

''Ere,' Mr Stapleton grunted. ''Is un.' His arthritic finger, lined with age and sun damage, tapped on a photo. Shakily he tried to pull the photo from the plastic covering but

Sassi gently put her hands on his arthritic fingers and did it for him.

Kim looked and saw them together as a couple now; the woman was dressed in a simple white cotton dress, gloves and hat, while the man stood looking solemn and smart if not uncomfortable in his formal clothes.

They stood outside the town hall, just the two of them. No one else.

'No' 'ast.' His eyes didn't leave the picture and his voice was soft.

'What was that?' Abe leaned forward.

Mr Stapleton spoke slowly and what Kim assumed he thought was clearly, but the noises were only part words. 'No' 'ast.'

'No' 'ast,' she repeated silently to herself. 'Oh, do you mean no last? Not last? Something like that?' She looked around. 'Is there a notepad and pen he can write it down on?'

'His right hand doesn't work too well either,' Abe said. 'But now you've said that, I know what he means. Mum's parents told him that they wouldn't last as a couple. Said that Mum was too good for him and she'd get sick of not having any money.' He patted his father on the shoulder as he took the photo and looked at it, a soft smile on his face. 'That was taken fifty-plus years ago, wasn't it, Dad? So I reckon they were wrong, don't you?'

CHAPTER 8

After everyone had left and the dishes had been washed, Sassi lay, exhausted, on the faded rose-patterned bedspread, a gift from Granny and Pa one birthday.

It wasn't the year her mother had left; that had been a few years before. Sassi chose to forget how old she'd been when Amber had announced she'd fallen in love with a farmer from South Africa and was moving there. Leaving Sassi behind.

The argument that had followed, from behind closed doors and in hushed tones, had set her heart racing. She hadn't really understood what all the words had meant, but she was old enough to realise they were about her, and her mother going to live somewhere else without her.

'How can you choose a man over your child?' Granny had asked.

Sassi had pressed the side of her head to the door and listened very hard. She could still feel the coolness of the wood beneath her ear and how the door had rattled a little when her pa had thumped his fist on the table.

'She'll have a better life here,' Amber said, her voice low. 'It's dangerous over there.'

'Then why are you going.' It hadn't been a question.

'Because I love him.'

'But you love your daughter, don't you?' Pa had stood, Sassi was sure because there were heavy footsteps rounding the kitchen table.

She imagined him standing in front of her mother. Tall, imposing. His shock of unruly grey hair and dark navy eyes made anyone feel like he was penetrating their soul when he was angry.

'Of course I do. But the education system is better here. Sassi has her friends here—'

Pa broke in over the top of her excuses. 'A woman is supposed to raise her children, not give them away because they don't suit her anymore.'

The scraping of a chair on the wooden floor had made Sassi shrink back from the door and press herself into the darkness, in case someone came flying out. She shouldn't be listening.

'You listen to me, Father, and listen well.'

Sassi clamped her hand over her mouth to stop a gasp escaping. Her mother had never raised her voice to her pa before. He'd never allow such behaviour in his house.

'He loves me. I would have thought you'd be happy to get rid of me considering the shame I've brought on your family name. Oh yeah, I've heard you praying to your God

at night, asking for forgiveness for my sin. For my illegitimate kid. The disgrace you must feel when you turn up to
church and know that everyone is aware that your daughter
has a bastard child. Now you're not going to have to worry,
because I won't be in your house, and I won't be in your
face. You can forget about me and pretend that Sassi is
yours. It's not like there's much of an age gap between her
and Abe anyway.'

'Amber.' Granny's tone was pleading now. 'Don't. We
can work something out. Dad's right. A mother's place *is*
with her child.'

'No matter the circumstances, apparently. No, Mum.
I'm leaving and you can raise Sassi the way you want to.
Hopefully, she won't be the disappointment I am, and you
can support her the way you haven't supported me. That's
all there is to it.'

Sassi had scrambled to her room and picked up a book,
pretending to read. Back then, the words her mother had
spat at her grandparents had been jumbled to her young
mind, but a few years later they had sunk in and the hurt
was still close to the surface.

Now, here on the rose-patterned bedspread, she curled
into a ball, still hearing her mother's voice. *She'll have a
better life here.*

Sassi hadn't been given a choice.

When Sassi's feelings overwhelmed her, the devil's advo-
cate voice in her head always asked if she would have
wanted to live in South Africa with her mother. The
short answer was she hadn't been given a choice so how

could she know? The long answer was that if her mother hadn't wanted her when she was in Australia, she certainly wouldn't have given her any extra time living in another country with a new love. So yes, she'd been better off with her grandparents.

A few moments later, she got up. Her chest of drawers was next to the door; Granny had kept all her things in the move to town and made sure this room was ready for her whenever she came back. The top drawer was filled with large hair scrunchies, all in loud colours. There was also an old brush and a tin of hairspray. Her Discman was in the second drawer and she reached for it, clicking open the deck. The large, loopy letters of her younger, immature writing told her the songs were from the top ten hits from the local radio station 5CS—the program had been streamed from Port Pirie.

She'd loved Sunday afternoons, lying on her bed with her sketchbook listening to the top ten countdown. Sassi wondered if the radio station was still in existence. Maybe she'd tune the radio in her ute tomorrow and see what happened.

Her scalp tugged where the stitches were and she remembered there wasn't a ute anymore. It was totalled. The insurance would have to go through before she could even look at buying another one.

Moving her attention to the bookshelf, she ran her fingers along the spines as she read the titles. *Sweet Valley High*, *Trixie Belden*, *What Katy Did*, *The Baby-Sitters Club*. Back then, she'd been jealous of the characters in these books, having a father in their lives, but those books had given her many hours of pleasure.

And they had made Granny put her hands on her hips and outright laugh at Sassi when she'd declared that she wanted a phone in her room, 'like Elizabeth and Jessica from the *Sweet Valley High* books'.

'Is that really what you want?' she'd replied.

'Can I please, Granny? Everyone else has phones in their own room.'

'Do they now?' She sounded vaguely incredulous.

Sassi remembered nodding vigorously. 'They do!'

Oh, how silly she'd been!

'Well, I'll just give Mrs Trapper a call and see if Holly has one in hers,' she'd said, picking up the receiver. 'Then we can talk about it.'

Heat had flooded Sassi's cheeks. Her friend didn't have a phone in her bedroom. She knew that. Granny knew that. Only the girls in *Sweet Valley High* books did.

'Don't worry about it,' she'd huffed and flounced out of the room, covering her embarrassment with annoyance.

She'd gone back to the books and lost herself in the world of Todd Wilkins and basketball and creative writing, because she'd always liked Elizabeth's character more than Jessica's.

Sassi chuckled to herself at the recollection, her eyes swinging around, searching for the next memory.

A class photo hung on the wall. Her Year Twelve class. Only ten of them. Three boys and the rest girls.

Holly stood at one end of the first row and Sassi at the other. They'd been the shorter ones. Rick Patman had been in the middle because he was the tallest. Sassi remembered when Granny had rung to tell her he'd been killed in a car accident a year after they'd left school.

And what a scandal there'd been when Courtney Wilson had become pregnant at eighteen while studying medicine.

She wasn't sure where any of the others were now. Except for Holly. She knew where Holly was.

Holly, her smart and clever friend. They were the bookish ones, not popular or sporty. Spending time in the library together, or in a quiet corner of the playground, talking about the books they'd read or what sketches or stories they'd created overnight. They'd had a secret society with a badge. Just like the Secret Seven, except they weren't about solving mysteries.

Not that there were any mysteries in Barker.

They were the CC. The Creative Collective. Only people who loved art, writing or photography were allowed to join and that was just the two of them. Everyone else in the class loved footy, netball, collecting sports cards and wanted to be either nurses, teachers or shearers.

Where was that badge? Sassi wondered, turning to look through the drawers of her desk. Pens, pencils, pretty pencil cases. Her sketchbook. How long had it been since she'd sketched a picture? Probably the same length of time since she'd laughed properly.

Opening the pages, she saw the black-and-white portraits she'd drawn of Uncle Abe; Granny feeding the chooks;

flowers, trees, hills. All from the farm where Abe lived now. Where she had grown up. A sketch on another page brought back memories of exactly where she was when she'd drawn it, and how she'd felt.

A familiar surge of anger hit her in the chest with such force she drew a breath.

The night she'd drawn the picture, Sassi had sat on her bed, smarting with fury, abandonment and fear. It had been some time after her mother had left, but all those emotions were still as raw as they had been on the day Amber had walked out. Sassi had drawn quickly, dark and angry slashes across the page. She'd drawn from memory, and it wasn't of her mother's face.

It had been Amber's back as she'd walked away, holding a suitcase.

That day, her mother's kiss goodbye had been brisk and dry. No hug, no 'I love you'. Pa hadn't been in the house. He'd taken off to the back paddock and, given his temper, everyone knew that was for the best. Granny had been standing next to the car, stony-faced. Hands on hips. Her lips were moving as Amber had thrown her suitcase on the back seat and jumped behind the steering wheel. Sassi couldn't hear what her granny was saying.

Amber had ignored her mother and driven down the road without a backwards glance.

To Sassi's knowledge, since then Pa had only spoken to his daughter on birthdays and at Christmas. He said he was too busy for small talk but Sassi suspected he was still angry he and Granny had been left to raise their grandchild.

Granny had sent letters every month and Amber replied with long newsy ones back. Life was so wonderful in South Africa, and she and Zola were very happy. The farm was doing well, and she was running the house with the help of servants. Zola was farming macadamia nuts and green maize.

Oh, she asked about Sassi, sent her presents and rang her every month on top of the letters. But Sassi noticed the joy in her mother's tone and the fact that she never said she missed her or invited her to stay.

After Amber's calls, Granny had always hugged Sassi a little more tightly than other days and told her she loved her a little more often.

Sassi threw the sketchbook back into the drawer and dropped back onto the bed, her hand under her head as she stared at the dull white ceiling with the dull white light glowing.

Her relationship with her mother had been strained for sure, and she'd often daydreamed about her father. A tall handsome man who had a nice car and shiny shoes. He'd call for her one day and take her away to a big house with a pool. Granny and Pa would visit, and she would have a parent who loved her. Her dream changed as she grew older, but she always saw him with a house and as a parent who loved her. The dream never came true. At twenty-eight, she still didn't know who her father was.

In the other room, the hum of the TV was muffled as Pa watched the late-night news.

Abe had asked her to stay with Pa for a few nights and Sassi had readily agreed. There was no way her grandfather would be able to look after himself.

'He'll be glad of the company,' Abe had said. 'I'll be back first thing in the morning. Will you be okay?'

'I'll get some sleep if I stay here,' she'd said. 'Your two ferals will probably come and jump on my bed in the middle of the night and scare the crap out of me! Can you feed Jarrah for me? I had dog nuts in the back of the ute . . .' Her voice trailed off. Only her phone, purse and duffle bag had been salvaged from the vehicle.

'Don't be concerned about Jarrah. We've got dog food at home.' Abe had given her a hug before leaving.

She wondered what time her grandfather usually went to bed and if he needed help. When she opened the door, the smell of bourbon hit her.

The lounge was quiet, save for the TV, and the house suddenly felt lonely. There wasn't the usual clicking of Granny's knitting needles, or the whistle of the kettle as she made the nightly cups of tea.

There was Pa, napping in his chair. Sassi hoped he was just asleep. There were stories of couples who had been together for years and years and then died within hours of each other.

She felt even more sadness as she looked at the small, shrivelled man sitting in the rocking chair. Now she was closer, Sassi could see his chest rising and falling steadily. His cane was hooked over his arm and his chin had dropped to his chest.

A side table, next to the chair, held a bowl of nuts and the latest copy of the *Farming Journal*. The magazine was dog-eared and had coffee rings on the front cover. An empty glass and a bottle of bourbon with more than the neck out of it.

Sassi sat down on the couch and looked at the man who had loved her in his own way, but never let her get too close. Funny how people seemed to diminish as they got older. Gravity could shrink even the most imposing person.

Granny's chair, on the other side of the table with a blue and white crochet rug thrown over the back, sat empty. It seemed to make the room feel extra lonely.

On impulse she leaned over and ran her hands over the worn arms. The pile had rubbed almost bare from years of Granny resting her elbows there. Poking up from the pocket on the side of the chair was a gardening magazine, the cover pulled open to the page she'd been reading last. Her glasses were resting on the other arm of the chair, where she'd left them before going to bed. Granny couldn't have known that she was never going to put them back on again.

Another lump in Sassi's throat as her hands touched the cold frames.

God, what a day! Fifteen hours ago, she was upside-down, trapped by the seatbelt in her smashed-up ute, and now here she was sitting next to her sleeping grandfather and her grandmother's empty chair. Her body was aching. Panadol and bed would be a good idea, but there was Pa to consider first.

Sassi's hand dropped to the left-hand side of the couch, where, if she'd been in her own home, Jarrah would have been curled up. Here the floor was empty. She missed her dog.

Her phone vibrated in her pocket with a text message. She ignored it and put her hand back on the arm of the chair. Back and forth, she rubbed her fingers, watching the plush pile darken then lighten each time.

Granny's fingers had rested here, in this exact spot. Sassi ached to feel her grandmother's hand on hers. Long fingers, stroking her hand, pushing her hair back from her forehead, telling her everything was going to be okay.

She felt as if she was watching her life through a surreal filter. Empty and numb.

Granny. Her mouth formed the word silently.

Sassi's phone reminded her there was a message and this time she dug it out, inhaling sharply when she saw the name on her screen.

Ewin?

It had been more than six months since he'd spoken to her.

With trembling fingers, she opened the message and stared at the words.

I'm sorry.

For what? Sassi wondered. *The fact you left. That you didn't love me anymore? Or have you heard about Granny?*

There are too many things you could be sorry for!

The phone told her it was nearly ten o'clock. It was still early in Western Australia where Ewin was.

Carefully she put the phone down.

How to answer?

The noise of a car swished past outside, and lights cut across the room. She should get up and shut the curtains. Granny would have done it hours ago.

Sassi closed her eyes. There was such a heaviness in her arms, head and legs that she felt like she couldn't move from the chair.

'What say we stay right here tonight, Pa?' she whispered and let her head fall back against the couch.

The phone buzzed again, but Sassi didn't open her eyes, even though her brain screamed at her to look at the message and see what Ewin had sent this time.

'Not tonight,' she told the now silent phone. 'No more tonight.'

Moments later there was a loud rapping at the door and Sassi shot out of her seat, heart pounding. Pa jumped, snorted and rearranged himself without waking up.

Sassi stood in the middle of the living room, her hand to her chest. A visitor at ten pm didn't seem right. Maybe it was some kids playing silly buggers.

Silence strung out across the house.

The clock ticked.

Nothing.

Sassi went to the window. The driveway was empty, only the moonlight lit up the garden.

'That's it, bedtime,' she decided. She went to touch Pa's shoulder when the rapping sounded again. This time it was more impatient, and Pa opened his eyes.

'Wha'?'

'It's okay,' she soothed. 'I'm just going to answer the door.' Sassi stepped into the passageway, her heart beating a little faster. 'Who is it?' she asked through the door.

'Open up, Sassi. It's me.'

Sassi blinked and her mouth opened slightly. Even though she hadn't heard that voice for a long time, she'd know it anywhere.

Opening the door, Sassi stared straight at her mother.

CHAPTER 9

My dear son,

I hope you're well. It seems such a long time ago you visited and I'm wondering if you have plans to come back and see us any time soon?

I'm not getting any younger and would love to see you! But you already know that, just as I understand you're happy and have a satisfying life where you are.

Dave put the letter on his lap and looked out across the dark landscape, lit only by half a moon. The night was quiet, save for the bleating of the sheep that were in the paddock two roads away. Noises carried such distances on clear, still nights like this one.

After the heat and fierce wind during the day, the stillness was a relief.

Dave didn't feel relieved though; there was a tug of war going on inside him.

Smoothing the page out on his lap, he went back to his mother's words.

Darling, I know you found your last visit difficult. And I don't believe there are words for you to explain to anyone how much you must miss Bec and Alice. Not seeing or knowing your children is devastating.

Giving a grim smile, Dave acknowledged the irony in that sentence. If Kim had read it, she would have highlighted the words with her bright pink highlighter so he couldn't miss them.

Still, I have some news on that front. In the paper's social pages there was a photo of a Miss Rebecca Burrows announcing her engagement to a Mr Justin Martin. I've enclosed the cutting.

I'd love to see you, Dave, dear, I really would. But I'll leave that to you.

Now holding the newspaper cutting, Dave looked into his daughter's face. So familiar and yet so unknown.

Her little upturned nose, which he used to love to kiss, was still the same, just a little bigger, as was her mouth. Her eyes had darkened from the blue grey that had mirrored his own to a greeny, hazel colour. More of Mel in those.

He thought the reflections of Mel and him in Bec were almost fifty-fifty. He craved to see Alice. To see what she looked like.

Bec would be twenty-four and Alice twenty-three now. It was ten years, three months and five days since he'd last seen the girls. They were old enough—and had been for many years—to choose if they wanted to spend time with their father or not.

Alice's words had echoed in his mind for years; he'd even dreamt about them at times. 'It's not that we don't want to see you, Dad, but you're busy and we've got sport and friends and a life, you know . . .' Her teenage shrug had been careless, not realising her father's heart had just been shattered into pieces.

Three years ago, he'd stopped writing to them. He'd laboured over weekly letters to the girls for years. They'd never been sent back, but they'd never been answered either. He suspected that either Melinda, his ex-wife, or Mark, her father, gathered the letters before the girls ever saw them. So he'd stopped writing.

Much to Kim's disappointment.

Kim had wanted him to keep going, to keep reaching out, but three years ago he'd decided his daughters would most likely have moved out of Melinda's house by then. They would have been living their own lives, going to uni, meeting new friends, exploring the world.

Getting engaged.

Dave's attention turned to the young man standing next to his daughter. He studied his face. Justin, according to the paper, was the son of Mr and Mrs Ian Martin and was a lawyer at a firm whose name Dave didn't recognise. Rebecca was the daughter of Mrs Melinda Grundy. Granddaughter to Mark. No mention of who her father was.

Dave had caught up with the news that Melinda had married again. He was glad for her. Really, he was. They hadn't been right for each other, and Dave had caused Melinda's family a lot of pain. Even twenty-two years later, he could hear the gunfire that his nemesis Bulldust had let off and see Ellen, his mother-in-law, ricochet backwards as the bullet hit her. Bec's pale face as her arm bled from where she'd also been hit, and Melinda as she ran from the house, screaming for someone to help them.

Justin looked as if he might be a few years older than Bec. His face seemed open and friendly. There was no sign of the inscrutable features that were usually stamped on a lawyer's face. Heaven forbid if they let an expression through that could be misinterpreted by another human being!

The tug of war inside him intensified and the urge to snarl was strong.

He wanted to be happy for Bec. But he wanted to meet Justin, to walk his daughter down the aisle, to see her engagement ring.

Neither Bec nor Melinda had bothered to contact him and let him know his eldest daughter was getting married. Not even Alice. It was like being punched in the gut.

He'd left his address in Barker with Melinda and Mark. If the girls ever wanted to contact him, they could. He'd never hidden away. But he seemed to have slipped silently out of their lives without anyone except him noticing.

For the first time in a long time, he wanted to hit something so very hard that, whoever or whatever it was, didn't get up. He needed to run, to move like he had when he was younger and having marriage troubles. Get the heat out of his body. His hands opened and closed, balling into fists then uncoiling.

He carefully placed the letter on the patio table and walked to the fence, slapping one fist into an open hand.

Dave had punched his ex-father-in-law once.

It had felt good.

But now that he was older and had lost some of the hot-headedness he'd been known for, Dave wouldn't recommend punching people. He hadn't regretted it at the time, even though it had led to the end of him and Mel, but now his preference was to talk someone down, rather than confronting them physically.

But it had been Mark's doing that Dave had lost contact with his girls, and that was unforgivable. Mel had been under her father's spell and too weak to stand up to him. So, Dave had an axe to grind as well.

The moonlight was gentle on the earth after the scorching day and Dave could almost feel the land breathing a sigh of relief. Some of the gum tree leaves had been burned. Dry and shrivelled, they fell from the tree and skittered along the path and road.

Dave tried to imagine Bec in a wedding dress. The squirming bundle of personality he'd held in his arms when she was born.

He hadn't been there for Alice's birth. A case had taken him to the north of Western Australia and by the time he'd got the message Melinda was in labour, his second daughter had already entered the world. The first time he'd seen her, she'd been sleeping in a crib next to Melinda's bed and his wife hadn't been speaking to him.

He brought his clenched fists down on the fence now and turned back to his house. The bedroom light had been turned out. Kim had known he needed time to process the letter his mum had sent and she had left him alone.

The mobile in his top pocket buzzed and Dave closed his eyes. Shit. He was on call.

He didn't want to see or talk to anyone.

Maybe he could throw the bloody phone far out into the paddock.

Instead, he took a deep breath and answered it. 'Hopper, what's happening?'

The noise from the pub came through the phone line.

'Get the fuck off me. What the bloody hell do you think you're doing?'

Dave didn't wait for Hopper to reply to his question before jogging into the house to pull on his uniform.

'Got trouble?' he asked again.

'Yeah, got a blow-in who's given your girl a bit of a headbutt. You'd better get here, Dave, the boys have got him on the floor. Better get an ambo here, too.'

'Mia? How?' But Hopper had gone.

Dave swore and sent a quick text to Hamish before leaning over the bed and giving Kim a kiss. She stirred.

'Going to the pub. Mia's been hurt,' he told her.

Kim sat up blearily. 'What's happened? Does she need help?'

'Don't know yet. I'll call you.' He gave her another kiss and Kim reached up to grab his hand and hold it to her face.

'Be safe,' she told him.

Dave took the police car, without putting the lights on. The drive was less than five minutes, and he was soon parked at the front of the pub.

'Get off me!'

'Mate, you're in so much shit, I'd shut your mouth if I was you.'

Dave thought that might have been Hopper, but he wasn't sure. Could be Kane Spencer or Russell Wood, blokes who spent most of their evenings in the pub.

A moment later and Hamish pulled up.

'We seem to be having some busy nights,' he told Dave as he got out. 'What have we got?'

'Your guess is as good as mine. Let's go.'

Dave pushed open the pub door. The first thing he saw was Mia sitting at a table with her head tipped backwards. Hopper was standing alongside her, holding an icepack to her nose.

Three men were restraining a stranger, two had hold of his arms while the other was grabbing the collar of his shirt. He was lunging away from them, twisting and turning, constantly moving, trying to break away.

Dave went to Mia.

'What happened?'

'He was being a dick, so I just tried to shut him down and he reacted.'

'Ah.'

Mia could be hot-headed and was still inexperienced; in fact, she reminded Dave of a female version of himself.

Dave nodded to Hamish, who took over from Hopper, applying a cold towel to Mia's nose and cleaning the blood away.

'And who do we have here?' Dave asked, moving to stand in front of the angry man.

'What's it to ya?'

Dave cocked his head to the side. 'Well, you've assaulted my constable and I don't like that. Caused trouble in my town and I don't like that either. Don't know if you've been here long, but you've worn your welcome out already. What's your name?'

'John Smith.'

'Really?' An eyebrow rose. 'I'll ask you again. What's your name?'

'I just fucking told you.'

'Right.' Dave took his handcuffs from his belt and indicated to the locals to swing the man around.

'He's got a smart mouth, this one,' Kane told Dave as he took a stronger hold on the man. 'Didn't think twice before headbutting Mia.'

'What caused the problem?' Dave asked as he snapped the cuffs on and felt in John Smith's pockets for some ID.

'Mouthing off to Mia. Telling her she had nice tits and they'd feel good against him. That sort of shit.' Hopper was standing behind Dave now. 'Told him to have a bit of respect but that didn't work out so well.'

'And Mia?'

Hopper grinned. 'Well, our Mia isn't backwards in coming forwards, is she? She gave back as good as she got. Told him if that was his pickup line, his dick must be small and she wasn't interested in anything so tiny.'

Dave let out a groan.

'He turned a bit like a crazed bull after that—didn't you, *mate*?' Hopper's sarcasm wasn't lost on anyone in the room. 'Snorted and bellowed, could almost see him pawing the ground. Got a bit closer and gave Mia a headbutt.

'You know, *mate*, in my experience women always respond best to a bit of loving, not violence. You'd be black and blue if I had my way with you.' Hopper spat at his feet.

'Hopper, that's enough,' Dave warned. 'Okay, John Smith, you're coming to the station with me.'

'You need help, Dave?' Kane asked. He was a big, strong, burly farmer and Dave could use an extra pair of hands.

'Just to get him in the car, thanks, Kane. I can take it from there. Can you hang onto him for a minute?'

Dave went to Mia. 'It's sounding like you had a bit to say just now.' He turned to Hamish. 'Broken nose?'

'Nah, just bruised. You might have a black eye tomorrow, Mia, but you'll be fine.'

'Sorry, Dave,' Mia said, her eyes seeking his. Her voice was nasal.

'Think we're going to have to get you a thicker skin. Or at least stop you reacting so quickly,' Dave said with a gentle smile. 'I know you've got to stand up for yourself, Mia, but . . .' He stopped. Now wasn't the time.

'I know, I know,' Mia said, hanging her head.

'Nuh-uh.' Hamish gently put his hands on her forehead and tipped it back again. 'Let's keep that blood where it belongs—inside the body!'

'Right to go, Dave?' Kane asked, pushing John Smith towards the door.

'What are you going to do with Mia?' Dave asked Hamish.

'I'm going home,' she said before the nurse had a chance to respond.

Hamish nodded. 'What she said. There's no concussion, just a bit of a bang on the nose, so she'll be fine by herself tonight.'

Dave turned his attention to Mia. 'Do you want Kim to come over?'

Mia shook her head. 'I'll be okay,' she said in a small voice. 'But thanks.'

Patting her shoulder, Dave grabbed the other arm of the man who was still telling everyone what he thought of Barker's hospitality and shoved him out the door.

'Oi, settle down, copper, or I'll report you.'

'I'm going to charge you with assaulting a police officer. That's the only reporting that's going on here,' Dave told him grimly.

Silence.

'She's a police officer?'

'Yes, Mr Smith, Mia is my constable. I told you that before, but you were too busy talking over the top of me to hear.'

Another silence then the man quickly recovered. 'Don't tell me you have haven't wanted to give her one yourself.

Hot, tight little bod she's got. You're either jealous coz she hasn't let you in or because you're already banging her.'

Bec flashed into his mind. What if some arsehole had done something similar to her? Or Alice. Dave wouldn't even know. He hadn't been there to help protect them.

The burning white-hot anger he felt reading the newspaper article earlier rose in his throat like bile. 'You are one of the most charming people I've had the pleasure of meeting,' Dave said and opened the back of the car. 'Get in. I'm looking forward to getting to know you better.'

'You sure you're going to be right with that prick?' Kane asked as Dave slammed the door shut. 'He's off his tits. Reckon it's more than booze.'

'I think you could be right,' Dave said grimly. 'It'll be okay. I've managed one or two of these over my time.'

'If you say so. Catch you later, Dave.' He paused as he looked at the man in the back seat. 'Make sure you give us a bell if you change your mind.'

Dave got into the driver's seat and started the engine.

'What's she like in the sack?' John Smith asked. 'She go off or what?'

Reaching forward, Dave turned up the radio so he couldn't hear the vile words the man was spewing out. He was thankful that the trip to the police station would take less than two minutes.

Instead of pulling up at the front of the station he drove around the back to a stone building detached from the main station. The heavy iron doors of the cells would make sure this bastard wasn't going anywhere.

From his belt he took a bunch of keys, opened the door and switched on the light, giving the first cell the once-over before he got John Smith out.

'Are you for real?' John Smith looked at the cell. 'What, just coz I gave your connie a compliment?'

Dave took the cuffs off his wrists and gave the man a shove. 'I'll see you in the morning.'

John Smith turned on him. 'Smelling like her?'

Dave didn't stop to think. The first punch landed on the man's jaw and the second on his nose.

CHAPTER 10

'You're here already?' Sassi stood back and held the door open, while her mother breezed in by her, not stopping for a hug or a kiss.

A sweet scent hung in the air as Amber passed by; a scent that Sassi had never smelt before. Watching her mother walk by, she realised that since they'd last seen each other Amber had put on weight.

'Of course I am. Did you think I wasn't going to come?' Amber parked her suitcase underneath the family photo on the wall, but didn't stop to look at it.

'Probably not so soon,' Sassi whispered to herself, glancing out into the dark, wishing there was someone who could come and moderate between them all tonight.

Shutting the door quietly, Sassi turned back to her mother, who was now standing in the doorway of the lounge room.

'Hello, Dad, I came as quickly as I could.' The words were the right ones, but Sassi thought her mother's tone was too brisk. 'Going all right, then?'

'Ugh,' Sassi heard Pa reply.

'I'll put the kettle on. Did you want a cup of tea, Mum?' Sassi still called her mother Mum but she rarely thought of her that way. She was Amber. 'Or something to eat?'

'I think I'll take a nip out of Dad's bourbon here and go to bed. I've been travelling since yesterday and I'm in desperate need of a shower.'

Opening the kitchen cupboard to get out a glass, Sassi heard the puff of the couch as Amber sat down.

'It's awful news about Mum,' she said to her father.

Pa grunted.

In the lounge room, Sassi handed over the glass and sat down at the other end of the couch and observed her mother. Sassi felt her body grow cold as she realised Amber didn't look like she had in previous visits. Gone was the youthful skin and bright eyes, replaced with deep lines around her mouth and furrows between her brow. Her sky-blue eyes were dull and didn't appear to hold anything but a bitter coldness. Not sympathy, not love, not compassion. Just annoyance and ice.

'How was your flight?' she asked.

Amber upended the bourbon into her glass and took a large gulp before answering.

Pa stared at Amber as if he couldn't believe she was drinking a hard spirit. Or that she was sitting in his lounge room. Maybe he was aghast, as Sassi was and doing her best to hide it, at the loose jowls under her mother's chin and the flecks of grey through her hair. The woman who sat in front of them was almost a stranger compared to the photos that hung on the wall, taken many years ago.

'Long,' was the only answer. Another sip. 'Are there any funeral arrangements yet?'

Making a distressed sound, Pa put his hands to his eyes. From underneath his gnarled fingers, a couple of tears slipped down his cheeks. Sassi wanted to bundle him up in a fluffy blanket and hold him until the pain went away. How amazing to have love that lasted so long, across such a span of years.

'We've made a few arrangements. Chosen . . . ah, things.' Sassi waved her hands around, not wanting to say the word 'coffin' where Pa could hear. 'But we have to wait until the autopsy's been done. The doctor is ninety per cent sure her heart was the problem, but he said he has to do everything by the book.'

Amber tossed her hair. 'Sounds a bit ridiculous to me. Of course it was her heart, what else could it have been?'

Sassi lifted one shoulder, not answering. Between the shock of seeing her mother, her accident and the exhaustion that was seeping through every part of her body, she didn't have the energy to answer.

Quietness fell over them as Amber took another sip, and then another, before she rested her head against the back of the couch with a sigh. 'Doesn't look like too much has changed here,' she said, holding the glass in the direction of the sideboard. 'They've had that crystal drinks set since I can remember. It sat there on the sideboard out at the farm, too.'

Pa reached out a hand towards Amber, but she didn't notice as she got up to look closely at a photo on the wall.

'These are the twins? They've grown since the last photo I saw. Got their father's cheeky grin, haven't they?'

Do I smile like my dad? Sassi opened her mouth to ask but then closed her eyes and shook her head. Not tonight.

'You must be really tired, Mum. I'll make up the bed in the spare room if you like.'

'Thanks, Sassi, I'd appreciate that. The drive up here was longer than I remembered.'

In the laundry, Sassi grabbed clean sheets and towels. She went into the spare room and pulled the bedspread back from the mattress, then spread out the sheets, carefully making the envelope corners the way she'd been taught.

Her head ached now, and her shoulders were stiff.

As she tucked the top sheet in and put the pillows into the cases, she realised her mother had not said one word about the bruising on her face.

⌐

The next morning, Sassi glanced over at her mother, who was sitting at the kitchen table with a cold piece of toast and a magazine in front of her. Amber had already complained that the coffee wasn't any good and the house needed a good clean—'*Mum must've let it go as she got older.*'

Abe had walked in a few moments earlier and thrown his hat on the floor beside his chair. When Sassi had placed a coffee in front of him, he'd whispered, 'How's it all going?' Sassi just grimaced and felt the ache of her muscles pulling in her face. She would have rolled her eyes, but that might have hurt, too.

She was in a bit more pain today than she had been yesterday. The muscles in her legs ached and her shoulder throbbed from where the seatbelt had held her in so tightly. Still, she'd swallowed a couple of Panadol, got Pa his toast and sat on the verandah giving the drugs time to work before her mother arrived demanding coffee, which hadn't been until way past breakfast time.

'We need to get someone in to give Dad a hand here,' Abe said when Amber looked up from the magazine she was reading. 'Not just the house, but him.'

'Yes, that's very true. I'm sure a nurse won't fall out of the sky in a small town like Barker though,' Amber said. 'Still, we'll have a little breathing space while I'm here. I'll be able to organise and interview a live-in helper. But I will need to head back once everything is sorted. Zola isn't very good at communicating with the servants,' Amber said. 'And we have many who need to be organised.'

Abe pressed his lips together and breathed in through his nose, while Sassi blinked. Amber would have to be very careful talking like that in Australia.

'No,' Pa said from the head of the table. He stamped his cane once as an exclamation mark.

Sassi hid a smile as he took his teacup and poured the steaming liquid into the saucer to let it cool. He'd been doing that for as long as she could remember and even the trembling in his hands didn't stop him.

'Unfortunately,' Sassi said gently, 'we will have to get you a bit of extra help, Pa. Even if it's only around the house. But home care would be great, too. You know, someone to help you shower and get dressed. Do your washing.'

Pa blanched at the thought of someone helping him get dressed and violently shook his head. 'Ma do.'

Abe took the old man's hand. 'She can't do it anymore, Dad. She's gone. Remember?'

The old man nodded, looking down at the brown liquid in the saucer. He pursed his lips to blow, then tried to pour it into the cup, the tea sloshing over the edge and leaving a mark on the table.

'Let's get that cleaned up,' Amber said. 'Sass, can you get the dishcloth?' To Pa, she said, 'You'll have to stop doing that. You might burn yourself and we can't have that. Old skin takes a long time to heal.'

Sassi grabbed the sponge and leaned over Pa's shoulder. His body was tense and quivering as if he was trying to control his annoyance. He looked at his daughter as if she was a stranger talking out of turn, then raised his cup to his lips. Sassi patted his arm in a calming manner even though she was feeling edgy. Sometimes, her mother had the same effect as fingernails scraping down a blackboard.

Abe nodded to the verandah, and Sassi washed and wrung out the sponge then picked up her coffee and headed outside.

'Good to see nothing has changed between those two,' Abe said as he sat down and took a sip from his cup. 'Can you remember the fights they used to have? What is there, five years between us? I'm sure I was a mistake; that's why you and I are so close together in age. Eleven years between Amber and me.'

'I probably can't remember their fights as well as you, but there're some that stick in my memory. Like the day she left and didn't come back.

'Mum was sixteen when she had me, so Granny kept telling me over and over.' Sassi paused, looking out over the garden. It needed a good watering. 'I always felt so sad for Granny and Pa, being lumped with me. In hindsight, I'm sure they felt like they were at the end of their child-rearing days, and then there I was.' Sassi paused again. 'I've always been so grateful, though. They could've put me in a home for kids without parents!'

'They never would've done that.' He broke a stick into small pieces and tossed them towards the fence. 'How old were you when she left?'

'Six. Granny raised me from when I was six and you were eleven.'

'Have you met him? Zola?'

'If she's been back to Australia with him, I've never been told,' she said. 'I don't even know how they met. Isn't it strange how none of us have been introduced to him and she seems to want to keep us all at arm's length?'

The door opened and Amber came out, pulling on a large straw hat. Again, Sassi felt dumbstruck. How was this woman, this *older* woman, her mother? The change in her physical features from when Sassi had seen her last was immense.

How long had it been? Two years? Three? Maybe longer. Amber came and went at times that suited her; and Sassi hadn't seen her every time she'd visited Barker.

A dull ache started in her heart. There was something different about Amber now. She seemed harder. Tired. Worn down.

'Talking about me?' Amber asked as she swept her long skirt up and sat down on the front step.

'Yep,' Abe said without apology. 'How was your flight?'

'Long, and the drive up here was longer.'

'Well, we're glad you're here,' Abe said.

'I am, too. Even if it's for such a sad reason.'

Sassi wasn't sure Amber meant it, but the words sounded good.

'How's the farm?' Amber asked Abe.

'Waiting for the opening rains. Forecast said they shouldn't be too far away. Want to come out for a look?'

Amber paused and a shudder seemed to run through her body. 'No. I don't miss anything about that place.'

'Right.' Abe grabbed at more twigs and kept breaking them into small pieces, while Sassi searched for an open question, then settled on an easy one. 'Zola didn't come with you?'

Amber paused. 'No, he's busy on the farm. There's been a few—' she paused and looked out across the street '—issues and he can't leave. And I thought it would be better if only I came as he never met Mum or Dad.' She looked out over the garden. 'It's weird to see the house without Mum here. And Dad has certainly gone downhill since I saw him last.'

'You don't come very often,' Abe said.

'It's hard to get away.' Amber changed the subject. 'And your children? How are they? They've grown, I could see from the photos I saw in the lounge room last night.'

'They're great. Jimmy and Harry. Real farm kids. Always out and about with me or driving their mum insane.'

Amber's lips curled up at the end in a resemblance of a smile. 'They're five, aren't they? You always seemed to be a mischief-maker when you were little. Actually, I always thought you were a brat. Talking over people, trying to help out in the shearing shed, when all you were doing was getting in people's way.'

Frowning, Abe answered, 'They'll be five next birthday.'

A sadness crept through Sassi. Not the sadness that came with death, or when a partner ended a relationship, this was a cold, bottomless sadness that came from watching her family try to navigate around each other. Thrust together by death but clearly happier apart. The distance between them all had been a thorn in Granny's heart and, now, Sassi felt it, too.

She would try, for Granny, to fix this awfulness between them. Forget the pain they'd all felt and start afresh.

'Tell me about your farm,' she asked, putting her coffee cup down. 'How many hectares do you have?'

'Oh, it's large enough,' Amber said dismissively. 'Enough to keep us all very busy.'

Sassi glanced at her own work-worn hands and then looked at her mother's. Well-moisturised and white, Amber's fingers were long and slender, like Granny's had been. Her wedding ring moved loosely around her ring finger. Maybe Amber drove tractors or did some kind of work that didn't make her hands look as old as Sassi's already did.

'I love living over there, though. Something about the country gets under your skin,' Amber said, reaching down to pull off a dead geranium head and crushing it with her fingers. 'It's home. Barker never felt like home for some reason. I didn't fit in.'

'Doesn't matter where I live or how much I love where I am,' Sassi said, 'Barker and the farm is always home for me.'

'You'll have to carry me out in a box,' Abe said, then shook his head as if he realised why they were all sitting on the verandah having this conversation.

'How long before we can set a date for the funeral?' Amber asked.

'I'm not sure if it's the police or the doc who will get back to us on that,' Abe said. 'Probably Dave since he had to organise the coroner's report.'

Amber looked at her watch. 'Hopefully, it won't take too long. I would have stayed home if I'd known I wasn't going to get here before she died.' Her gaze slid across to Sassi. 'You're quiet, Sass. And you haven't told me what you've done to yourself to be all black and blue like you are.'

'I had a car accident.'

Amber's mouth opened then she shut it again. She started to move towards her daughter, then she pulled back. 'Oh.' The pause became an awkward silence. 'When?'

'Yesterday morning. Early. I was trying to get here before Granny died, too.' Her voice became soft. 'I didn't make it either.' She reached out her hand.

Amber took it momentarily then let it go. 'Well, I'm glad you're okay. Your face looks like it could be sore.'

'I'm okay,' Sassi said.

'Her car was a write-off, Amber. Shit, you should have seen it—the roof is all caved in and they couldn't open the doors. Had to get the jaws of life to cut her out. And you didn't ask anything until now?' Abe got up and walked to the front fence. 'Sometimes I wonder about you.'

'I'm sorry,' Amber stood up. 'I assumed someone would tell me what was going on if it had anything to do with me.'

'It's okay,' Sassi said. She reached forward and tugged at Amber's skirt, trying to get her mother to sit back down again. 'Please, let's just all get along. For Pa, for Granny. She'd want us to work together.'

Amber swayed, then sat down. 'I'm sorry you had an accident. That would have been frightening.'

'It was,' Sassi said, watching as Abe hurled a few more sticks towards the ground with a lot more force than was needed.

Amber turned to Abe, a frown on her face. 'So, what are we going to do with Dad now? You don't think he's able to live by himself?'

'No, we'll need to get some type of help in and—' he spread his hands around to take in the town '—Barker doesn't offer a lot of options when we need assistance with older people.'

'He's certainly unsteady on his feet, and his speech will be a problem. I can stay for a couple of weeks but that's all. Around-the-clock care would be ideal.'

Abe laughed, but it was without humour. 'Around-the-clock care? In Barker? Have you forgotten how small this place is?'

'Well, I—' Amber broke off. 'We could hire a nurse from another town.'

'You seem to have thought a lot about poor old Dad, considering you only got here last night.'

'Is there a home he can go into here? Somewhere that caters for oldies.' Amber shrugged. 'You can't look after him and neither can I. I'm not . . . I can't stay. I have responsibilities.' Her glance slid across to Sassi. 'I assume you can't give up your job to care for him either.'

Sassi spoke up. 'There's a nursing home in Broad River.' She paused. 'Do you think we should talk to Pa about this? He might have his own ideas. I really don't think he'll want to leave here.'

'I—' Amber didn't finish her sentence because Abe was talking over her.

'Yeah, I reckon this needs to be Dad's decision, with our input. He's not a child and Mum has managed to help him live independently in his own home until only a couple of days ago. Sassi, I agree with you, I doubt he'd want to shift from this house. And to move him from his home town, where he's lived all his life? I think that would kill him quicker than mourning Mum. Let's include him in the decision-making. His mind is still alert and active, even if his body is a bit dickie.'

Sassi picked up her empty coffee cup, wishing there was more caffeine in it. Although there mightn't be enough coffee in the world to sustain her today.

Amber's face flushed red. 'Sorry,' she said quietly. 'Sorry, you're right, I'm out of line. This is all such a shock. I feel like I've just got to do something. Get *things*—whatever they are—organised. Shock can be strange like that.'

They were silent, watching the sun continue to climb into the sky and the willie wagtails darting in and out of the sprays of water from the retic on the council side of the fence.

'I should have come back sooner.' Amber had tears on her cheeks now. 'There just was never a right time. We were always busy and now I've missed my chance.'

'Granny understood. She had the biggest heart,' Sassi told her. 'She never stopped missing you, but she understood.'

Amber wiped her hands across her cheeks. 'But Dad never did.'

Abe walked over to face her, put his hand on Amber's shoulder. 'Everything will be all right, Amber. You've got time to talk with Dad while you're here. Maybe you can sort things out with him. And, look, I'm sorry if I'm a little brisk. We're all feeling sad. It's not just the loss of Mum.

Dad is getting frailer and suddenly we're the ones who are having to make sure he's looked after.'

'Big changes across the board,' Amber said. She took a few deep breaths and tried to smile, although it looked a bit wonky. Then she held out both her hands to Abe and Sassi. 'Yes, of course you're right, Abe. I'm sorry. Sorry to both of you. And I hear what you're saying about including Dad.' They gripped each other's hands in some kind of unspoken agreement and then let go.

'Sounds like part of it is decided then.'

Amber got up and went inside.

Abe looked bemused as he ran his hand through his hair.

The sides were grey; Sassi had never noticed that her uncle was getting older, too. Then she realised what he'd said, and a tiny hysterical giggle escaped. Who were they now? These kids who had grown into adults way before they were ready. She wanted to turn back the clock to when she and Abe were pretending to muster sheep, but they were really racing each other on motorbikes. Or when Abe had been helping her jump over the rushing water in the creek below the house. The weight of responsibility rested heavily now and she became serious. 'You know what I think?'

'Tell me.' Abe walked over to the lawn near the roses and started to pull off the dead blooms.

Sassi followed him and began helping. 'Regret and guilt are awful things.'

They stood side by side, looking at the roses that Granny had lovingly tended year after year. The stalks were so thick and Sassi vaguely remembered being a small girl when her grandmother had planted them.

Her grandparents had lived on the farm until Abe had married, but they'd always owned the house in Barker. Granny had often talked about their plans when they retired into town, and she'd kept the garden as beautiful as if she lived there always. And as most farmers did, Pa hadn't really retired—that was just a word. Not until the stroke, anyhow. He'd driven out to the farm in the morning, and back in the evening, most days.

'Do you remember my friend Rose? The girl I shared a house with when I was working in South Australia?'

'Vaguely,' Abe said. 'I don't think I met her.'

'Her mum had been terminally ill for ages. Years. And every time she got close to death, she seemed to rally and come back. I remember Rose used to say that none of the family ever thought she would actually die.'

'I think I know where this is going.' He grimaced.

'Yeah. Her mum had taken a bit of a dive and the doctor had thought maybe the family should come. Rose didn't go and neither did her brother. Too busy. Thought her mum would live another day like every other time.' She shook her head. 'Rose was riddled with guilt for years. Went to Bali for six whole months afterwards, you know, to one of those wellness, holistic retreat things to try to deal with it.' She looked at her uncle. 'Best way to deal with guilt and regret is not to have it at all.'

'In an ideal world, Sass.'

'Maybe that's what's hitting Mum now. I think we should all try to behave as if none of us want regrets. I mean if the roof of the ute had caved in a few more inches, I probably wouldn't be here either. I don't want to die having regrets, do you?'

'Like I said, in an ideal world.' Abe broke off another dead rose head. 'I'm glad you're still here, though.'

Sassi threw him a look.

'All right,' he said. 'I'll try. Talk about the tables being turned, it's usually me calming you down about your mother.'

The silence stretched out between them for a while.

Finally, Sassi asked, 'Are you going okay? You've hardly said anything about how you're feeling about Granny dying.'

Abe looked down at the roses. 'If I let myself feel anything now, I won't be able to get through what we have to, so I'm concentrating on the logistics, and I'll deal with the rest later.' He paused. 'Maybe I'm a bit like Amber, I need to organise things to feel as if I'm helping.'

'Hmm, maybe.' She pushed her shoulder into his.

'You coming out to stay at the farm?'

'You think you can keep me away? Now that Mum's here, I can leave Pa and come out. Plus I need to make sure your terrors aren't corrupting Jarrah.' She stopped talking for a second as a truck rumbled past. 'When are you starting seeding?'

Abe looked up at the clear sky. 'There's rain forecast for next week. Hoping to get at least twenty mils. If we get another follow-up after that in a week or so, should be able to go in then. The bloody weather pattern is looking more like summer than autumn.'

'It is that.'

'What's going on at your place?'

'I spoke to my boss this morning. The feedlot is full. As the manager, I should be there, but he's given me a month off, if I want to take that long. I've got another couple of weeks owed on top of that, too. Trouble is we'll start to truck the yearlings out every fortnight next week. I should be there to oversee it all. Still, the blokes I've employed to do the feeding are pretty good, so I might play everything by ear. See how Pa goes. See when the funeral is.

'And this bloody weather pattern is the same over there, so I don't think the boss will want to seed anything dry like we did last year. We got a fricking caning—too dry then too wet. We ended up with a wet drought.' She huffed a little. 'Yields were right down and we had to buy in grain to feed the cattle, which wasn't ideal. Who would've thought that a wet drought was possible in Australia?'

'It's not up here, that's for sure. We're always hand to mouth when it comes to rainfall.'

'Have you got someone to help with seeding?'

Abe shook his head. 'Finding anyone who wants to work is difficult at the moment. Don't know where all the workers have gone since Covid. I mean, all the borders have opened back up again and we're still short. Not just agriculture. Every industry is stretched. Dunno where everyone has gone.'

'I know.'

They continued to deadhead the roses in companion-able silence.

'Hey, Abe?' Sassi said as she collected the cuttings into a bucket. 'Despite everything, it's really nice to be home.'

'I reckon we can put up with you being here for a bit.'

CHAPTER 11

'Do you want me to take John Smith some breakfast?' Mia asked Dave, who was making a coffee in the station kitchen. Kim had sent a tray of food over and it was waiting on the table to be delivered.

'John Smith is Mr Nathan Woodbridge and, no, I'll do it.' Dave sounded grim. He turned around and assessed her face. 'Not as bad as I thought you'd look this morning. Don't think they'd take you as a cover model but, hey.' He shrugged.

Mia gave a little laugh, trying not to move her mouth too much. 'No, they wouldn't.' She opened the locker and peered at the mirror inside the door, before touching her face gently. 'The bruising doesn't do justice to how it felt last night, though. I thought he'd split my skull open!'

A small humph from Dave. 'Often smaller injuries don't give us the satisfaction of looking as bad as they feel. The real bad ones, sometimes they don't hurt until the adrenalin has worn off.' He added the coffee to the tray.

'Do you want to tell me what happened last night?'

Mia had been waiting for this. 'He was being a pig. That's really all there is to it. He made some obscene suggestions about what he'd like me to do to him and I reacted.' She looked down, knowing she would have disappointed her mentor.

'Reacted, how? Tell me in your words.' Dave's voice was low, but not judgemental.

'I, ah,' she coloured, 'made some suggestions that his dick probably wasn't a good size if he needed to speak like that.' She looked Dave in the eye as she spoke and caught just a tiny indication his lips wanted to twitch into a smile, but he couldn't let himself.

'I'm really glad you weren't in uniform.'

'I probably would have said the same thing if I was.'

'What am I going to do with you?' Dave replied. Gone was the hint of amusement Mia was sure she'd just seen. 'I thought we'd been through this before. Your mouth engages before your brain. As a copper, you can't do that. Just calm down a little bit, okay? Not everyone is the enemy.'

'But he was being—'

Dave held up his hands. 'I know, and this is a bad example of why you need to calm down, because he's such a wanker, but seriously, Mia, you're going to get a reputation as someone who flies off the handle too quickly. People won't want to come to you to report things. Okay?' He didn't wait for her to answer. 'Do you think this

Woodbridge was high? He didn't seem to calm down at all when I turned up.'

Mia didn't hesitate in her answer. 'I'm sure he was. He had no fear and kept coming. Don't know what he was on, although it was stronger than weed. Maybe ice or something similar.'

'Right, well, I guess there'll be others around who will be taking the same stuff. We'd better keep an eye out. Those types of drugs make policing more difficult because it's uncertain what you're going to get personality-wise. Have you noticed anything that would indicate there're any hard drugs around?'

'Nope. Nothing. But he's a blow-in. No one's seen him before.'

'He might've been here drumming up business. We'll have to keep an eye out. We don't want that shit in our town.' Dave picked up the tray. 'Can you please open the door?'

'Sure. Need help with the cell door?'

'I reckon you should stay well away from this bloke, don't you?'

Joan bustled in and gasped when she saw Mia. 'What in heaven's name have you done to yourself?'

'Got a guest out the back,' Dave said before Mia could answer. 'He seems to have a problem with females, so you two are to stay away from him.'

'What? He did this to you?' Joan stepped closer to Mia, inspecting her face.

'Yeah, the bloke out the back got up close and personal with his forehead last night.'

'Oh, Mia, have you been to the doctor?'

Mia quickly relayed what had happened and Joan clicked her tongue. 'Gosh, that's nasty behaviour.' She eyed Mia and the young constable saw a questioning look cross the older woman's face. 'Does it hurt much?'

'Not too bad.' Mia went to the door and watched Dave carry the tray down the path to the cells. Her partner wasn't himself this morning. He'd been quiet and withdrawn since she'd walked in.

Joan was shaking her head. 'Oh dear, Mia. You seem to attract this type of incident, don't you?'

'That's what I told her she needs to be careful of,' Dave called out over his shoulder.

Mia's eyes followed her partner, making sure Nathan didn't come out swinging.

The door opened.

Nothing. Not a sound.

'Morning. I've brought you some breakfast,' Dave said. His voice carried up the path towards Mia.

At first she couldn't hear what the prisoner said, then his words were loud and clear.

'Mate, I'm really sorry. I shouldn't have behaved like that. I never normally would do something so stupid or disrespectful.'

Mia raised her eyebrows. She'd never had anyone she'd arrested apologise to her.

'You were being a right dick last night, mate. Why should I think you're not going to do it again?'

Moving closer, Mia looked over Dave's shoulder. Nathan was sitting on the bed, his hands in his lap, his head hanging down. He certainly looked remorseful.

Dave had planted himself in the middle of the entrance, arms crossed, the tray at his feet.

'I don't know what to say other than sorry.'

'Were you on something last night? Drugs?'

'Nah, just angry. Had some shit go wrong yesterday and got meself a skinful. Your constable riled me. Still, I shouldn't have reacted like that. Me dad would be real disappointed in me.'

'Your boss from Hunter's Shearing is coming to get you. He's going to take you to the hospital and get you a drug test.'

The man looked up. 'No court?'

'Not if you get a negative drug test and don't do this again. I've looked you up and you don't have any priors.'

Mia's mouth dropped open. That wasn't the way this should play out. Nathan Woodbridge should be heading to Port Augusta for a date with the magistrate but instead Dave was about to bail him?

'I really do promise not to act like that again.'

Dave ran his hand through his hair and sighed. 'For some stupid reason, I believe you. Don't make me regret doing this, Woodbridge.'

'I won't.'

Dave stood in front of the cell door for a moment longer, seeming to weigh up his decision, then stepped away.

'You definitely didn't take any drugs?'

Nathan shook his head. 'No, no drugs.'

'Right-oh, have your breakfast and then you can head off. Go and get that test, do a day's work and get the shit off your liver, got it?'

'Sure, mate. Thanks.'

Mia strained to look over Dave's shoulder.

She stared.

Nathan had about a week's worth of growth on his face, but there was something . . . Was that a bruise under the stubble? Was his nose swollen? Her eyes flicked to Dave who hadn't moved. He cut an imposing figure in his uniform. Tall, lean and fit. Strong, too. If this bloke decided to do anything stupid, Mia had no doubt that Dave would be ready for him.

Joan called out from the main building, 'Mr Woodbridge's ride is here.'

Mia saw Dave's shoulders relax slightly.

'Want your breakfast or not? Coz it sounds like you're out of here.'

The man picked up the coffee and a piece of toast and walked towards the entrance. 'Thanks for making me realise I'd fucked up, mate,' Nathan said to Dave.

Silence.

Trying to appear as if she wasn't studying the man closely, Mia dropped her eyes to the ground and followed behind as if it was perfectly normal for her to be doing so.

One of Nathan's eyes was bloodshot, Mia noticed.

Still, that could be from a wild night at the pub then not sleeping well in the cell. And that purply looking thing that ran from his chin, up one cheek and to his eye could be a horrible birthmark. The nose? Hmm.

Dave was silent as he marched Nathan into the station, handed him back his wallet and watch and made him sign for his belongings.

'Even with all your apologies, I don't want to see you around Barker again, hear me?' Dave said. 'Not in the pub, not in the main street, not even in the grocery store.' He turned to the shearing boss who was holding the front door open. 'You make sure he doesn't come back here, got it?'

'Right.' Nathan grabbed his things and gave them both a nod, before leaving.

'Really am very sorry about this, Dave,' the shearing contractor said. 'He's never caused me an ounce of trouble before, so I'm not sure why last night was a problem.'

'Maybe we were all having a bad day,' Dave said. 'And I'm serious when I say he's not to come back here, Riley.'

'Do me best.' The old man raised his hat and left.

Mia raised her eyebrows at Joan and hurried after Dave.

Standing at the filing cabinet, he was putting his paperwork away. He turned to Mia with a smile that wasn't quite as broad and carefree as normal. 'So, you're good to go for today? Don't need any more time off? No headache?'

'Nope, I'm good. What did you want me to do?'

'You can finish that paperwork from Sassi's accident, and then we'll see what's going on after that.' He gave the cabinet drawer a push, then went to sit at his desk.

Mia quietly made her way to her own desk and sat down, pushing paper around for a bit.

Then she jumped up again and went back to Dave. 'Um, Dave?'

'Hmm?' he didn't look up from the emails he was checking.

'That Nathan bloke, did he, ah . . .'

Dave faced her.

'Did he have an, um . . .' Mia realised she didn't know how to say what she suspected out loud. How could she? This was Dave Burrows! The bloke who'd been shot under-cover and solved too many crimes to count. A legend.

Dave who had brought her to Barker to work with him. Dave who believed in her.

'What, Mia?' he asked patiently, his eyes regarding her coolly.

'Nothing. No, it's okay.' She gave a half smile, before heading back to her desk, confused at what she was thinking.

The report she had began to write up about the car accident was partly completed on her desk and she started to reread her words.

Joan came down the hall and put a coffee in front of her with a smile then continued on to Dave's office.

Mia listened as they talked.

'Joan, the lady at your church who has just moved to Barker from Adelaide, what was her story again?'

Mia heard the puff of air leave the vinyl chair as Joan sat.

'Rasha? Oh, she is a lovely lady and her two children are delights. She's settled into Barker really well. Doing a few

124

hours at the IGA both behind the counter and restocking the shelves, you know, that sort of thing. It's lovely seeing some diversity coming into our town, isn't it?'

'Yeah, it is. But why did she come to Barker in the first place? What makes a single mum turn up here with no family support or reason to live here? I mean Barker is four hours from Adelaide and it's not like we're a thriving metropolis!'

'The same reason that so many people are leaving the city now. It's too expensive to live there, or they can't find rentals. And they're trying to get away from Covid.' Joan gave a heavy sigh. 'Rasha told me she can live here for half the price. They've moved into that little house behind the silos, the one that's been empty for years. The owners reduced the rent in return for her getting it clean and tidy.

'Life is tough for a lot of people right now, Dave. Rasha was working four jobs in the city and one of them was at night, so she'd rush home in the afternoons just to spend a bit of time with the kids before they went to bed, then head out to do night stocking at one of the supermarkets. That's not as irresponsible as it sounds—the oldest child is ten and had access to a mobile phone.

'Rasha would be home by midnight and there in the morning when they woke up. As soon as they'd had breakfast and gone to school, she'd head to her next job, then the next. One thing she's not afraid of is hard work.'

'And what's different here?'

'She doesn't need as much money to pay the rent so here she can be home with her kids every night. And I'm sure you know how much easier it is to create a community around yourself when you live in a country town, compared to the city. Rasha is getting a lot of support from Barker, and she hasn't had that elsewhere.'

'Hmm.'

Mia imagined Dave pushing the silver-framed glasses up on his nose, his elbows on the table and hands tucked under his chin, as he thought.

'What work did she do in Adelaide?' he asked Joan now.

'Like I said, restocking the shelves every night. Then she'd do a few shifts at McDonald's. The rest were cleaning jobs. I think she cleaned a school and some hotel rooms. I know she was trying to get work at a nursing home because there was one near where she lived. All of the work she did had to be close to where she lived, for the kids.'

'And why didn't she get work in the nursing home?'

'Don't think she was able to find a position that worked in with her other jobs.'

There was silence from Dave's office and Mia started to type on her computer. The keys made loud clicking sounds in the quiet.

'Why do you ask?' Joan finally said.

'I'm wondering if she might be interested in caring for Mr Stapleton. When Kim and I dropped some food around last night, Abe said he thought his father was going to need some extra care; someone to come in and clean, do the washing. You know, all that sort of stuff. I think there might have been some personal care involved, too, but I don't know the details.'

There was another long silence and then a rustling as Joan pulled a tissue out of the box on Dave's desk. Her voice sounded like she had a cold when she spoke. 'Dave, Rasha would jump at the opportunity, I'm sure.'

'Great, I'll ring Abe and put the idea to him.'

Mia swallowed. Dave always looked out for the people in his town, always had everyone's best interests at heart.

How could she possibly think he'd done something bad to Nathan Woodbridge?

CHAPTER 12

Sassi looked around the spare room at the farm and listened to her cousins playing happily outside the bedroom window.

A cool change had blessed Barker overnight and she was glad to sit in the chair next to the window with gentle sunlight streaming through. Her watch told her it was nearly 9 am. She couldn't remember the last time she'd stayed in bed that late.

Her face hurt today. Ached. And her stitches were pulling and itchy, so she figured her body had needed the extra couple of hours of sleep. She was also bloody glad that Abe had suggested she spend a few nights at the farm to let Pa and her mother have some time.

Amber hadn't been so keen. She'd told Sassi she'd wanted to spend time with her, too. Sassi had smoothed that over by telling her she would drop in every day.

'Sassi. Sassssssseeee?' A shrill tone was now outside her door. 'Are you awake? Come on, get up and play with us.'

She was sure that was Jimmy, but both boys sounded similar. Instead of answering, she crept over to the door and stood behind it, knowing there was no way either of the twins would be able to hold back from opening it when she didn't answer.

'You boys stay away from Sassi's room,' Renee called. But it was too late.

The door handle turned and slowly, slowly the door moved inwards. Sassi held her breath.

'She's not here,' Jimmy whispered.

'Are you sure? Where is she?' Harry asked.

'I don't know.'

Sassi grinned, still hiding, waiting until the time was right. She saw a foot, then Jimmy's body. Harry was close behind.

They took a couple of hesitant steps into the room and Harry turned to Jimmy with a confused look on his face.

'But she's not outside. Where is she?' he asked again.

Just then, Sassi let out a loud roar and jumped out, her hands up and fingers curled like a cat. She grabbed both of the boys, one in each arm. The aching across her whole body disappeared as they squealed with mixed delight and horror.

'What are you two doing in my room?' she asked, laughing. She dropped a kiss on each head and let them go. 'Were you going to wake me up?'

'No.' Jimmy's face was schooled into a mask of innocence.

'I don't believe you. I think you were going to wake me up by jumping on my bed.'

Harry's face broke into a cheeky grin. 'Maybe.'

'No maybes about it,' Sassi said. 'That's exactly what you wanted to do!' She took each of their hands. 'Now, is there any breakfast? I'm very late, so maybe we should skip breakfast and go straight on to smoko? What are your mum and dad up to?'

'Mum is doing the washing and Dad has gone to check the sheep in the paddock across the creek,' Jimmy said.

'Yeah, he said they didn't have any water,' Harry finished.

Sassi smiled at the twins' knowledge. They were so young yet knew so much about farming. The stab of envy she'd expected to feel towards these two beautiful little boys wasn't there. They would go on to take over this place; the farm where Sassi and Abe had worked alongside each other as they'd grown up. The five years between them had never felt like much of a gap.

Except when Abe had friends over and they'd tried to get away from Sassi, who had desperately wanted to hang out with them.

'You can't, you're a girl,' Abe had said.

'Why does that matter?'

'You can't ride motorbikes like we can.'

At ten, Sassi had crossed her arms and glared at him. 'Watch me.' Then she'd practised and practised and practised, and one afternoon, when all the boys were out riding, Sassi had grabbed her pa's bike from the shed and followed them out. Keeping up, crossing creek beds and manoeuvring around rocks and trees.

Abe hadn't ever said she wasn't as good as a boy again.

Sassi was glad the farm would stay in the family and be loved as much as she and Abe loved it.

It had taken time, but Sassi had come to terms with the fact she wouldn't get a look-in on the farm. Abe was the son, and he had sons of his own. The old adage was the eldest boy in the family gets the farm. And that was okay. She'd made a life for herself in New South Wales, running a feedlot. Her friends were there, she loved the area and she'd been gone from Barker so long that it was just a place for her to visit, with mixed feelings.

'You two are awful!' Renee stood in the doorway, hands on her hips. 'I asked you to leave Sassi alone!'

'She scared us, Mum,' Jimmy said earnestly.

'Yeah, she jumped out from behind the door,' Harry agreed.

Renee's lips twitched then she rearranged them into a straight line. 'Well then, I think that was very clever of Sassi.' Her eyes moved in the direction of Sassi's. 'Coffee?'

'Yes, please. But I can get it. Come on, you two. You can show me where the cereal is so I can have some brekkie. Where's Jarrah? And why aren't you at school? Today is Wednesday, isn't it?'

'It's Saturday!' they chorused together.

'And we only go to kindy on Tuesday and Thursday,' Jimmy told her. 'Jarrah's gone with Dad. He said she needed a run.'

'Oops, silly me.' She let the boys lead her to the kitchen.

Renee had changed the farmhouse since she'd lived here, in a good way. The tired green curtains that had been full of spider webs and sun rot had been replaced with bright blue ones, tied back with white ribbons. The table that had sat in the middle of the kitchen floor for as many years as Sassi could remember had moved into town at the same time as her grandparents. In its place stood a dark wood eight-seater table with grey leather chairs. There were gum leaves in a vase in the middle, next to the salt and pepper shakers.

'New carpet?' Sassi nodded to the plush grey pile that lined the passageway and sitting room.

'Oh my god, it's been sooo nice since that other carpet was replaced. I don't know how long it had been there for, but most times I walked on it with bare feet the staples would prick me! Do you like the new colour?'

'Yeah, I do.' It matched the picture frames on the wall, which were filled with baby photos of the boys all the way through to the present.

'And we had the house painted as well. I felt like it needed a refresh. Arctic white.' Renee seemed anxious, as if Sassi might not like the changes that had been made to her childhood home.

'The fact that Abe spent money on something that wasn't the farm is amazing!' Renee continued. 'You know what farmers are like. Always needing a new tractor or boom spray or something. Just so long as the house is livable, everything is all right!' Renee rolled her eyes as she switched on the kettle. 'I swear some farmers would sleep under a broken barbed-wire fence, providing they have their stock and operational machinery!'

Sassi laughed. 'You're spot on! But this all looks lovely.'

'And I'm lucky,' Renee continued. 'A couple of my friends haven't been able to change a thing in the houses they moved into once they were married.' She peered closely at Sassi. 'How are you feeling today? Those bruises look worse now, they've come out yellow and blue.'

'I can count four colours on your face, Sassi,' Harry said, reaching up to touch her cheek.

Sassi caught his hand. 'Nuh-uh. Don't touch. My face is still a bit sore. Do you have jobs to do this morning? Got to feed the chooks or something?'

'We've done them already,' Jimmy said.

The sound of a ute pulling up distracted them. 'Here's Dad!'

In a tangle of legs, hair and arms, they both raced out to meet Abe.

Sassi laughed. 'Are you permanently exhausted with those two?'

'You wouldn't believe how much,' Renee said, setting out three mugs and two plastic cups on the bench. She put some Milo on the table and two spoons in the places that Harry and Jimmy sat.

'Can I do anything?'

'Nah, all good.'

They lapsed into silence, listening to Abe telling the boys that the windmill hadn't been pumping properly, which is why the sheep didn't have any water. The sounds of their voices came closer as they neared the house.

'How'd you fix it, Dad?'

'Did you have to climb to the top?'

'I want to climb to the top.'

'Me too.'

'Boys, I've told you before, you are not to go anywhere near those windmills and you're certainly not to climb up the ladder. You could fall.'

'I wouldn't.'

'Me either!'

Their words came out at a dizzying speed; almost as fast as they seemed to move. Sassi came to the conclusion they had two speeds: fast and stop.

Abe and the twins walked in. Jarrah was at their heels, her tongue lolling to one side while she puffed hard. She saw Sassi and took a flying leap to land on her lap.

'Oomph! Jarrah! Stop it.' Sassi tried to fend off the licks and love that Jarrah was heaping on her. 'Stop it!' Grabbing the dog around the collar, she pulled her gently to the ground and made her sit, until finally Jarrah stopped wriggling and looked up at her mistress with delight.

'There's a good girl,' Sassi soothed and patted her head. 'I've missed you, too.'

Her tail thumped on the floor and Jimmy sat down next to her, his arms around her neck.

'I love Jarrah,' he said. 'Can she stay with me?'

'Don't be silly, Jimmy,' Renee told him. 'Jarrah is Sassi's dog and she loves her, too.'

Renee was pouring the drinks now; Sassi still hadn't got used to seeing her in the place that Granny had always stood.

'I remember Granny used to make these shortbread biscuits and leave them cooling over there,' Sassi said, distracting the kids from Jarrah.

'She did,' Abe said. 'And her chocolate cake was legendary. Couldn't leave it out when these two were around, because they'd eat it before it was cool!'

'Do you miss her?' Harry climbed up onto Sassi's lap. 'Sometimes Granny would let us have ice cream with Milo on it after lunch when we visited her and Pa.'

A moment passed before Sassi could answer. 'I do. Very much.'

'Why is your voice croaky? You sound like a frog,' Harry told her.

Sassi cleared her throat. In the three days she'd been back in Barker, she'd gone to ring her grandmother every day. Each time she'd remembered Granny wasn't there to answer the phone anymore and that numb feeling had crept across her insides.

Harry sat at the kitchen table and, grabbing a spoon, he started heaping Milo into the milk that Renee had put in front him.

'One spoonful is enough!' Abe told him.

Sassi turned to the boys. 'I'll tell you a secret,' she said, leaning in towards them. 'Ice cream and Milo is my favourite dessert, and Granny used to let me have it when I was your age. And Milo and milk is still my favourite drink and I'm nearly as old as your dad.'

'It's my favourite, too!' Harry declared and took a big mouthful, leaving a rim of milk and chocolate malt around his mouth. When he grinned, there was some Milo on his teeth.

Her heart melted. These boys made it hard to be sad for long. Their laughs were infectious, their thirst for knowledge and love of life irresistible. Sassi decided that every grieving family should have four-year-old twins, because they wouldn't feel too sad. Or if they did, it wouldn't be for long.

'Right, boys, can you take your drinks outside, so nothing is spilled on the table, please?'

'But—'

'No buts,' Abe interjected before Renee had the opportunity to. 'Out you go. I'll finish my coffee then how about we take Sassi and Jarrah for a drive around the farm?'

'Sounds good to me,' Sassi said over their cheers. 'You'd better take Jarrah outside with you, so she doesn't make a mess here.'

The door banged behind the kids and dog, and peace took over the kitchen. Renee sank down, a cup of hot tea in her hand.

'You would not believe how blissful it is when there's no noise,' she said to no one in particular.

Abe reached out and took her hand, giving it a squeeze. Sassi noticed he smiled at her in a way that said so many things: you're an awesome mum; I know you're tired, hang in there; I love you.

Had Ewin ever looked at her like that? Perhaps in the beginning, when they were learning everything about each other and going everywhere together.

In the middle of the busy season, when they were sending steers off every second weighing, weighing them twice a week and feeding them every day, Sassi had managed to get pneumonia and had been banished to bed on two different types of antibiotics.

Ewin had googled chicken soup, then driven to town after work to buy all the ingredients. By eight o'clock that night, he was spooning the soup into a bowl and delivering it to her bed.

She'd known he loved her then; he hadn't had to tell her with words, his actions had showed everything he felt.

When had it changed? Sassi wondered. The thought reminded her of the text message she still hadn't answered. Along with the second one she hadn't read yet.

I'm sorry.

Ewin hadn't really done anything wrong, so Sassi didn't think he had anything to apologise for. Except he'd changed his mind about them. That wasn't a crime, even if it had broken her heart.

'Dave the copper rang this morning,' Abe said, breaking into her thoughts as he heaped sugar into his cup. 'He thinks he's found a lady to help Dad out. Maybe we could have a yarn with her. What do you think?' He looked at Sassi.

'Oh wow, that was quick. Is it someone we know?'

'Nah. Well, at least, I haven't met her. She's just moved to town with her kids. She's from Sudan.' He turned his attention to Renee. 'Have you met her, love?'

Renee shook her head. 'But I have seen a lady who's been stacking shelves at the IGA. Maybe that's her? Dark-skinned with the most beautiful thick hair.'

Sassi blinked. 'She's a person of colour?'

'If it's the woman I've seen in IGA, then yes.'

Abe put his spoon down. 'Shouldn't make any difference, should it?'

'No, of course not! There's no way it should, but this is Pa we're talking about and he's not known for moving with the times.'

'Let's cross that bridge when we come to it. I rang Amber to tell her, but only got her message bank. I want to have a quick chat with her before I organise a time.'

'I think you'll find he'll be okay,' Renee said, taking a sip of her tea. 'Maybe you two are remembering what he was like, not who he is now. We seem to do that as families, don't we? Remember how someone was and don't make allowances or see who they can or do become. When they change. I think we keep our childhood perceptions of our whole families.'

Sassi opened her mouth to say something, then shut it again. She had noticed a difference in Pa. The gruff, angry man wasn't as angry. He was still crotchety. Abrupt. But not the burning anger that Sassi remembered from her childhood. Maybe his changed behaviour was because he was grieving for Granny. *But,* she reminded herself, *I haven't spent a lot of time here so I wouldn't really know what he is like now.*

The FaceTime calls to Granny never really showed her exactly what was going on. The visits she'd made were only long enough to make sure she remembered what everyone looked like and to allow her to have a relationship with her cousins that she never would have had otherwise.

'The stroke changed him,' Abe said. 'I know he can't talk very well, but sometimes he gets the boys to sit with him, grabs a book and points at the words then the picture that matches. It's almost like he's trying to teach them words.'

Sassi was astonished. 'He used to look at me as if he didn't know who I was. I was never sure whether that was because he was worried that I was going to do what Mum did, or he didn't want to know me *because* of what Mum did.'

'I don't think it was either,' Renee said. 'I'm sure his behaviour was the only way he knew how to cope with the grief of his daughter leaving. Not the fact Amber had disappointed him, more so that he had lost her. And he was ashamed of himself for playing a part in that. Let's not forget that anger is a symptom of hurt.'

'That's true,' Sassi said. 'Anger is a manifestation of lots of different emotions.' She paused as she looked around and saw a photo of her grandparents hanging on the wall. Taking her coffee with her, she assessed the image. It had been taken under the tall gum tree near the machinery shed, tables close by, filled with food and a birthday cake.

Both the kids were dressed in their Sunday best. Amber and Abe looked as if they were in primary school. Pa had his hand on Granny's shoulder and was looking at her, while she crouched down, talking to the children. To the left there was a table with a birthday cake, twelve candles were lit.

'Where did you get this photo? I haven't seen it before.'

Renee came to stand beside her. 'I found it in one of the drawers in the spare room after we moved in together. I think it says a lot about the family.'

'Look at the way Pa is looking at Granny. There's so much love in his expression.'

'And that is mirrored in the way Mum is looking at us kids,' Abe said. He put his arm around Renee's shoulders.

'I think love is supposed to fix everything, isn't it?' Sassi asked quietly as she thought about the angst between her mother and Pa and her mother and herself.

She turned away from the photo. 'I might take Jarrah and go back and stay with Pa tonight. Talk to Mum and see if I can crack that armour.'

CHAPTER 13

Half an hour later, Sassi, Abe and the twins piled into the dual-cab ute and set off towards the back of the farm. Jarrah leaned out from the side of the tray wagging her tail.

A quick glance in the side mirror showed her ears pushed back in the wind and her cheeks blown out. Just a dog enjoying her life.

'The neighbours and I have put in a new boundary fence,' Abe said. 'We were having all sorts of trouble with sheep going back and forth. Not that either of us have stock with lice or any diseases, but the time we took to load them up and run them back to each other's place was dead time.'

'How long is the new fence?' Sassi asked.

'Eight point nine kay ems,' Harry said from the back seat, sounding pleased with himself.

Sassi turned. 'How do you know that?'

'Dad talked about it a lot. Eight point nine, eight point nine kay ems.' Jimmy tapped his head with his pointer finger. 'Costs lots of money to put in a fence that long.'

'Are you meaning kilometres?'

'Kay ems.' Harry nodded.

'Are you sure you two are only four?'

Sassi shot Abe a glance.

He had been watching the road with a wide grin on his face. When he saw she was looking over, he pushed his hat back and scratched his head. 'Must've complained about the length and the price a bit more than I thought I did,' he said.

In the back seat, the boys giggled and peered out of the windows. 'There're eight hundred sheep in that paddock there,' Harry said pointing to a gate that was closed.

'Sorry, old mate,' Abe said. 'I've shifted those sheep and forgotten to tell you. There's zero in there now.'

'Where'd you put 'em?' Jimmy wanted to know.

'Why do you think we're heading out the back?' Abe asked.

'Ohhh.' Both boys looked at each other and then at their father.

'How many sheep are here all together?' Sassi asked, pretty sure it was the boys who were going to answer.

'Fifty million,' Jimmy said.

'No, there's not.' Harry sounded as if he'd just discovered his brother was an idiot. 'Only fifty hundred.'

'Fifty hundred?' Sassi echoed. She tried not to laugh at

the little boys imitating their dad—they were so serious she didn't want to disappoint them.

'I think what you're both trying to say, is one thousand, five hundred,' Abe broke in, laughing. 'We have one,' he held up one finger. 'Five.' A whole hand. 'Zero, zero.' He clenched his fist to indicate a zero.

'You're pretty good at this farming stuff, boys,' Sassi told them. 'Do you know what crop Dad is going to seed this year?'

'Wheat.' They said the word together, completely sure of that answer.

'I look after the same number of cattle as you've got sheep here, in a feedlot. Do you know what a feedlot is?'

'Where you feed cattle?' Jimmy asked.

'Yep, in small pens so they don't walk very much. We try to get them to put on a nice amount of weight so we can eat them later. Look.' She got out her mobile phone and brought up some photos she'd taken about three weeks ago.

Beautiful glossy Angus steers being brought into the finishing pens. Their feed would consist of high protein, energy and roughage now, plus some mineral mix. She looked at them proudly.

'These cattle probably only have another ten days on feed,' she said.

The ute bounced in a rut and the boys pretended to bounce higher than needed.

'We haven't got any cattle,' Harry told her.

'It's not really cattle country here, is it? Not enough rain to grow grass for them.'

'Who do you sell your cattle to?' asked Abe.

'A family-run abattoir who like to buy from family farmers. The Tilfords, who I work for, are one of the oldest farming families in the state. Bennetts are the abattoir owners and they sell the meat into independent butchers and grocery stores. They've had a long association.

'You know, the agricultural industry is different from here. Lots of private buyers have started up their own businesses, for stock and wool. Makes for a lot more competition, which is fantastic. We don't have to use the main agribusinesses like we have done in the past.'

'Out here, I'm stuck having to use the stock agents everyone else uses,' Abe said as they drove through a creek. 'If I've only got one hundred lambs to sell at the time, well, that's not going to fill a truck so I have to rely on the agent to put a whole truck together using people around here so we don't get slogged too much in freight. Bloody annoying, especially when I know I could get better prices if they went to the sale yards.' He stretched his arms out, still holding on to the steering wheel and pushed his body back in the seat.

'I've thought about buying my own truck and carting them there,' he continued, 'but I've got enough to do without adding another job to the list.'

'You know what Pa would say,' Sassi said. 'We're farmers, boy, not truck drivers.'

They laughed and fell into a comfortable silence. There wasn't a peep from the back seat.

'Doesn't take long to wear those two out.' Abe glanced in the rear-view mirror.

Sassi turned around and saw the twins leaning against each other, eyes shut.

'How do you know if they're really asleep?'

Abe grinned and mouthed, 'Watch this.' Aloud he said, 'Hey, Sass, see those roos over there?' He made his tone urgent. 'Over there, under the saltbush.'

'Where?' Sassi copied his tone and leaned forward. 'I can't see them.'

Abe pushed his foot on the accelerator and the ute shot forward. Jarrah gave a bark and leaned even further over the side, pulling the chain that tied her safely to the ute.

With no sound from the back seat. Abe started to slow.

'They're asleep,' he said. 'For some reason, they just love chasing roos. Get all excited. You'd think they were puppies!'

'Jarrah wouldn't mind having a go,' Sassi said with a grin. 'They're gorgeous kids, Abe.' Another glance to the back seat filled her heart with love. 'I wish I had half as much energy as they do. And the way you've taught them so much about our land and business—well, they'll be farming before they can add up their sums!'

Abe looked over at her. 'What about you, Sass. Any chance of you having any kids anytime soon? Got a bloke on the horizon?'

'Ewin's only been gone six months,' she said. 'I'm nowhere near ready to get mixed up with another man. And I'm not sure I want to, anyway.'

'What happened there? You never told me.' He brought the ute to a stop. 'Just before you answer that, look at this.' Pointing to a large mound of dirt he continued to talk. 'I've dug two new dams. One here and one a bit further to the south. See how I've got them in the gully of the hills?'

'They're huge. How much will they hold?'

'Hopefully, when they're full, they'll give me three years' worth of water between them, if we don't get any rain during that time. I'm really trying to drought-proof this farm.' He ran his hand along the dash to wipe the dust away. 'The last few years have been good. The break of the season has been on time and we've grown good crops. The wool price has been high so everything has been going along well.

'But Dad has always reminded me that there are always bad years and sometimes the bad times last longer than the good ones. That's why I decided to spend a bit of money on the house while I could and do some capital improvements on the farm. I don't want to get caught out.'

'That's a really good idea,' Sassi said. 'We've had three bad seasons and low yields, and prices cause problems quickly. We're in an industry where, as the farmer, we are the price taker not the price setter, unfortunately.'

'Don't I know it! Anyway, sorry, I asked about Ewin.'

Sassi huffed through her nose. 'I'd rather talk farming.'

'You don't have to tell me if you don't want to.'

Sassi chewed the inside of her cheek, then realised doing so pulled her skin and made it hurt. 'To be honest, Abe, I'm not sure what happened. I thought we were happy. Both living on the farm. He was overseeing the cropping part of the business and I had the feedlot. I think we stopped talking, you know, got so busy with what we were doing.

'I noticed he'd seemed withdrawn for a while and I asked him if anything was wrong.' She shrugged, pushing down the hurt that still seemed to overtake her unexpectedly at times. Then she told Abe the rest.

One day the boss had pulled up at the feedlot office and asked her if she was staying on.

'Staying?' she'd replied, confused. 'Of course, I am. Why wouldn't I be?'

'Well, if Ewin is buggering off, I assumed you would be, too.'

'I'm not going anywhere. Where is—' Sassi hadn't had a chance to ask any questions because her boss had kept talking.

'Oh, I understand why he has to go back to Western Australia. Sons have to go home, don't they? Start taking over the reins before the old man gets too old. But, geez, he's going to be sorely missed here. How come you're not going, anyhow?'

Her boss's hands had been hanging over the edge of the window as he'd spoken to her. His faded gold wedding band had caught Sassi's attention. Had it been three months earlier that she and Ewin had talked about tying the knot? Somewhere thereabouts, anyway.

'I . . .' Sassi had tried to speak, but she found she couldn't.

'I'll be sorry to lose him, Sassi. Ewin is a good manager, but I have to say I'm glad you're not going. Trying to replace both of you would have been a nightmare.' He'd put the ute in gear and driven off, not realising he'd just broken Sassi's world apart.

She had actually been feeling disbelief until she saw Ewin had rounded a nearby corner. He'd seen the exchange and stopped, guilt flooding his face.

And then she had known. What her boss had said was true. He was going and she wasn't invited.

The humiliation and sadness still burned.

'Why wouldn't the move have included you?' Abe reached out and touched her hand in sympathy.

'Who knows!' Sassi flipped her other hand as if it really didn't matter now. 'His dad always ruled the roost. Maybe he set some parameters down. Anyhow, Ewin didn't tell me.'

She looked out the window and drank in the familiar sights of the farm. The tall, purple hills covered in rocks and trees could look harsh to some, but she loved every rock, nook and cranny. And she knew this land like the back of her hand. It was home.

'Ewin and I had our differences,' she said. 'Although I did think for a while we might get married. But something changed for him, and once he'd made the decision to go, he was gone within two weeks.'

She remembered their awkward goodbye, Ewin just saying, 'Catch you later,' and then the ute revving, spraying a bit of gravel before the dust from the driveway had engulfed him.

'Do you miss him?' Abe asked gently.

'For a while I couldn't feel anything. Must've been the shock, because him leaving really blindsided me. Then slowly I started to . . . I missed him more than I could explain. When you're used to having someone in the house all the time—doesn't matter if they don't make much noise, or if you are in different rooms—but when they go, the house seems to know and becomes silent. So silent.' Her voice trailed off. 'Then that silence sort of seeps into everything around you.' She sighed and looked at him. 'Time moves on, doesn't it? I worked and worked and slowly forgot that I felt like my body was in a million pieces. Mostly, I'm pretty good these days, but it's taken a while. We were together for six years, you know.'

'I'm sorry you had to go through that, Sass.' Abe touched her hand again.

'Yeah, we all have to have a bit of heartbreak, apparently. Well, that's what every country music song tells us anyway!'

Abe laughed softly.

Sassi turned to look at the twins. They were still sound asleep.

'What about you and Renee?' she asked. 'Even though these two seem to run you both ragged, you and Renee look happy.'

'I think we are,' Abe said simply. 'I think we are. And we're having another baby.' He winked at her. 'Without help this time.'

Sassi's eyes grew wide and a smile erupted on her face. 'Oh, Abe, that's so exciting! Congratulations.' She leaned over to grab his hand and squeeze it.

'Yeah, it is, although—' his voice cracked '—I wish Mum had known.'

CHAPTER 14

The church was decorated with gum leaves and Geraldton wax.

'We're sorry we can't do anything else,' the woman organising the church had told them. 'That heatwave really took its toll on all of our gardens and we just don't have any flowers left. Thank goodness it's much cooler now.'

'Isn't there a florist?' Amber asked.

Sassi had looked at her mother in disbelief. Had she really forgotten how small Barker was?

'We can get them over from Port Augusta, if you like?'

'Don't worry,' Abe had butted in. 'Mum wouldn't mind. She'd make do with what was in the garden.'

Amber had apologised and offered to fold the order of service booklets that had been printed from the council printer.

Now, Sassi sat in the church, Jimmy on her knee and Harry cuddling underneath her other arm. The scent of gum leaves wafted through the church combining with the wax from the burning candles, while lavender drifted in from behind. There must be a lady wearing perfume that smelt like the sort that Granny used to wear.

A rubber band squeezed around her heart.

'Why is Granny in that box?' Harry asked, pointing to the coffin at the front.

The gold handles reflected a flame from one of the candles, dancing and blurring in front of her eyes.

Sassi gently pushed Harry's hand down. 'Don't point,' she whispered. 'It's rude.'

'Why are there so many candles?' Jimmy wanted to know. 'And why are they in a church? We have candles on birthday cakes. Can we blow these ones out?'

Sassi wanted them both to be quiet so she could concentrate on not crying. The church behind her was full; she'd had no idea that Granny had touched so many people in the town.

'Do you think they're all just here to stickybeak?' she'd asked Abe earlier when they'd pulled up at the front of the church.

'I don't think so. Mum got pretty involved in a lot of community groups when she moved into town. There was some garden committee she was on and she'd been volunteering at the library a couple of mornings a week.'

'What was her favourite thing to do?' Amber's lips had trembled as she'd asked and her hands had twisted the tissue she was holding.

Sassi had thought how sad it was her mother didn't really know the woman who had raised her. Amber seemed hungry for information about her mother. The previous evening, when Sassi had returned from the farm, Amber had been in the lounge room looking through photo albums. She'd tapped at a photo of Granny and Pa in the sheep yards. It had been a black-and-white photo, Granny wearing her standard uniform of blue overalls and Pa wearing baggy pants held up by a set of suspenders. His little cap looked out of place in the yards and certainly wouldn't have done anything to stop the sun damage they could see on his face now—and Granny wasn't wearing either a cap or a hat!

'Look how close they are,' Amber had said to Sassi. 'He's even got his arm around her. In the sheep yards!'

'I think they were always great friends,' Sassi had said, sitting down next to her mother. 'Abe has one up on the wall in his house, showing all four of you, and Pa was looking at Granny like she was the only thing in his world.'

'Hmm, maybe.' Amber didn't sound convinced.

'It's such a shame Zola couldn't come over,' Sassi said, trying to keep her mother talking. 'He didn't want to?'

Amber shifted on the couch and turned the page. The next photo showed the first poles being cemented in for the tennis court that was next to the farmhouse.

'I told him it wasn't necessary,' Amber said, not looking at Sassi. 'He means everything to me and it would have been wonderful to have him here, but it just wasn't possible.' There was a pause.

'I'm sure you would have loved to have his support right now, though?'

'Of course, and I guess it might have been nice for you to meet him, but like I said, we weren't able to make it happen.' She changed the subject. 'I remember when they put the tennis court in. On Sundays after church, Mum and Dad would invite people back to play. There was some fierce competition.'

'Did you like playing tennis?'

'No.' Amber shook her head. 'I used to head for the hills when everyone turned up.'

Now, in the church, Amber, dressed in a dark pants suit with her hair pulled back into a low ponytail, was sitting next to Pa who was on the end of the row, his cane stuck out into the aisle. Sassi hoped it didn't trip anyone over. Abe and Renee were next, then Harry, Sassi and Jimmy.

There were some familiar faces in the crowd: the policeman and his wife and the young constable, who Hamish had told her had driven the ambulance back to town. She couldn't remember her name. Instead, she'd smiled and nodded when she saw her at the back of the church. She would try to catch up with her afterwards to thank her for her kindness.

Some of the parents of the kids she'd gone to school with were there; older of course, but not as old as Granny had been.

She became aware of Harry poking her.

'What?'

'You didn't answer my question.'

'Which one?'

'Why is Granny in the box?'

Tears pricked Sassi's eyes, but she tried not to let Harry see. 'Well, when someone dies, they can get buried in the ground and, to do that, they have to be in a special box called a coffin. That's what Granny's in now.'

'We don't bury the dead sheep,' Jimmy told her. 'Just drag 'em to the tip.'

'That's right,' Sassi agreed. 'But people we love are different from sheep and we all loved Granny, didn't we?'

For a second there was blissful silence and Sassi took a breath, trying to control her feelings. Was it wrong to let her cousins see that she was upset?

Grief was normal when someone died. But she wasn't sure she had the energy to explain her tears to the twins.

A quick check of Renee, who had a tissue curled up in her hand and a box full of sultanas she was trying to get Harry to take to keep him quiet. Harry was studiously looking away from his mother.

She touched Renee's hand to get her attention and then pointed to the lollipops she had sticking out of her pocket. Renee nodded gratefully.

Now that Sassi knew Abe and Renee were having another baby, she could pick the slight swell of Renee's stomach under the skirt. She reached in and got the lollipops.

'What's he wearing?' Harry asked.

The minister was now standing at the pulpit, a white gown over his suit. Surely he must be expiring wearing so many clothes. The fans were lazily spinning overhead, not doing anything to cool the church down, only spreading the stifling heat over everyone.

The congregation was silent except for the sound of pages flapping as people fanned themselves with the order of service and flies buzzed against the stained-glass arch windows.

'It's his, um . . . uniform,' Sassi said. 'He has to wear that when he's talking to us about God.'

Harry wrinkled his forehead. 'Isn't he supposed to be talking about Granny?'

Sassi pressed her hand to one of her eyes. There was a harsh ache behind it and, as much as she loved her cousins, they were making the pain worse.

'You boys need to be quiet now, okay?' Sassi told them. 'Because the minister is going to talk to us very soon. Here, would you like a lollipop?'

'Dad says that's bebry.'

'What?'

'No, it's bibery,' Jimmy said scornfully.

'Shh, you mean *bribery*, and I don't care what it is, but I'm serious now, boys, shh. Okay?' She handed them each a lollipop and put her finger to her lips.

Harry's next words were drowned out by the sound of organ music, playing hymn number 132 from the *Australian Hymn Book*. The congregation stood, books in hand, and started to sing.

Pa didn't though. Sassi watched as he stood, shakily hanging onto his walking stick, his arm tucked through Amber's.

He tried to make his lips move in time with the words, but there was no noise coming out and there was a tiny bit of dribble on his chin.

Sassi wondered what had happened between Amber and her pa for them to be so cordial today. Pa was even looking to Amber for help now and there wasn't the disgust Sassi had noted the previous day on Amber's face as she wiped his chin. Maybe the time alone, and Granny's death, had shown them that age was against them both. If they were going to reconcile they had to do it now. Forgiveness set people free.

She hoped that's what it was. Like Sassi was trying to do with Amber. That's what she was also trying to do with Ewin. He should be here holding her hand. They should have been sharing the driving the morning she had the accident. Did the last six years mean nothing to him? *It mustn't*, common sense told her. *Otherwise, he'd be here now.*

The stabbing pain behind her eye started to move down her cheek and into the roof of her mouth.

Don't think about him, she told herself. A thought popped into her head: she and Amber were both missing and wanting their partners, and neither was able to be there. Different circumstances, of course, but perhaps they had more in common than Sassi had realised.

Blinking a couple of times, she refocused on the little warm bodies surrounding her and their hair, which smelt like shampoo and love. Giving Jimmy a gentle squeeze, she rested her head against his.

The music had stopped and the minister was quiet, walking forward with a hand outstretched to help Pa, but Amber shook her head and took a step forward, making sure Pa's hand was holding her arm.

Together, they stood next to the coffin and faced the crowd.

'For those of you who don't know, I'm Amber Stapleton. Dad has asked me to read this to you.' She cleared her throat.

'Fifty-something years ago, I met Cora at a dance,' she said. 'I knew right from the start she was the girl for me, but it took some time for her to agree to have the same thoughts.'

There was laughter.

Abe was staring ahead, his jaw working overtime. Sassi wanted to touch his arm, to take away some of his pain. Renee laced her fingers through her husband's and he glanced at her gratefully.

Sassi felt the intense loneliness that chased her in the early, empty hours of the mornings.

'We had a good life. We loved each other, and if you've got someone who loves you, even when you're not on your best behaviour, then you should hold on to them.'

Amber folded the piece of paper and then took something from her pocket and gave it to Pa.

He bent towards the coffin and placed something sparkly on the top, then leaned down. Whispering to his wife, something no one could hear, he stayed like that for a moment, then stood up, looking for Amber's arm.

The cool wind whipped around the headstones as the mourners walked in twos or groups away from the freshly turned earth. They were making their way to the hall next to the church for coffee and cake.

Sassi was sick and tired of smiling and thanking people for coming. Sick of hearing: 'How nice you were able to make it here for the funeral.' Annoyed with the small talk that didn't matter. She wanted to go home and sink into bed with an icepack on her head, take a Panadol and maybe cradle a glass of wine.

'Sassi, it's nice to see you back.' It was a low female voice behind her. 'I'm sorry about your grandmother.'

Holly's mother, Michelle Trapper, stood there holding a bunch of flowers. Lavender and a white flower that Sassi didn't know. 'Your granny loved these flowers. I thought you might like to take them with you. They're all I had left in my garden. Leaving flowers on a grave is a waste of something beautiful. They're better brightening up the house.'

'Thanks,' Sassi said. 'That's a lovely thought and—' She held the bunch up. 'These are lovely. How are you? And Mr Trapper?'

'Oh, we're fine. We miss Holly, of course, but she is doing very well. Did you hear she's getting married?'

Sassi shook her head. She hadn't had a conversation with Holly in years. Not since Holly had left for New York, where she'd secured a job in a law firm. 'That's wonderful. Who is she marrying?'

'A partner in the firm where she works, apparently. We haven't met him. Such a long way to travel, isn't it? And, expensive. Holly is incredibly busy with work . . .' Her voice trailed off and Sassi saw the sadness touch her face.

'When did you see her last?'

'Gosh, it must be four or five years ago, I suppose. They work them very hard when they first join the business.'

'Yes, I think new lawyers are a bit like doctors-in-training. There's never a spare moment in the day. Or night! There wouldn't be much time to catch up with old friends. I haven't heard from her in ages.'

'It's easy to lose touch, isn't it? Would you like her email address?'

'That would be nice.' Sassi stood awkwardly, realising most of the crowd had left, except the constable who had driven the ambulance. She was crouching down at the end of what looked like a new grave. Her shoulders moved a little and Sassi wondered if she was crying.

'Here. I'm sure she'd love to hear from you.' Michelle gave her the piece of paper she'd finished writing on. 'Maybe you'd like to come around for a drink before you leave? We'd both like to hear what you're up to.' The wistfulness in her words hit Sassi; she wanted to hear about Holly, not Sassi, but she would make do with Sassi because she was a link to Holly—they were the same age, and perhaps, they might be doing or feeling the same kinds of things.

'Sure, that would be nice. Are you still in the same house?'

'Oh yes!' She smiled. 'Nothing much ever changes in Barker. I think you'd be able to knock on the door of any of the kids you went to school with and find their parents still living there. Anyway, looks like we're the only ones left, so I'll let you go to the wake. But please,' she reached out and put her hand on Sassi's arm, 'do come and see us before you head off. There must be lots to catch up on.'

'I will, and thanks for the flowers.'

Michelle walked away.

Sassi missed Holly. When her friend had told her she was moving to New York, Sassi had been thrilled for her. They hadn't caught up a lot since they'd finished school. Holly was busy studying and Sassi had been working on farms across Australia. Staying as far away from Barker as she could, still smarting from knowing she wouldn't have a place on the farm.

Why do kids not come home enough to see their parents? she wondered. There really is very little time in life.

'Hi, Sassi. You look a bit better than the last time I saw you.' Now the policewoman was talking to her.

'I feel much better,' Sassi said. 'Thanks for driving the ambulance to get me to the hospital. I'm so grateful.'

The police officer smiled but her eyes strayed to the grave she'd been standing at only moments before. The dirt hadn't settled properly yet and it was covered in wilted, dead flowers.

'You've lost someone recently?' Sassi asked.

'Yeah, my grandmother. Same as you.'

'I'm sorry.'

'It's tough, isn't it? Well, I'm finding it is. Nan raised me. Both of my parents are dead, so I feel like I'm an orphan now. And I don't really like that word very much.'

Without thinking, Sassi reached out and touched her arm. 'Granny raised me, too,' she said simply. 'What's your name?'

'I'm Mia. Mia Worth.'

'We could be twins, Mia, although your face doesn't look quite as bad as mine! What happened to you?'

'Oh, this?' she pointed to her nose. 'Perks of the job.'

'Doesn't look like a perk.' Sassi paused. 'Do you want to see if we can find a drink? I've had enough of today and what they're offering in the hall isn't going to cut it for me!'

CHAPTER 15

'I've just got to pop into the IGA and grab a couple of things,' Mia told Sassi as she came to a stop in front of the shop. 'Are you okay to head to the pub by yourself? I won't be far behind you.'

'Sure, see you there.'

Mia pushed the door open and went inside. The lights had been dimmed and the shop was being readied for closing.

'Hi, Mia. You've got half an hour,' the man behind the counter said. 'Can you do a shop in that time?' He smiled broadly.

'Watch me power shop,' she told him, knowing it would take less than three minutes to pick up the milk and washing powder she needed.

Quickly walking towards the fridge, she saw a woman placing the last few tins of sweet corn kernels on the shelf. Mia gave her a friendly smile as she walked past, and the woman ducked her head as she picked up the cardboard box and started to crush it.

Mia heard whispering as she opened the fridge door and reached in to grab a litre of milk.

'What's she even doing here?'

Looking around, Mia tried to see where the voices were coming from.

'She doesn't belong here.'

'And she certainly shouldn't be taking jobs away from locals.'

'Such a terrible thing to do when I know of two women who have lived here all their lives who could do with this job. I don't know what our world is coming to.'

Mia stuck her head around the end of an aisle and saw two elderly ladies with their heads together, speaking quietly. She recognised one of them as Pauline Simpson. The other lady she wasn't sure of.

Annoyance flared in her chest. She desperately wanted to dress them both down, but to what end? They were elderly women who had grown up in a different time.

Unless they were harming the woman, Mia probably couldn't do anything.

'Excuse me, ladies.' Mia came up behind them and reached for the washing powder they were standing in front of. 'Isn't it lovely to have fully stacked shelves here?' She grabbed a box, gave them both a smile and left them to their small-minded thoughts.

'G'day, Mia,' Hopper said as they walked into the pub. 'How's that face?'

'Better,' she told him. 'Just don't take any photos of me. I'm not back to model looks just yet.' She gave a cheeky grin.

'And what happened to our mate?'

'Dave cut him loose. His boss came and picked him up the next morning. Don't know where they ended up. Hopefully nowhere around here. Dave told him not to come back to Barker. Have you ever seen him before?'

Hopper shook his head. 'Hope I don't have to again, either. What's your poison?'

She reached into her pocket for her phone and looked at Sassi who was already waiting at the bar. 'What would you like to drink?'

'Just a wine, thanks.'

'Two SSBs, thanks, Hopper.'

'Coming up. Who's your mate?' He aimed his next words at Sassi. 'You look like you've been in the wars, too, love.'

'Just a little argument with my car and a kangaroo. I'm Sassi Stapleton.'

'Ah, that explains it. I heard you were back. Good to meet you. Sorry to hear about your grandmother. Her funeral was today, wasn't it? Took a while to get the okay to go ahead, so I hear.'

Sassi laughed a little hysterically, Mia thought.

'Everyone knows everything here, don't they? But yeah, there were a few hoops to jump through before we could hold the service.'

'I certainly don't miss much,' Hopper said and waved away Mia's phone. 'First one's on the house.'

She thanked him then ushered Sassi to a table in the corner, away from the noise of the bar.

'How long are you staying in Barker for?' Mia asked as they got comfortable.

'I've got a month off work so I can stay that long. I thought Pa might need a bit of help. It sounds like Mum is only staying around for another week, but I mightn't be needed if we can get Pa some home help before she leaves. If that's the case I reckon I'll give Abe a hand to get ready for seeding. He's got some machinery that needs servicing and the like.'

'You're a farmer?'

'Well, I've always wanted to be, but there's no room at home, so I took off and went working around Australia. Ended up in New South Wales, managing a cattle feedlot. So, I guess I am, just not on my own place.'

'Ever thought about buying your own piece of dirt?'

Laughing, Sassi held up her glass. 'Cheers. I wish I could, but land is worth a squillion dollars these days and I don't earn anywhere near that amount!'

'Cheers.' Mia clinked her glass to Sassi's. 'Must be hard knowing you can't come home to the place where you grew up.'

'Yeah, it took a while to get used to the idea but, really, I don't have any call on that land. Abe is my uncle and the son so it would automatically go to him, and only to me if something happened to him. And now he has twin boys, so there's no chance that I'll get a look-in.'

'That type of mentality sounds so old-fashioned.'

Sassi took a sip of her drink. 'Just the way it is for our family. I love working at the feedlot and I can't see me leaving there any time soon.'

'You and Abe must be pretty close in age, huh?'

Sassi smiled just enough to let Mia know she knew she was being quizzed and then nodded. 'Five years. My mum had me when she was sixteen.'

'Was it good fun to grow up with someone close to your own age? I'm an only child.' She rested her chin on her palm and regarded Sassi. 'You would have had your own playmate.'

'Yeah, Abe and I always got on really well. Used to raise a bit of hell when we were in our teens, but we were guns on motorbikes mustering the sheep through the hilly paddocks!'

Mia laughed. 'I can only imagine. Never been on a motorbike myself.'

'Would you like to go for a hoon sometime? If you don't mind being dinked. Come out to the farm, Abe and Renee won't mind. I'll take you for a ride and show you round.'

Mia widened her eyes and smiled at the same time. 'That sounds scary, dangerous and really awesome all at the same time.'

Sassi let out a laugh. 'There's nothing too scary about it.'

'Changing the subject and weird question—are there many women at the feedlot where you work?'

'A few. There's definitely more women working in agriculture compared to when I first started looking for work about ten years ago. I'm twenty-eight now.' She took a sip and regarded Mia. 'Always found it a bit awkward when the blokes were around and I had to find a bush to go to the loo. But I worked out pretty soon that they were fine, just so long as I knew my way around a set of yards. Which of course I did, having been on a farm since I was born.' She tipped her head to the side. 'You must find it hard being the only female cop in Barker.'

Mia gave a shrug. 'I've been in worse places. Broad River Station was pretty bad, but I was only there for a couple of days, thank god. I've really enjoyed my work here with Dave. The difference between the two stations is incredible.'

Her phone beeped on the table and their eyes flew to the screen.

Chris. Mia turned it off. Then quickly typed out a text saying she'd call him later.

'Boyfriend?' Sassi asked.

Shaking her head, Mia explained how she and Chris had been through the academy together.

'Kim, that's Dave's wife, she's sure Chris wants to have a relationship with me, but who's got time for that when we're trying to make a name for ourselves at work? Anyway, he's more like a brother. What about you?'

Sassi shook her head. 'I had a partner for six years, but he shot through about six months ago, so I'm footloose and fancy-free.'

'I don't think you'll change that status here in Barker,' Mia said with a grin.

Sassi spluttered into her drink.

They were quiet for a moment.

'What made you want to become a police officer?' Sassi twirled her glass around. 'Especially here.'

Mia shrugged. 'It was just a job I always wanted to do. I like helping people and there're a lot of opportunities to do that in a country town. We all know each other so it's harder when something horrible happens, but it's also more rewarding. I was born here and I was very keen to be close by to my nan when I came out of the academy. And, honestly,' Mia leaned forward, 'I'd rather be here than dealing with the shit that happens on the streets in the city. With the amount of drugs around, honestly, city cops have no idea what they're going to face on the streets each shift.'

'And your nan? She agreed with your job choice?'

Mia laughed. 'Well, yeah, but that didn't mean she wasn't worried. Especially when I first started at the academy. By the time I was stationed at Broad River, her memory was deteriorating, and I don't think she thought about the dangers we face as coppers. Or maybe she didn't think anything bad could happen in the country areas.' Mia took a sip. 'I don't think it crossed her mind by the end.'

'Here's to grandparents,' Sassi said, raising her glass.

'Yeah, to the grandparents who raised us.'

They clinked glasses.

'Hey, did the kids tease you when your grandmother turned up at school for parent–teacher interviews?' Sassi asked. 'Because they were so much older than all the other parents.'

Mia threw back her head and laughed. 'Yes! And I'd always get weird sandwiches. Everyone else would be having chicken and salad and I'd have corned beef and pickles. Chicken, according to Nan, was a special treat for a Sunday lunch after church or on Christmas day. The generation gap was huge!'

'I know, right? I was never allowed a lunch order from the canteen.'

'Me neither. Nan always cooked a roast on a Sunday so we had enough cold meat for the week. Usually mutton. Then we'd have to eat that for the rest of the week, and right at the end, she'd hack off what was left on the bone and make a curry. The dog would get the bone. Nothing was ever wasted.'

'"Waste not, want not," Granny used to say. And it sounds like they both did the same. She used to get out of sorts if I snuck some pocket money to school to buy something from the tuckshop. Even if it was something she didn't make. "If you take care of the pennies, the pounds take care of themselves," was another saying she had.'

Mia wanted to reach over and hug this woman who'd had the same unusual upbringing she'd had. How nice it was to have someone who could understand what her life had been like as a child. She grinned then touched her nose. 'God, that hurts. Stop making me laugh!'

'What about sport?' Sassi asked. 'Granny never liked me playing sport much. Thought it was a waste of money and fuel to be driving all over the district to run up and down a netball court. But I wasn't naturally sporty so I didn't mind. I preferred books and art.'

'I left Barker when I was still in early primary school so it was easier for me to play sport when I went to school in Adelaide.'

'I reckon we were lucky, Mia,' Sassi said. 'Lucky that our grandparents wanted to raise us. We could've ended up anywhere.'

'Isn't that the truth.' Mia took another sip of her drink. 'So, you said your mum was here. Why did you end up with your grandparents, if you don't mind me asking?'

A loud burst of laugher came from the bar and they looked over their shoulders. A young man was weaving his way towards them, beer in hand.

''Lo, ladies, can I buy you a drink?'

'We're good, Troy,' Mia answered immediately. 'But thanks for the offer.'

'Did you two fight each other?' Troy looked at them through his beer googles and then grinned. 'Wouldn't mind seeing that. Lovers' tiff?'

'Fuck off, Troy,' Mia said mildly. 'Don't be a dick.'

'But, Mia. You know I've been pining for you.'

'You and every other bloke on the footy team. Sorry, you're all out of luck.' She winked at him. 'Head back over to your mates and leave us alone, okay?'

'You're breaking my heart.' He clutched his hand to his chest, but turned away and started to stumble back across the floor. Then he spun around and squinted at Sassi. 'Do I know you?'

'Maybe. Not sure.'

'Ah, an exotic stranger.'

'I think your mates are calling,' Sassi told him, just as the door pushed open and the woman Mia had seen stacking the shelves at the IGA walked in with two small children. She pushed the kids towards the dining room with a nervous glance at the bar.

Everyone who was leaning on the bar turned to watch their path into the next room. Hopper picked up three menus and followed them through with a welcoming smile.

A couple of people put their heads together and spoke as they watched the newcomers.

'God, I get so sick of this shit!' Mia said, frowning.

'Must be a curse being pretty and having a uniform,' Sassi quipped. 'Every man's dream, I'd think.'

'What? Oh no, I don't mean that. Those blokes are harmless—all footy club fellas. I even play tennis with some of them. They know they're not going to get anywhere with me. It's all a big joke between us now.

'No, I mean this.' She indicated the people at the bar, who were still observing the family who were making their way to the restaurant. 'People don't seem to like newcomers. That family moved from Adelaide to have a better life here, and I keep seeing people talk about them. Just because they don't look like they fit in around here. As much as I love small towns, the small-mindedness gets to me at times.'

'The barman looked like he was being friendly,' Sassi said.

'Hopper loves everyone,' Mia told her. 'No, I mean the people who gossip and say nasty things, forgetting these people are just like them. They have feelings and family and a life.' Mia told Sassi about the old women she'd overheard in the IGA only a half hour before.

'They didn't really say that?'

Mia nodded. 'They did.' She could hear some local women speaking nearby now.

'I hear the children are going to school but they're having trouble speaking English. No one understands what they're saying. And I've never seen someone with skin so dark!'

'I thought there was an English test foreigners had to do before they were allowed into Australia.'

Sassi looked over at the restaurant. 'They must be the family Abe told me about. Apparently, Dave suggested the mother might be interested in helping to look after Pa.' She indicated her wine glass. 'Want another?'

'Why not? I don't have to work tomorrow.'

CHAPTER 16

'I'm going to the city for a couple of days,' Amber announced at the door of Granny and Pa's house.

Sassi noticed a suitcase at the door, already packed. Amber held the car keys in her hand. She must've been watching for her.

'What, now?' Sassi looked at her watch, confused. 'It's nearly ten pm. You won't get there until after two in the morning!'

'I know, but I have an appointment I must keep in the morning and it's easier to go now than to leave very early tomorrow. If I go now I'll avoid the roos around dawn. Let's try to avoid another accident in the family.' Amber put her hands huffily on her hips. 'If you'd been back earlier I would have left before now. Dad didn't want to be by himself after today. You know, Sassi, you can be very selfish at times, taking off the way you did today.'

Disbelief hit Sassi. Selfish? Her? What the hell did Amber think *she* was after dumping her only daughter with her parents and shooting through? 'Right, well, whatever you think you need to do,' Sassi answered stiffly and looked past her into the house. 'Pa in bed?'

'He's still up watching the news. I don't know why. It doesn't change from one hour to the next.'

'I guess it's company for him.'

Amber picked up her bag and tried to smile at Sassi. 'It's been a long day and the quicker I get to the city, the better it'll be. Look after yourself and Dad. I'll be back in a couple of days.'

'Sure.'

Amber left the house and Sassi heard the car door slam, then the engine start up. A flicker of doubt moved through her. Was this Amber's way of leaving without having to say goodbye? Would she come back?

'I guess you'll find out in a couple of days,' Sassi told herself, closing the door and heading to the lounge. The office light caught her attention and she popped her head in, to see if Pa was in there.

The room was empty.

She switched the light off and continued on.

'Hi, Pa. I'm back,' she told the sleeping figure.

He didn't answer.

Sassi fixed herself a Milo and sat down at the kitchen table, her head in her hands. When she'd gone to get drinks for her and Mia at the bar she'd heard two women talking. At first they'd been talking about the family who'd gone to the restaurant, but when Sassi walked past they'd dropped their voices lower.

'That's Amber Stapleton's illegitimate daughter,' one had said.

'Is she really?' The other woman had turned to look but her friend shoved her elbow.

'Back for her grandmother's funeral.'

Sassi had ordered the wine and shuffled closer to the women to try to hear more of what they were saying. She heard her granny's voice: 'Eavesdroppers never hear anything good about themselves.'

'She's quite pretty, isn't she? Looks like her mother. Not too much of her father in her, though, is there?'

Sassi had drawn in a breath. When she'd been young, she'd desperately wanted to know who her father was. She'd started by asking Granny, who hadn't answered her, then she'd gone to her mother.

Amber had shut her down as soon as the word 'father' had come out of her mouth.

She had whispered conversations with Abe about it when no one had been listening, and she'd found herself searching every man's face at school concerts and sports days. Did any of them look like her?

'Didn't think we ever knew who he was?' The woman had stared openly at her then, maybe looking for any resemblance to any of the men she knew in Barker.

'Carol from the hairdresser always thought it was the Year Four teacher. Highly illegal, of course, but then Jan from the caravan park told me it was Peter Benson's son. What's his name? Roger? Rory?'

'Oh yes, Roger. But don't forget, Amber was in Adelaide when she got pregnant. I don't think the boy could be local.'

'Well, it was a long time ago. Look at her, she must be nearly thirty.'

Sassi had picked up the drinks, feeling adrift in a room of people who seemed to have knowledge of a whole part of her life that she herself didn't know anything about.

Now, in Pa's kitchen, the words from the two ladies in the bar were still ringing in her ears.

Would Amber have told Granny who Sassi's father was? Pa wouldn't have known; he wouldn't have wanted to.

Her headache that had started at the funeral was back in force and she rubbed her temples, willing it away. A clear mind would be helpful if she was going to work through this father issue. It sounded like the whole town had an opinion on who her father could be, but who else could know, other than Amber?

'Illegitimate,' she said aloud, testing the word. Many years had passed since the kids had taunted her with that word. For a long time, she hadn't even known what it had meant, until Holly had told off one of the boys for saying it.

'That's a mean word and it's not nice to use.'

If Abe knew who her father was, Sassi was sure he would have told her already. Still, it wouldn't hurt to ask.

Would it?

But do I really want to know? she wondered. *How much would it change?*

Restless, she got up and walked the passageway, then down to the back of the house and out into the garden.

The moonlight was soft and the breeze picked up the scent of the rose petals on the ground. Wriggling into the swinging chair, her feet pushed off and she let the rhythmic movement soothe her.

She'd spent her whole life not knowing who her father was. Mostly she was happy and content without this knowledge, so perhaps it would be better for her not to try to find out now. She shook her head as if to try to clear it, and the urge to ring Ewin to talk it through flooded her body. She ached for his familiar hands and his gentle kisses.

Ewin. She hadn't read his second text message.

Bringing up the text app, she waited a moment before tapping to open the message.

I'm sorry.

And the second one: *Can we talk?*

Her head fell back against the chair and it continued the calming rocking motion, while Sassi let her thoughts run free.

Maybe she should call Ewin. They'd said so little when he'd left, maybe he needed to tell her why now. Why she hadn't been able to head back west with him. Why his family hadn't wanted her, and how he was able to give her up so easily.

Could she bear to hear his voice, though? Or would that set her back just when she was starting to find her own feet again?

Ewin's why, Sassi thought, *is a bit like trying to work out whether I want to know who my father is. The outcome will still be the same—Ewin and I are no longer together. And knowing who my father is probably won't change his role in my life either.*

She let the phone fall from her fingers.

Neither of those puzzles were going to get solved tonight, she decided. The day had been a long and emotional one.

When Granny's coffin had been lowered into the ground earlier that day, both the twins had gasped. For all their bravado and knowledge of farming and death, they hadn't understood why the woman who had made shortbread biscuits and played with them was being put in the ground.

Harry had started to cry first, and Jimmy had followed. Not long after that Sassi had started weeping, too.

Renee had gathered up the boys and taken them a little way away, while Abe and the pallbearers finished their duties, and the minister had said his final words.

Sassi had reached out to hold Pa's arm, to offer and receive comfort. There had been the glimmer of tears in his eyes when she did that, but when she looked again, his eyes seemed dry.

Only Amber had stood tall and erect, apart from the family group, appearing unaffected.

And only Sassi knew that wasn't the case.

Last night Amber had sat out here, in this exact chair, sobbing as if her heart was breaking her whole body in two.

Sassi had still been awake and had heard the spare room door open, then the floorboards creaking as they always did when someone was standing in front of the kitchen.

A few more moments of silence and the back door had swung open.

Sassi had got out of bed to see what Amber was doing. Then she'd heard the sobs.

And the words: 'I'm sorry. I'm sorry, I'm sorry.'

Right then, it had seemed to Sassi there were a whole lot of people apologising for things they could have fixed or not let happen in the first place.

Sassi shook her head. *Stop being a bitch,* she thought. *It's not like you've never made a mistake.*

From inside the house, Sassi heard the clump of Pa's walking stick on the wooden floor. He must have decided it was bedtime.

The crash of crockery startled Sassi and she shot out of the chair and towards the house. 'Pa?' she called. 'Pa?'

A thump and a thud.

Yanking open the door, she ran through the empty passageway, glancing into the kitchen and then the lounge.

Pa was on the floor, his hands trying to reach his walking stick.

'Pa? Oh my god, are you all right?'

He grunted at her, hands still reaching, searching. ''ick. Nee . . .'

'It's here, it's here.' She grabbed the cane that was lying on the floor just out of his reach and put it into his hands. 'Let's try to get you up. Does anything hurt?'

He didn't answer, only tried to turn over and get on to his knees. He rocked and rocked, but he couldn't get over.

Sassi fished out her phone and dialled Abe. 'Can you come? Pa's had a fall.'

~

It seemed an age before she heard footsteps on the verandah, and the front door opening and shutting loudly.

By then, Sassi had a pillow under Pa's head, a blanket tucked in around his frail body, and a hot water bottle underneath.

'We're in the lounge,' she called.

Abe's flustered face appeared and, two steps later, he was next to his dad, reaching down to grasp his hand. 'Dad.'

'Ah,' Pa said.

'I can't get him up,' Sassi told Abe.

'Do you think anything is broken?'

'No, I think he's just had a hell of a fright.'

'Be—' the old man's voice quavered. 'Berum.'

'Bedroom? We'll get you there.'

'Nah hom.'

Sassi looked at Abe, despair flooding her stomach.

'You're not going into a home, Dad,' Abe said. 'Let's not worry about that now. Let's try to get you up.' Hooking his hands underneath his father's armpits, Abe gently pulled upwards. 'Tell me if anything hurts.'

A bit more puffing and moaning and Pa was back in his chair.

'Do you want a cup of tea?' Sassi asked, desperate to do something useful.

Pa shook his head. His chest heaved with exertion, and he closed his eyes.

Sassi flitted from one side of the chair to the other, while Abe kept his fingers on Pa's wrist and an eye on his watch.

After a few minutes, Pa opened his eyes and stared at them.

Sassi was relieved to see his eyes were clear and free of pain.

'Be,' he told them. Bed.

'Are you sure you don't need to sit there a bit longer?' Abe asked.

The old man shook his head, so with Sassi on one side and Abe on the other, they slowly walked him to the bedroom and settled him on the edge of the bed.

Sassi slipped out while Abe undressed him. A few minutes later she went in with Panadol and a glass of water, as well as another hot water bottle. 'Here, take these.' She held out the tablets.

Pa reared back against the pillows, shaking his head violently and pushing her hands away. 'Na.'

Both Abe and Sassi stared at him. 'Pa, they're just normal Panadol tablets. They'll help with any pain you start to feel.'

Pa looked uncertain, as if he wanted to believe her but was not sure he should.

'Pa, you know it's me, Sassi, don't you?'

'Ass,' he said and blinked a couple of times.

'It's me.' She met Abe's eyes with a worried look.

Then Pa held out his hand for the tablets. "Anks.'

Breathing a sigh of relief, she handed them over and helped him drink from the glass, before tucking the blanket in around him.

'We should get the doctor,' Abe said.

The room smelt like the lavender hand lotion that Granny used, but over the top of that was a musky unwashed, old man odour. There was a pile of clothes on the floor and Sassi recognised them as the ones Pa had been wearing over the last week. Why hadn't her mother washed them? She gathered them up and started to leave the room for the laundry.

Pa's hand shot out to Abe's arm. 'Okay,' he said again touching his chest. I'm okay, he meant.

'Don't worry, Dad. We'll make sure you're looked after.'

Ten minutes later, Pa was asleep and Sassi had put a load of washing on. Abe was making cups of tea in the kitchen.

'Well, that was an interesting finish to a bloody long day,' he said when she came in.

'I think we've all had more than enough.' She sighed and let her head drop into her hands. 'God, I'm exhausted.'

'Me too.' He paused and took a sip of tea. 'How's your head?'

'Not so bad. Stitches are pulling a bit, but I'm okay. I looked in the mirror before and everything looks worse than it feels.'

'Still can't get over how lucky you were.'

Sassi shivered. Her dreams had been punctuated with the noise of crumpling metal and Jarrah's frightened yelp.

Taking a sip of her tea, Sassi screwed up her nose and added a sugar to the black liquid. 'Not too good at the bushman's tea,' she said.

Abe half-smiled, then his face became serious. 'Do you think he's going a bit, in the mind I mean?'

Sassi considered this, recalling the last time she'd been back in Barker. Pa seemed like an old, frail man, with the speech problems he'd had for a while now, but his mind still seemed as sharp as a tack. And if you added grieving into the mix, well . . .

'Probably more shock, if you're talking about tonight. I haven't seen anything to indicate there's a problem. Let's see what he's like in the morning.'

'We really need to organise meeting that carer.' Abe looked around and frowned. 'Where's Amber?' he asked as if he'd just realised she wasn't there.

'Gone to Adelaide.'

'What!'

'Yeah, when I came home she was packed and ready to go. I'd gone to the pub with Mia and I think she must've been waiting for me to get back, because she flew out the door without an explanation other than she had an early morning appointment and it was easier for her to go tonight than leave really early.'

Abe closed his eyes tiredly and shook his head. 'Crazy woman.'

They sat in silence. After a few moments, Sassi got up then tiptoed to the door of Pa's room and looked in.

They'd left the bedside light on and she could see her grandfather's face reflected in the light. The dark shadow of his stubble was beginning to show and his left hand was outside the bedspread, his wedding ring catching her gaze under the soft glow of the light.

'Must be so lonely when you're that age and you lose the person you've spent more than half your life with,' Abe said, coming to stand alongside her.

'Mmm-hmm, I haven't seen anything that's fun about getting old.'

'I miss Mum.'

Sassi glanced at her uncle and saw vulnerability in his face. Her strong dependable uncle, who was more like her brother. She leaned into him.

'It's us now, isn't it?' Sassi said quietly. 'We're the ones who have to look after our family.' Moving her elbow to give him a little dig in the ribs. 'Good thing we're stronger together.'

CHAPTER 17

Pa and Sassi were sitting in the backyard, enjoying the soft warmth from the sun, when the front door flew open and loud steps echoed down the hallway.

Jarrah, who was at Pa's feet, cocked her ears and got to her feet, leaning towards the noise.

Sassi put a hand on the pup's head and then glanced at Pa, who was looking curiously at the house. 'Guess, it's Abe,' she said and got up to see.

By the time she'd reached the back door, Amber was standing there, hand outstretched to open it.

'Hello, Sassi,' she said. 'Where's everyone?' She tucked her shirt into her jeans and patted down her carefully styled hair.

'Oh, you're back!' The words tumbled out of her mouth as Sassi felt both relief and shock. She'd been sure that Amber had packed up to leave for good when she'd disappeared so suddenly two days ago.

Amber smiled. 'Of course! I only had an appointment in Adelaide. Wasn't ever going to take too long. Where's Dad?'

'Outside. He had a fall on the night of the funeral, but he's fine. No broken bones, or even any bruising. Just a bit of shock, that's all.'

'Oh no, poor Dad.' She pushed past Sassi and went to Pa, crouching down in front of him. 'Dad, are you all right?'

Sassi watched for a moment, then went inside to give them some privacy. She'd been wondering about her mother's mysterious trip to Adelaide for the past couple of days. What sort of appointment would she have needed to go to Adelaide for, and so early in the morning?

The door was open into the spare bedroom and Sassi peered in. Her mother's suitcase was thrown on the bed. Beside it was a large bag from a pharmacy chain. Raising her eyebrows, she took a step inside, wondering what type of medication was in the packaging. Maybe Amber had left her home in South Africa so quickly she hadn't packed enough, including tablets. She wondered what kind of medication her mother could be taking. The swift trip to Adelaide fit in with the rest of her mother's secrecy act.

A noise from outside made her realise she should mind her own business, so Sassi went into the kitchen and started to plate up some biscuits she'd bought that morning, and put the kettle on.

Her watch showed it was nearly 10.30 am, and Abe and the lady from Sudan were due in about twenty minutes.

She headed outside with the morning tea, but stopped when she saw her mother bending over Pa.

Amber had her arms around his frail shoulders, giving him a hug. Pa caught Sassi's eye and drew back.

'You just need to be more careful,' Sassi heard Amber tell him as she sat down again.

'Mum?' Sassi walked out and sat at the outdoor table with them. 'How was your appointment?'

'Oh, you know, just normal run of the mill stuff. I thought I'd catch up with an old school friend while I was down there, so we went out for dinner last night.' She smiled brightly. 'Your face is looking better, Sassi. Do you feel okay?'

'Much better, thanks, although I'll be glad when these stitches dissolve. They're really annoying the way they pull. And they're itchy!'

'That must mean you're healing.'

'Hope so! Um, Mum, Abe is coming in about twenty minutes with the lady who might look after Pa. Just for a chat. We decided to get it organised ASAP, after his fall the other night. We talked to Pa, didn't we?' Her eyes cut across to her grandfather.

Pa had been looking down at his hands, which had a small tremor in them. His eyes were rheumy and, even though he didn't have any bruising from his fall, his normal confidence seemed to have disappeared.

'We talked about a lady coming to help you,' she prompted him. This time she looked over to Amber. 'We're sorry we didn't get to involve you in the first step. Pa's insistent that he doesn't want to go into a home.'

'Nah 'ome,' Pa said, above the galahs that had started to shriek from the trees above as a truck rumbled by.

'I'm glad you went ahead,' Amber said simply, reaching out for Pa's hand and squeezing it. 'We need to make sure Dad is safe, don't we?' Turning back to Sassi, she asked, 'Do we know much about this woman?'

'Not a whole amount other than she's from Sudan and is looking for work. She has a couple of kids.' Sassi reached forward and rubbed some bird shit off the table, then looked at Amber, seeing her stiffen.

'Sudan? She's a long way from home.'

'Yeah, she's been living in Adelaide but found it pretty expensive with rent and so on.'

'Has she got any experience in caring for the elderly?' Amber got up from her chair and walked over to the fence and back again.

'I guess we'll find out soon. But, look, from what I understand from Dave, she'll be great.'

'The policeman recommended her?'

'Well, I don't think it's a recommendation as such, more a "Hey, I've heard about this person and they might be able to help".'

Amber sighed and sat back down.

'Be 'kay,' Pa said, nodding vigorously. He seemed a little more alert now, his eyes sliding from Amber to Sassi to Jarrah. His hand reached for the comforting feel of Jarrah's head and the dog put her head on his knee.

'I think we need to talk to her seriously, Dad. We can't just have any old Tom, Dick or Harry looking after you.

We need to make sure she has a police clearance and some kind of training in working with—'

''Op.' Stop. Pa reached out and tapped Sassi on the arm, his eyes searching for hers, then turned towards Amber. 'Be 'kay.'

Sassi forced a sad smile. 'Let's hope so, Pa.'

⌒

Rasha sat at the table with her hands folded. She was the lady Sassi had seen with two children in the pub the night she had been there with Mia.

Rasha was observing everyone in the room—Pa, Abe, Amber and Sassi—carefully. A good once-over their face and then eye contact.

'Would you like a biscuit?' Sassi held the plate of melting moments out and the woman took one cautiously.

'Thank you.'

Rasha's voice was deep and soft like flowing caramel, Sassi decided, and she liked her very much. Her hair was short and black with tiny ringlets. She had dark brown eyes and dark skin. But it was her hands that fascinated Sassi. They had seen hard work for they were chafed along the sides of her fingers, but they were immaculately looked after, too. Not dry, and her short nails were shaped prettily.

'Your name,' Rasha said to Sassi, 'it is African.'

'Sorry?'

'In our language it means "she who speaks the truth". You did not know?'

'I . . .' Sassi glanced over at Amber who had a notepad in front of her so she could take notes. 'No, I didn't.'

'I can see you speak many truths. Your face is open and wise.'

Sassi wanted to laugh. Wise was the last thing she felt. 'Um, thank you.'

Amber interrupted. 'Let's move this along. We're going to make sure you're a good fit for each other.'

Pa's eyes were trained on Rasha, and Sassi couldn't work out if he was fascinated by her, or something worse.

'Can you clean a house?' Amber asked. 'What's your experience?'

'I can.' Rasha inclined her head. 'Very well. I have been cleaning for many years.'

'Yes, I would have thought you would have been. Now Dad's sheets will need to be washed once a week and his other clothes at least twice. We don't want anything hanging around making the place smell.

'And your children won't be allowed here. Understood?'

'I do.' Rasha answered Amber but she was only looking at Pa. Sassi really liked that. It didn't matter what Rasha's relationship with the rest of the family was like, just so long as she and Pa got along, and he was comfortable. That would be all that mattered.

'Can you make a decent cup of tea?' Abe wanted to know. Sassi knew he was trying to cover for Amber's brisk tone. She was being obnoxious.

Rasha looked confused. 'Tea? To eat you mean?'

Sassi laughed. 'Tea the drink.' She mimed holding a cup and sipping from it.

'Oh.' There was a flash of brilliant white teeth as Rasha gave a self-deprecating shrug. 'I see. Yes, of course, once I know how you like it. I have lived in Australia long enough to understand what your culture likes and dislikes.'

Abe grinned at that. 'Nothing to it. Tea bag and a bit of hot water.'

'Now,' Amber interjected, 'back to the subject at hand.'

Sassi wasn't sure who had appointed Amber head interviewer, but she seemed to have assumed the role. 'You won't have to worry about cooking as Kim from Catering Angels is going to keep up with that. She'll bring enough meals for a week and put them in the freezer.' She glanced up. 'Your cooking wouldn't be what Dad is used to anyway.'

Sassi kicked Abe under the table. They had to stop Amber being so rude!

'Obviously, the house will need to be cleaned and the windows washed monthly.'

Sassi blinked. Windows?

'Hang on,' Abe said. 'Rasha isn't a maid, she's here to look after Dad. A carer.'

'Cleaning is looking after Dad,' Amber said indignantly. 'Mum has always kept this house spotless and it needs to be kept in the same condition. For his comfort. And cleaning is what Rasha will be used to.'

Pa coughed a phlegmy sound and flapped his hands. ''Ay 'ere.'

'You'll stay here, we promise,' Sassi told him.

'I can clean well,' Rasha told them.

'Right.' Abe took a breath and leaned forward. 'Are you happy, Dad? Do you think you can have Rasha around the house?'

A short nod.

'Okay.' He turned to Rasha. 'When can you start?'

'Work?'

'Yes, here.'

'I can start now if you please.'

Abe nodded and brought his hand down on the table like a judge holding court. 'That's decided.'

'Wait!' Amber frowned as she ran her finger down the notebook in front of her. 'We don't know if she has a police clearance. What if she runs away with Mum's jewellery?'

'Do you have a police clearance?' Abe asked.

Rasha dug into her purse and pulled out an envelope. 'Police clearance, referees and my experience are in here. Along with the visa that says I can work in Australia.'

Amber took the envelope and drew out the documents.

Silence. Pa looked at Rasha and smiled, a little dribble ran down the side of his chin. Rasha nodded and smiled back, then took a napkin and dabbed at his face.

'Well,' Amber said huffily, 'that all seems to be in order.' She stood up and beckoned to Rasha. 'Come with me.'

Abe pushed his chair back as well. 'I gotta run, Dad. Hope you don't mind. I've got the seed cleaner coming this afternoon and I have to shift a bit of grain around.'

Another nod. ''Uch?'

'We're cleaning sixty tonne of wheat,' Abe answered, then turned to Rasha. 'If you need me, here's my phone number. You can talk to Amber or Sassi as well. And thank you. You've got no idea what this means to Dad. To us.' Abe held out his card.

Rasha took it with a bob of her head. 'Thank you,' she said. 'I am glad for the work.'

Amber was impatient now, tapping her foot. 'Come on.' She turned and went out of the room.

Quickly Rasha stood up and went to follow her, but Sassi put her hand out. 'Please don't be offended by my mother. She's being rude and we apologise.'

Rasha held her head up proudly. 'I am used to such words and I take no notice.' She left the room, walking towards Amber's voice.

Sassi heard her mother say, 'Now this is where the cleaning products are kept. When you run low, make sure you let Abe or Sassi know and we will organise for you to purchase more. I live in South Africa, so I won't always be here.'

'Which part of South Africa?' Rasha asked.

Their voices faded and Sassi put her hands on her grandfather's shoulders and leaned down to give him a hug from behind.

'Hopefully, you'll be happy, Pa.'

He reached up and patted her hands.

There was a knock at the door. From the backyard Jarrah let out a round of barking before falling quiet again.

'I'll get it on my way out,' Abe said. 'See you all later. Before I forget—Sassi, have you heard from the insurance company about your ute? I think I've found one for you to buy once the payout comes through.' He walked down the passageway, talking over his shoulder.

'Yeah, they've written it off, so I'll have the money in the next week or so, by the sounds of the email they sent.'

Abe pulled open the door. 'Oh, hi, Kim, I thought it might be you. Go on through. Sassi, I'll send you the link to the ute. Have a look and see if it suits, okay?'

'Yeah, thanks, I will. Hello, Kim. All of that food smells yummo.'

'Gosh, this is a busy place today,' Kim said, bustling through to the kitchen, an esky in one hand. 'How are you all? Hello, Mr Stapleton, I hear you had a bit of a fall. You don't look like you've hurt yourself, so that's great news.'

Pa gave a lopsided smile and cocked his head to one side, as if he was trying to work out who the new woman in his house was.

Sassi opened the freezer door for Kim and put out her hand for the container.

'He was really lucky, weren't you, Pa? I can't believe he didn't even get a bruise. He spent a little bit of time on the floor until Abe got here, but other than that he's come out of it unscathed.'

Pa pushed his chair back and put his hands to his ears.

'Ah, too noisy, are we? Sorry about that.'

Holding on to his cane, he took a few tentative steps towards the lounge, testing the floor underneath his feet each time he moved. It broke Sassi's heart to see Pa being so careful with an action she took for granted.

Kim gave a chuckle. 'Nice to see you, Mr Stapleton.' She handed more containers to Sassi. 'Here you go, love. There's a couple of trays of corned beef and a beef casserole. What do you think he might want left out for his dinner?'

'Whatever one you think,' Sassi said.

'Now, I'll need you to send weekly reports through to me,' Amber's voice could be heard down the hall. 'I'll give you my email address. My dad is very important to us and it's imperative that he receives the best care you are able to provide.'

'Visitors?' Kim asked.

'The lady Dave suggested,' Sassi told her. 'Rasha. She's going to come over every day and help Pa.'

'That will be lovely. He'll feel safer and more secure.'

Amber came into the kitchen, Rasha trailing behind. She stopped short when she saw Kim.

'Hello, Kim,' Rasha said. Her teeth flashed with her wide smile.

'Hello, Rasha. It's lovely to see you again.' Kim gave her a brilliant smile, while Amber looked between the two women. Then she frowned.

'Oh, you must be the one doing the cooking?' she said in Kim's direction.

Kim held out her hand to Amber. 'Yes, that's me. Kim Burrows. I remember you from when you were a little girl.'

A guarded look crossed Amber's face. 'I'm sorry, I don't think I remember you.'

'I'm a little older,' Kim said, while she kept handing containers to Sassi. 'I own the roadhouse. When you were a tiny tot, your mum would bring you in once in a blue moon for a treat. Around your birthday I think it was, and I'd make you a banana milkshake. You always used to ask for an extra scoop of ice cream.'

Amber blinked. 'I do remember doing that with Mum. Well, it's nice to see you again and thank you for cooking for Dad. As I was just telling the serv— ah, Rasha here, Dad is very important to all of us.' She turned to the lady who was waiting behind her, hands clasped together, her eyes inspecting each person in the kitchen. Watchful and waiting.

'As every person in every family is,' Kim answered.

'Of course, very true.' Amber ushered Rasha out of the room towards the front door. 'Be here tomorrow at nine am. No later.'

CHAPTER 18

'I'm going out for a walk,' Sassi called to Amber as she slipped on her sneakers.

The day had passed quietly once Abe, Rasha and Kim had gone. She'd sat with Pa for an hour or so and read the *Farming Journal* to him, although he'd slept through the article about a bull sale in Victoria.

Jarrah met her at the front door, tail wagging, jumping around on her hind legs, puffing happily.

'Sit down, you mad dog,' Sassi said gently as she made Jarrah sit quietly until she clipped the lead onto her collar. They'd been for enough walks now, to know what the routine was.

'See you when you get back,' Amber said, appearing in the passageway.

'You writing another list?' Sassi asked, indicating to the notepad her mother was holding. She seemed to have a love of long lists, asking everyone else to do jobs rather than doing them herself.

'Yes, a to-do list for Rasha when she starts tomorrow. Polishing the furniture should be at the top. I don't think it's been done in some time.'

Swallowing her anger, Sassi tried to think of a gentle way to say what she wanted to. 'Rasha is really only here to help Pa,' she said. 'You're treating her like the servants you apparently have in South Africa. This is Australia and what you're doing isn't appropriate.'

Jarrah pulled at the lead, and Sassi made her sit again as she frowned.

'She would have worked as a servant in her home country, Sassi,' Amber said dismissively. 'She would expect it.'

'No, she wouldn't! Don't you think she might've left Sudan for a better life? To be treated better?'

'You don't know what you're talking about when it comes to different cultures. I do.' Amber put her hands on her hips. 'Just leave this to me. Making sure Dad is comfortable is my main priority before I go, and I won't leave until everything is just so.'

A bubble of resentment sat in Sassi's stomach and she knew it would be better not to continue the argument. 'See you in a while,' she said, her tone tight with annoyance. She didn't want to have anything to do with anyone who spoke and treated another human the way she'd seen her mother treat Rasha.

Somewhere in the distance, she could hear Granny's

calming voice. 'Take a breath, dear. Don't let your mother get to you.'

That's easier said than done! Sassi thought.

The pavement radiated heat from the day as Jarrah ran as far as the lead would let her, then stopped to sniff at a power pole, or a bush, or anything that another dog had marked as its territory.

Across the quiet town, she could hear the squeals and shrieks of some kids enjoying the pool. Someone close by was cooking a barbecue, and her stomach rumbled at the smell of onions in the air.

She wondered where Mia lived and what she was up to. She'd mentioned that she loved to play tennis and read. Although it was not as hot as it had been the day of the accident, it still would have been a lovely day to be curled up inside underneath the air-conditioner with a good book.

Or sketchpad. Her fingers twitched a little at the thought of holding a pencil and drawing lines across a crisp white page. In her mind she could see the strokes needed to create Granny's face, her hands, her smile.

Glancing at her watch she saw that it was nearly five o'clock. If she hurried she'd be able to make it to the newsagency. They would have a sketchpad and pencils there, wouldn't they?

Tugging on the lead, she made Jarrah trot alongside her as she headed for the main street.

'Hey, Sassi.'

Sassi turned at the sound of a car engine slowing alongside of her and smiled when she saw Kim.

'Kim! Oh my god, your food is so yummy. I can't remember the last time I had corned beef.'

'What are you doing eating the meals, you minx.' Kim laughed. 'They're supposed to be for your pa.'

'I had to sample it before I gave it to him for lunch. Otherwise, how did I know that it was going to be okay!'

They shared a smile and Kim indicated the pub. 'Would you like to get a drink?'

'Yeah, I'd love to, except I've got Jarrah with me.'

'Hopper won't mind if you tie her up outside in the beer garden. We can take the drinks out there so you won't be away from her.'

'Great idea. Can I meet you there? I'm on my way to the newsagency to get a couple of things. I won't be long.'

'Sure, see you in fifteen.' Kim put the car in gear and pulled away only to flick her blinker on about ten metres down the road and turn into the street parking in front of the pub.

Sassi crossed the road, thinking how Barker-like it was to be able to stop in the middle of the road for a conversation without other cars banking up behind. Sassi waved to the man who'd just come out of the newsagency to start bringing in the posters and close up.

'Do you mind?' she asked, indicating inside. 'I know what I want so I won't be long.'

'Sure. I can hold your dog, if you like. She's a beauty. What's her name?'

'This is Jarrah,' Sassi said, handing over the lead. 'I'll be two secs.'

'Take your time. Carrie's in there, so she can serve you.'

'I'm Sassi Stapleton,' she said.

'I thought you were. Didn't want to say anything in case I got you mixed up with another girl. Maybe you remember me. Jason Foster. I went to school with your mum. She was always the life of the party, when she came home for exeat weekends. All the boys had a crush on Amber, and you look just like her.' He seemed super keen at the mention of Amber. 'I also gave your grandpa a hand out at the farm during school holidays.'

Sassi gave the man a once-over, wondering why he thought she should remember him if he was her mother's age. Jason's receding hairline made his skull look elongated, which in turn made his nose look like an eagle's beak.

Her fingers went to her nose and felt it. She knew hers wasn't as large as his, but she still wondered if his genetics ran through her veins.

'Um, no, I'm sorry, I don't remember you.'

'Not to worry. You were only a little tacker when I was out there. Is your mother here?' The words were too casual for the eagerness in his eyes.

'Ah, yeah, just for a short while. Would you excuse me?' She ran up the steps and away from his keenness to see Amber.

All the boys had a crush on her.

Why did Jason Foster think Sassi wanted to know that? What child wants to think about their parents having a life, fun, sex or otherwise, before they were born?

Sassi wiped her hand over her eyes as if she could wipe away his words, and assessed the inside of the shop. The magazines were inside the door and the aisle led towards cheap souvenirs, postcards and party decorations.

She made her way over to the wall with office and school supplies, where she found an A4 sketchpad and some lead and coloured pencils. They weren't what she would normally use, but they would do. She opened the book and touched the creamy white, blank pages still seeing the finished portrait of Granny in her mind. She would start on it after she'd caught up with Kim.

'Hello, that's the lot?' A woman with short frizzy hair stood behind the counter, her hand outstretched for Sassi's purchases.

'Thanks.' She glanced curiously at the woman to see if she recognised her, but came up blank.

'This for you?' the woman asked.

Sassi nodded, digging in her pocket for her phone so she could pay.

'You must be a bit arty, then.'

'Something I've always liked to do.' Sassi felt as if the woman was examining her, searching her face for some-thing . . . What?

'You're Amber Stapleton's daughter, aren't you?'

Knowing she was probably being oversensitive, Sassi wondered if the woman's question was leading—was there a man in town who was an artist? None of her family had ever drawn anything, except perhaps to design a new machinery shed or fence line. Her art came from another genetic pool, she was sure.

'Ah, yes, I am.'

A strange looked crossed the woman's face and her eyes slid to her husband on the street, squatting down and patting Jarrah, then back to Sassi.

Maybe Carrie knew Jason had the hots for Amber when they were in high school and still held a torch for her. Did she think Sassi could be Jason's love child?

Sassi wanted to roll her eyes.

'What do you like to draw?' Carrie asked.

'Oh, anything and everything really. I'm not as good with faces as I am with landscapes. I don't do it for a job, just relaxation.'

'Must be lovely to have that sort of talent.' Carrie checked the Eftpos machine and then grabbed a paper bag from under the counter. 'I haven't got a creative bone in my body. Wouldn't know where to start if I had to sketch something. Used to dabble in writing poetry, but I don't think I was too good at it.' She checked the payment had gone through and handed over the paper bag. 'There you go, love, all yours. See you next time, eh?'

Sassi took the bag and smiled her thanks. Outside she took Jarrah's lead from Jason and said goodnight, then crossed the road to the pub, before he could engage her in conversation again.

Kim was waiting with two glasses of wine.

'Hope you don't mind, I just ordered two,' she said pushing one towards Sassi as she sat down.

'This is lovely,' Sassi said, looking around the garden. Fairy lights were strung along the wooden beams of a structure that looked like a shed, but without any walls, except a back one to stop the prevailing winds. A wooden fence ran all the way to the perimeter of the garden and in one corner there was a swing-set and in the other a multi-play station that had a slippery dip, ladder, platform and cubbyhouse at the top.

'The best feature on that,' said Kim, holding her glass of wine and indicating the kids' play area, 'is the fireman's pole down the side. The kids just love it.'

'I've never seen a pub cater for kids like this,' Sassi said, holding her glass up in a cheers manner.

'Hopper enjoys it when families turn up. Of course, he likes the old blokes who turn up every day and hold up the bar for a while, watching the racing and that sort of thing, but there's beginning to be quite a few young families around the district and it's important to him that they come here for a meal and a drink. Enjoy some downtime.'

Kim gave a little laugh as if a memory had amused her. 'He would hate anyone to think he was soft, but he asked me if I'd make cakes for a mother's group he wanted to organise.'

'That's a great idea. Did it get off the ground?'

'Yeah, every Monday there're about ten ladies who come here. They've all got babies under two, and it's a real relief for them to have a safe spot to let the kids roam around. And it's so lovely that there's that many babies in the district. Some years there's none!'

'I love it!' Sassi said.

Kim took a swallow of her wine. 'How are you liking being home?'

Sassi took her time answering because she wasn't sure how she felt. 'I'm enjoying being with my family, especially seeing the twins and Abe and Renee. But it's weird being in a place that I recognise like the back of my hand, yet everything is different, you know? The main street with the trees and little shops are all the same, but there are kids I don't recognise walking home from school or getting an ice cream at the shop.

'My friend, Holly, her mum has grey hair now and looks heaps older—' Sassi paused and laughed, embarrassed at her words. 'Sounds ridiculous, doesn't it?'

'Not at all. I understand what you're saying. I guess you recognise faces but don't always remember names?'

'Yeah, that type of thing. And I really miss Granny—' Sassi broke off again and took another sip of wine.

'Of course you do, love.' Kim reached out and touched her arm, giving it a few little pats before sitting back. 'Life is just like the sea, I think.'

'Really?'

'Yeah, ever moving and ever changing. You never know what you're going to get, but the minute you're comfortable, it changes.'

'That is so true.' Sassi nodded her head emphatically. 'And occasionally there's a rogue wave that catches you from behind and dumps you good and proper!'

Kim laughed. 'And that, sweetie, is life!'

They clinked their glasses again and sat back, Sassi's hand straying to Jarrah's head. She stroked the dog's ears until Jarrah gave a contented sigh and flopped down at her feet, her chin on Sassi's shoes.

'Have you lived here all your life?' Sassi asked.

'Sure have. Born in the hospital just up the road. Guess I'll die in it or at home. You know, it's funny. When I was seventeen, I was on holidays at the beach, just over the way a bit.' She waved her hand south. 'I met this gorgeous bloke and we had a bit of a summer fling, then he had to go home to Western Australia and I had to come back here. My parents needed my help at the roadhouse and I loved to cook. Thought I'd hone my cooking skills before I tried to go and get a chef's apprenticeship. Anyway,' she cocked her head to one side and raised an eyebrow, 'as we were just saying, life happens and Mum and Dad died unexpectedly, leaving me to run the roadhouse.

'I'd fallen a bit head over heels in love with my summer fling, and we wrote letters for a while, but we lost contact, which really broke my heart. I was a bit fragile anyway, because of Mum and Dad, so I decided I was going to stay here, run the roadhouse, and if this man—' A cheeky smile spread over Kim's face. 'If this very cute man, wanted to find me, he'd know where I would be.'

Sassi leaned forward. 'Seriously? You didn't want to become a chef anymore?'

'I was run off my feet and cooking every day, all day, and I loved it. Loved living here. Only thing was, I was a bit lonely.'

Sassi smiled. 'And then Dave came along.'

'Well, then the gorgeous summer fling came back.' She raised her eyebrows and wiggled them.

'No!' Sassi was enthralled. 'Dave is that person? Are you *kidding*?' Her voice raised in disbelief.

'Dave was sent here to investigate a case years later. My niece, Milly, had been involved in a carjacking. She'd been carrying the night's takings from the rodeo and a few fellas hit her car and pushed her off the road.

'Dave turned up, and it worked out for us—we rekindled our romance and the rest, as they say, is history.'

Sassi sat there staring at Kim, shaking her head. 'Now that is a story!' she said softly.

'Yeah, it's pretty cool, isn't it?' Kim smiled again. 'And he's still gorgeous.'

Laughter bubbled out of Sassi. 'Now I know why he looks at you the way he does. I saw it the other day when you both came over. He wouldn't ever want to let you out of his sight now he's found you again.'

'And I don't want to let him out of my sight either.'

Sassi held up her glass. 'And may that never happen.'

CHAPTER 19

An hour later Sassi jumped when she looked at her watch.

'I'd better go. Mum might need a hand with Pa,' she said.

Jarrah had sprung up at the same time and looked at her expectantly, while Kim had reluctantly stood, too.

'Yeah, I'd better head home and get Dave some dinner. This was lovely. Let's try to do it another time.'

'I'd like that.' They walked to the footpath together. As Kim was getting into her car, Sassi spoke. 'Kim, do you remember much about my mum when she was younger?'

Draping her arm over the car door, Kim pursed her lips thoughtfully. 'I know a little,' she said and waited.

Jarrah looked up at Sassi and decided she wasn't moving anywhere anytime soon, so flopped at her feet with a groan.

'I was wondering if you'd ever heard anything about my father?' The words came out in a rush and they surprised

Sassi. She hadn't even been sure she was going to ask the question until she did.

Kim didn't seem at all surprised. 'You don't know who he is.' A statement rather than a question.

'Not something we've ever discussed.'

'Oh, sweetie, I'm not sure I can help you. I remember when Amber was pregnant with you, because she came home from school for the last couple of months. She lived out at the farm, so we really didn't see her very much, although when we did, she always had you in a pram. And then a few years later, Amber just wasn't here. There was never a goodbye party or an announcement your mother was leaving as far as I can remember. We just started seeing you with your granny.'

Another silence.

'You could ask her,' Kim said.

Shaking her head, Sassi grimaced slightly. 'Not a question she likes to hear. I thought Granny might've known, but she never mentioned it.'

'Do you want to know?'

'I'm not sure. It's strange, isn't it? I'm happy with a family who loves me, yet . . .' Her voice trailed off and she leaned down to pat Jarrah. The words she wanted to say were just out of reach.

'Would I be right in thinking you'd like to have the *option* of knowing?' Kim asked. 'But to have that choice, someone you trust must have this information and you're not sure if they do. Other than Amber, of course.'

Sassi almost sagged with relief. 'Yeah, that's exactly right. How do you know how to put all these mixed-up emotions into words?'

'I guess that's just what I'm here for,' Kim answered, softly. 'To make sure all you girls who need a bit of love and support get just that.'

There was a wisdom behind Kim's words that seemed to come from a long, aching pain. Maybe Sassi would be as wise as Kim in time.

'Think on it a little more,' Kim finally said. 'You might come to the conclusion that you don't need to know.'

'Maybe.'

'Or the need to know might drive you to distraction and then you can do some research into your family history, get some DNA tests done. You know, all that sort of stuff.'

'Do you remember any rumours about who he was?'

Kim shook her head. 'Sorry, sweetie, it was a long time ago.'

'Twenty-eight years!'

'Well, there you go. I try not to listen to gossip at the best of times, so I'd have no hope remembering anything from back then.

'Anyway, I'd better get home. See you a bit later. Make sure you're kind to yourself.'

Sassi waved and set off down the footpath towards her grandparents' house, Jarrah trotting alongside her ankles.

The street was familiar, like she'd said to Kim earlier, but she took it all in this time. The stock agent's shopfront had a new coat of paint and the soldiers' memorial in the median strip had been cleaned. The grass around it must get a lot more water than any of the other lawns around town, Sassi decided. It was rich and thick. When she'd been little, she'd loved to dive her fingers into it and do cartwheels.

A person wearing a bright high-vis T-shirt and a hat was jogging towards her. When she'd lived here, she didn't remember too many people running for fitness. Not down the streets anyway.

The footy oval and the pool had been the places to keep fit.

Now the person slowed, wiped their brow and walked the rest of the way to Sassi.

'Out for a walk? And how are you going?' A voice that was vaguely familiar spoke, then bent down to pat Jarrah. 'Good to see you again, Jarrah.'

Sassi squinted and realised it was Hamish under the hat. His bright red hair had turned dark with sweat.

'Hamish! Sorry, I didn't recognise you, your cap blocked you out. I wouldn't have picked you for a runner.'

'Oooh, look at you, Sassi. Those pretty colours all over your face. Purples and yellows. Looking a million bucks.' Hamish grinned at her and then his voice became serious. 'Actually, you look a whole lot better than you did when I saw you last. Looks like everything is just about back to normal.'

'I feel fine, thanks. How far have you run?'

Looking at his watch, he tapped the screen. 'Brilliant. PB today. Nine kilometres. I've been working up to that.'

'You've run *nine kilometres*? Why?' Sassi was astounded.

Laughing, Hamish wiped his face with the bottom of his T-shirt. 'It's a great way for me to unwind after a day at the hospital. There are no bells or buzzers or machines beeping. Just me, my thoughts and the music. If I run in time to the beat, I seem to forget everything other than my breathing and steps.' He grinned and pushed his hat back.

'On your way home?'

'Yeah. Going to help with Pa.' She adjusted the bag that held her shopping.

'How's he going? Have you managed to find some help?' Hamish put one foot forward and lunged down, stretching his muscles.

'We have. Rasha. I'm not sure of her last name. Moved here not that long ago. A Sudanese woman.'

'Oh yeah, I know her. She's a lovely lady. I imagine she'd be great at helping out around the oldies. Is it working out okay? No problems?'

'She's starting tomorrow, but after meeting her this morning I think she'll be wonderful.'

'Good. Well, let me know if I can do anything at all.' He swapped legs.

'Sure.' She smiled and tried to think of something else to say.

'Right, well, I'd better get on before I cool down too much,' he said. 'Guess I'll see you around. Especially if you're going to be walking this gorgeous girl at night.' He leaned down to pat Jarrah. 'How long are you staying for?'

'I'll just see how Pa is managing, plus Abe could do with a hand at the farm, and that's the sort of work I love, so . . .' She shrugged. 'Suck it and see, I think is the phrase.'

'And an excellent one at that! Right-oh, I'll see you later.' He tapped at his watch and gave her a flick of his wrist as a wave and jogged on.

Sassi watched him for a moment then turned back towards the house.

It didn't take long to make it back. The front gate swung open silently. Pa had been a stickler for keeping things well maintained when he'd been able, and Abe had taken over after Pa had the stroke, making sure everything was just so, especially on the farm. The farm shed had to be swept out daily, doors kept closed when it wasn't in use so the wind didn't cover the cement floor with dust and leaves. The cabs of the machinery were kept clean and debris free, gate handles oiled and spare parts labelled and stored in separate containers so they were easily found.

She pushed opened the front door just as Amber came out of the office and into the passageway.

'Hi, Mum.'

Amber started at Sassi's entrance, her hand flying to her chest. 'Sassi! You gave me a fright.' Smiling, she dropped her hand. 'Did you have a nice walk?'

'Yep, Jarrah and I have had a lovely time, checking out the Barker pub with Kim.' Bending down, she unclipped Jarrah's lead and let her out into the front yard. Checking

Jarrah's water bowl, then food, she patted her goodnight and went back inside.

Amber was switching off the light and shutting the door into the office. 'You had a drink with Kim? You hardly know her.'

Sassi shrugged. 'Guess that's the lovely thing about small towns—everyone is friendly.' Choosing her words carefully, she went on: 'And people who have been here a long time often know things about families that the younger generation don't.'

Brushing off an invisible bit of lint from her shirt, Amber continued down the hallway with purpose. 'Well, it's nice you were able to spend some time with her.'

'How's Pa?' she asked, slipping off her shoes.

'I'm just about to heat up his dinner. I had a piece of toast a little while ago, do you want anything?'

'I can cook myself an egg on toast. I'm not that hungry.'

There was a cry from outside and Sassi yanked open the door to check that Jarrah was okay. What she saw was two little people dressed in pyjamas, with grins and bare feet.

Renee hadn't even managed to get herself out of the car yet.

'Sassi, there you are. I've got lots to tell you,' Harry said, throwing himself at her. 'Dad nearly got a fox. It was in with the chooks!'

'Meee too,' Jimmy called out. 'It killed three of our layers!'

'Woah, hold up.' Sassi put out her arms and hugged them to her. This time her bruises and stretched muscles didn't ache. Her body was healing. 'Gosh, you've got me all mixed up you're talking so fast. Should we go and sit with Pa and tell him the story, too?'

'Yeah, he would've shot it if he could,' Jimmy said.

'Who would've shot what?' Amber asked, coming out behind Sassi.

The twins fell silent and shied behind Sassi a little.

'Hello again,' Amber said to them. 'Did you mean your dad was going to shoot the fox? You've had an adventure by the sounds of that.' She smiled encouragingly, but Harry and Jimmy ducked their heads into Sassi's jeans.

Amber seemed to take the hint. 'I'll be in the kitchen,' she said, almost a little huffily, Sassi thought.

Renee finally caught up with the boys and handed Sassi a magazine. 'Abe couldn't send you the ad for the ute. Bloody internet is playing up again. I've marked the page for you.'

Sassi waved it at her. 'Brilliant, I'll have a look in a sec.' She followed the twins into the lounge room and saw they had parked themselves on the couch. Pa was awake and waving his hands around, indicating for the boys to tell their story.

'We heard clucking. It was *reaallly* loud so Jimmy and me went running out to see what was going on.'

'And there was a fox. In the chook yard!'

'Dunno how it got in there.'

Shotgun-sounding sentences, but Pa kept up, looking at each boy as he spoke.

Renee was now in the doorway. 'I'm sure the gate must have been left open.'

'I shut it, Mum,' Harry said earnestly as he turned to her. 'I made sure I did.'

Renee nodded and ran her hand over her stomach, looking tired.

'Can I get you anything?' Sassi asked quietly as the boys continued to talk at the top of their voices and enact the fox's dinner expedition.

'I wouldn't mind a whole night's sleep.'

'Don't think I can help with that.'

'No, probably not.'

'But the boys could stay with me at some stage. To give you a break.'

'I might take you up on that offer, before you leave.'

Amber came to stand alongside them and Renee gave her a tired smile.

'They're balls of energy, aren't they?' Amber said.

'No other word for it.'

'I can remember when Sassi was that age. She was so quiet. Sometimes I could have forgotten she was there, always curled up on the couch looking at a picture book or colouring. So different from your boys.'

'None of us is the same. Granny said Abe was like this. Always wanting to go out on the farm with Pa and racing around on his bike.'

'Yeah, I remember that. And Sassi was keen to be outside as well, she just didn't have the noise factor that Abe did.'

'Maybe she's more like her father,' Renee said, absently picking some Weet-Bix off the front of her shirt.

Sassi froze and Amber stiffened.

Renee put her hand to her mouth.

Not that Renee would know who Sassi's father was. Her home town was more than six hours from Barker.

'Right-oh, boys, it's time to head home. Make sure the rest of the chooks are still alive.' To Amber she said, 'Sorry, I just said that without thinking.'

Amber forced a smile without answering.

'Come on, boys,' Renee repeated and started to walk towards the door.

'Bye, Pa,' the boys chorused and gave him a high-five as they left.

Sassi shut the front door behind them and turned to Amber. 'Can we talk about my father?'

CHAPTER 20

Mia walked into the station and leaned over the counter to Joan. 'How is he today?' she asked.

'Just like he was yesterday. A little sharp and distracted.'

Frowning, Mia punched in the code and let herself in behind the desk. 'Got any idea what's wrong?'

Shaking her head, Joan raised her eyebrows. 'Nope, but something is certainly amiss.'

'Well, I'd better go and face him. I'll see if I can get to the bottom of his mood.'

'You'll only get there when Dave is ready to let you in on whatever's bothering him, so you might as well leave him be,' Joan said quietly.

In the kitchen, Mia poured herself a coffee then knocked on Dave's closed office door, another sign her boss wasn't himself.

'Come.'

'Morning,' Mia said, putting her head around the door. 'Want a coffee?'

'No, thanks.' Dave looked up from the computer and over the top of his glasses, without smiling. 'Your face is looking better.'

'Feeling better, too,' she said. 'What's happening? Any news from our friend Mr Woodbridge?'

'Dead air,' he said. 'Not a bad result.' Dave slipped his glasses down to the end of his nose.

The words were out of Mia's mouth before she could stop them. 'He seemed to have a horrible birthmark on his face, didn't he? Under his stubble. Could've almost been a bruise.' She wanted to put her hand over her mouth and take back what she'd just said.

Dave leaned back in his chair. 'Really?' He sounded glacial.

God, she'd opened a can of worms and there was no going back.

'Just something I noticed . . . Guess people have unfortunate birthmarks in all sorts of places.'

Dave raised an eyebrow and crossed his arms, waiting.

Her backtracking wasn't working. 'Anyway, doesn't matter.' Mia made to leave.

'Sit down. Now you've brought it up, I have something to say on the subject of you and Mr Woodbridge.' He looked down at the desk as if gathering his thoughts. 'I was hoping I wouldn't have to speak to you, but I can't let this incident go by. Especially since I've mentioned this to you before and you haven't taken any notice.'

Silence filled the air, but the undertone of anger was palpable. Mia slowly sat, her hands in her lap, her eyes on his face.

'See, Mia,' Dave stood and started to pace the room, 'as your boss, as the *senior* officer in this station, I have a problem with your reactions to certain incidents. It's not only this one, but I could list four or five others that had the potential to end as badly.

'You really do seem to have a chip on your shoulder when it comes to people questioning your authority and I'm not sure why. You were only at Broad River Station for a limited time, so the behaviour of the boys over there shouldn't have affected you too much.'

Mia wanted to crawl through the floor. She'd never seen Dave this angry.

'I couldn't charge Nathan Woodbridge with assault, Mia, because you didn't declare you were a police officer. And your behaviour left a lot to be desired.'

Mia reared back as if he'd slapped her. 'Sorry?'

Dave rounded on her. Icy, grey blue eyes that were furious. 'Your behaviour at the pub.'

Heat flooded through Mia and a cold sweat broke out on her brow. Her mate Chris had always told her that she spoke without thinking about the consequences. And she'd been too sharp, too cutting, too often.

'I've been back and spoken to Hopper, to Kane, to other people who were there. Your behaviour isn't befitting of a police officer. You got into an argument with Woodbridge.' He threw up his hands. 'Remember how you wanted to haul Aiden Galloway down to the station because you didn't like the way he treated you? Joan spoke to you after that, and so did I.'

Now Mia bristled and shot to her feet. She wasn't going to take this and Aiden Galloway had nothing to do with what they were talking about now.

'Have you forgotten?' She pointed at her face. 'Nathan Woodbridge did this to me.'

'Sit down!'

For a moment she stood defiantly, glaring at the boss she respected so much. Then slowly, Mia sank back into the chair.

Dave continued. 'I am not condoning his behaviour, but Nathan Woodbridge doesn't work for me and I am not responsible for him. But I am responsible for your conduct. In any other posting, it's likely you would have been hauled before Standards. You can't trade insults with members of the public.'

Under the desk, Mia clenched her fists and then let them go again.

Dave shook his head as if his star recruit had disappointed him in a way he didn't think was possible. 'And your veiled accusation about Woodbridge's birthmark is way out of line.'

'Let me tell you, Mia,' his voice was low and measured, 'you're just out of the academy and you've still got a lot to learn.

'You're living in a small country town and your job as a copper puts you in the line of sight of every single person who lives here. You cannot, I repeat, you cannot behave like the people we arrest.'

Mia couldn't believe what she was hearing. She wanted to put her hands over her ears and block out the sound of his voice. She'd never heard Dave speak to anyone the way he was talking to her now.

'But I . . .' Mia stared at her boss, trying to find words to defend herself.

'No buts. When you are a country copper, you are on duty twenty-four seven whether you like it or not. Behaving like you did is only going to give you a bad reputation. And if you keep this up, you're going to have a very short career. Understand me?'

Mia dropped her head, devastated. Her behaviour wasn't the problem here. Nathan Woodbridge's was. Why was Dave turning it onto her? Dave was as bad as those sexist pigs at Broad River Station.

It was as if Dave had read her mind.

'I'm sure you think I'm being a prick. That I'm having a go because I'm a shithead and I don't think women should be coppers. That isn't the case. You know me better than that. But fuck . . .' He ran his hands through his hair, as he always did when he was frustrated and felt helpless. 'Mia, you need to understand that you have to be above reproach.

'I'm angry at the whole situation, and I certainly don't like what happened to you. But you cannot be reactive. You're in the public eye. I'm not saying this because I don't think you're good at your job. You are. But pull your fucking head in and behave like a copper. All right?'

The clock ticked loudly, in time with the beats of her heart. Then she realised Dave was waiting for her to respond.

'Yes, Sarge.'

Mia needed to get out of the station now. She wanted to cry and run. To not see Dave for a long time. To ring Chris. Still, she wouldn't give him the satisfaction of seeing her tears.

'Good. I want you to concentrate on being the best copper you can be.' He took a breath. 'Now get in the car and go and conduct some speed checks up towards Blinman, okay?'

'I'm sure you're angry with me, but if you think on it, you'll work out I'm right.' He stood by the door and held it open for her.

Mia shot forward, wanting to be out of the room as quickly as she could.

Maybe she should apologise to him. Had she really behaved badly? Cutting people down to size was the way they'd done things in the academy. Sure, it was the trainers doing it to the coppers. Yelling at them the way the movies portrayed. Teaching them to harden up. But, she had to admit, it wasn't the way she'd been taught to deal with the public. And she'd watched Dave talk people down. Words were important, she knew that.

Mia dashed for the restroom and let out a sob as the door banged shut behind her. Her chest heaved as she tried to control the noise she was making; she didn't want anyone to hear or see her right now. Putting her back to the wall, she slid down onto the floor and rested her head on her knees, hot tears scalding her cheeks.

'Idiot. Fucking idiot,' she muttered, not sure if she was talking about herself or Dave.

Wasn't it ironic that he was ripping her a new arsehole for her behaviour and yet Dave's behaviour was on show here, too?

His knuckles were a funny shade of yellow, just as if he'd punched someone.

'Fuck you, arsehole,' she muttered. Now there was white-hot rage surging through her. She should go back in there and confront him. Yeah, that's what she'd do. Confront him. Tell him she knew what he'd done.

Where's your proof?

But it's obvious.

Is it? Nathan didn't make a complaint. In fact, he apologised. Why would he have done that if Dave had punched him?

Mia stilled. Her voice of reason was right. There was nothing to prove what she suspected.

Voice of reason was back. *Let's not forget who Dave is.*

But who is he really?

Her phone buzzed. She pulled it from her pocket and looked at the screen.

Joan.

Ignoring the message, she took a few hiccuping breaths.

Joan had probably heard the whole conversation. How embarrassing. No, it was more than embarrassing. The humiliation burned in the back of her throat.

The phone buzzed again.

Chris.

Shit. She hadn't returned his call from the other night when she'd been with Sassi. Mia got to her feet and ran the tap, washing her face with cold water, then patted her face dry. Staring at herself in the mirror, she wondered what Nan would have had to say about Dave's dressing-down.

Reactive, not proactive.

How did she appear through other people's eyes: a young woman demanding authority, because she was frightened she'd never get it otherwise?

Mia swallowed. Maybe Dave was right.

Her mobile buzzed. It was Joan again.

Mia remembered what Joan had told her when she'd first started at Barker Station: 'Take a breath and remember you are a police officer and you'll be setting an example for everyone—man, woman and child. Prick, Prick-ess, Prince or Princess.'

CHAPTER 21

In his office, Dave wiped his brow. He was furious.

Furious with Mia, with Nathan Woodbridge. Even with Mel and Bec.

But mostly he was furious with himself because for the first time in a very long time, he'd let his private life affect his work.

Not that he regretted a word that he had said to Mia. She had behaved unlike a police officer and he needed to nip that in the bud. She was very good at her job, mostly. But her temper and spontaneous emotional reactions did not bode well for the level head a copper needed. Her impulsiveness would see her pull a gun when it wasn't needed.

He slammed his fist into his palm. He should get out of the office. Go for a drive. Check on Mr Stapleton and make sure that he was being cared for. That was all part of the community policing he liked to do.

Instead, he sat down at his desk and opened the web browser. With two fingers he typed the name 'Rebecca Burrows' into the Google search bar and hit enter.

There were lots of hits. It seemed that Rebecca Burrows was a reasonably common name. The link to Facebook looked like the best one, because he knew she was the one he was looking for by the photo. His daughter, surrounded by smiling girls, their arms around each other. His daughter standing on the edge of a vivid blue sea and white sand. His daughter next to Melinda.

He gave Melinda a cursory once-over. Time had been kind to her, but he could tell there was a lot of money behind her appearance. Her hair was carefully styled, while foundation hid the blemishes that age didn't stop.

No sign of Bec's fiancé or grandfather. That was good because the way he felt at the moment he might put his fist through the computer just at the sight of Mark's contemptuous face.

Clicking through photo after photo, looking for one of Alice now. Instead, he found that Bec had been to Uluru. There she was, smiling with the giant, red rock behind her. She'd holidayed in New Zealand, dressed in ski gear. Smiling broadly at whoever was taking the photo.

Dave knew neither of the girls would have ever wanted for anything. Mark had so much money, he assumed that the girls would have got whatever they wanted.

Just not their father's love. Their father's guidance and protection.

Have you forgotten? A voice sneered inside his mind. *You couldn't protect them. In fact, you put them in danger. That's why Mel's mum died. You couldn't protect them. You couldn't protect them.*

Over and over, the words he hated, the words he'd spent years saying and thinking. The words that had been thrown at him by his ex-wife and ex-father-in-law.

He wanted the memories to stop. They'd been put to bed a long time ago, so why were they coming back?

Because Bec is getting married.

Looking back up at the computer screen, he pushed the mouse so the screen changed to the next photo.

With a quick intake of breath, Dave leaned back in his chair. There they were together. Bec and Alice.

'Oh.' The word was a soft sigh. 'Look at you two.'

Both were standing in front of a Christmas tree, decorated with candles and lights. The heavy jumpers and jeans told him the photo had been taken in a different country. One where it was cold for Christmas.

He searched for a date. There next to the comment section. The photo had been taken last Christmas. Smiling, he reached out and touched their faces. *My girls, almost as they would look today*, he thought. Both had long brown hair, their faces oval-shaped like his, eyes like their mother.

Dave leaned in closer and assessed them both. Alice looked a little like Mel's mum.

He liked that.

Was there any way he could print this photo off and keep it? They both looked so happy and he wanted to grab hold of that happiness and put some of it inside him. To have a little piece of them.

He didn't know much about Facebook, but he guessed that Alice would have a page, too. How would he find it? When Kim finished cooking later today, she would help him.

Are you going to write to them? He could hear her question already.

'No.' As he said the word, he realised that's exactly what he was thinking. No, he wouldn't. They looked too happy for him to interfere in their lives.

No, he would just admire them from afar. Love them from a distance.

Looking away now, the blinding anger he'd felt before had dulled slightly, but he was still breathing heavily and his heart was thumping hard.

His daughters.

What he could do for them was check out that bloke Bec was marrying. Justin Martin. That would give him peace of mind that his daughter would be safe and happy and cared for.

What the hell are you going to do if he has a record? he asked himself. *And what you're about to do is prohibited.* Ignoring the voice, Dave tapped on the computer and, hesitating only for a moment, he put a search in through National Crim Records for Justin Martin.

As he hit enter, he shook his head. 'You fucking idiot,' he said. But it didn't stop him.

He typed another name: Ashley Bennett. And hit enter again.

Ashley Bennett. Bulldust. His nemesis from another life-time ago. The man who had threatened his family, murdered his mother-in-law and injured his tiny daughter. He needed to know where he was. With any luck he was still in jail and Dave's family was safe from the brutal cattle thief.

He wondered if Bec still had a scar on her arm from where the bullet had nicked her. Perhaps it was a faded white now.

There was a knock at the door. Dave frowned at the noise, thinking he really should leave the bloody thing open. It usually was.

'Hello?' he called out.

The door opened slightly and Kim put her head inside. 'Can I come in?'

Dave swallowed his rage and sadness then took a breath. 'Hi, honey, sure.' He waved her through. 'Come and sit.' Shifting some papers from his desk, Dave smiled at her. 'I didn't expect to see you until I got home. Thought you were busy cooking.'

'I'm nearly done,' Kim said. 'And I was passing, so I thought I'd drop in.' She reached up and wrapped a blonde curl around her finger as she looked at him steadily across the desk. 'You don't usually have your door shut.'

Dave flicked his hand. 'Had a bit of work I needed to do and I didn't want any interruptions. How's your morning been?'

'Fine. I've just delivered some meals at three different houses. I saw Rasha going for a walk with Mr Stapleton.

It was lovely to see them out and about, even if he's very slow on his feet.'

'Nice.' He didn't smile. His gaze went back to the screen and he read what was there.

'What are you working on?' Kim asked. 'I thought things were pretty quiet.'

Pressing his lips together, Dave shook his head. 'Jesus, Kim. I'm an idiot.' He pushed his chair back as if he needed to be as far away from the computer as he could be. Then he bent over at the waist, his arms around his legs, and stayed there.

'Shit. Dave? Are you okay? What's wrong, honey? Do you have a pain in your chest or something?' Kim ran around the other side of the desk and dropped to her knees, putting her hands on his. 'What's wrong?'

'I've fucked up, Kim.' He looked at her now, his eyes sad.

'I'm sure whatever it is can be fixed.' She ran her fingers over the bruises on his knuckles. 'It's not just work though, is it? The news about Bec has brought everything back up for you.'

She knows, he realised. There was no point in hiding anything from Kim. She knew him too well. And loved him no matter what.

'I'm so angry at Melinda and Mark again, but that paper clipping, it's—I miss the girls.'

'Of course you do, but if you write to them or give them a call, I know they'll be happy to hear from you. Does it frighten you that you won't hear back from them or they won't want you? Is that why you don't write anymore?'

'They haven't answered in all the years I did write.'

Kim shifted and frowned. 'You know Melinda was taking the letters before the girls saw them.'

'We're assuming that and I've always been taught not to assume anything. Here, look at this.' He brought the photo of both girls up on his screen. 'Don't they look happy?'

Kim studied the picture for a minute. 'They do. That's good.'

'Yeah, except I'm not in their life and they're *that* happy.' He pointed at the screen and left the rest unsaid.

Kim just rubbed his hand and kept looking at him, waiting for Dave to continue.

'That night the letter arrived, when I had to go to that disturbance at the pub.'

'Hmm.'

Dave felt Kim's supportive hand rubbing his, and took a deep breath. 'I was so angry. Been years since I've felt like that and, let me tell you, it's not something I want to feel again. It's not who I am anymore. Not since . . .' He wanted to say, since I've been with you.

'Anyhow, you know from what I said before that the Woodbridge bloke was going off his nut. He hurled one too many insults once I got him in the cell and I reacted without thinking and punched him.'

Kim drew in a breath, but again, stayed silent.

'I don't think anything will come of it, but if he wanted to, he could make a complaint about me. And then internal affairs would get involved and they'd go through me like a dose of salts, because that's what they do.' He paused and looked back at the computer. 'And then they'd find this.'

Dave wiggled the mouse and showed her the search he'd performed only moments before his wife had knocked on the door.

And the results.

'Oh, Dave. You're not supposed to access the police database for your own research.' Kim looked at him despairingly. 'And why hasn't the police department told you that Bulldust was released from prison last year?'

'I fought for those girls all my life,' he told her. 'You know how much I've tried to stay in touch with them. Then that article turns up and they haven't even bothered to let me know about the wedding. I'm not even an afterthought. Their *father* isn't even an afterthought. And now this. I can't return to their lives now that I know Bulldust is out on the street.'

'This is why you've been so out of sorts. I thought as much,' Kim said. 'Joan rang me. She said you lost it with Mia today. Really dropped the bomb on her.'

'I did, but in my defence, she needed it.'

Kim gave him a soft smile.

'All right, yes, I could have handled her better,' Dave agreed at her unspoken suggestion.

'Maybe you should tell her that next time you see her. Joan says she's pretty upset.'

'I'm not apologising for what I said, only the way I did it.'

'Good. Now what about this guy you punched?'

Dave shrugged now, and he stood, helping Kim to her feet. He put his arms around her and held her close. 'Like I said, I don't think anything will come of it. But if it does, then I won't have a leg to stand on.'

Kim tightened her arms around his waist. 'Well, there's nothing you can do about it now, honey. You'll just have to live with whatever happens.'

'I know. I'm pretty bloody angry with myself.'

'That saves me having to be.'

Dave gave a small laugh and kissed her head, resting his chin there.

'Do we need to be worried about Bulldust?' Kim asked.

Letting out a long breath, Dave considered her question. 'I wouldn't have thought so. That case was a long time ago and Correctional Services would have been in contact if they believed there was any risk when he was released.' What he didn't say aloud was that he knew Bulldust wasn't the kind of bloke to let go of a grudge, no matter how rehabilitated the powers that be thought he was. Bulldust, or Ashley Bennett as they would know him in jail, was a great actor and an even better manipulator, although he didn't have the brains his brother, Scott, had before Bulldust had put him in the ground.

Kim spoke again. 'Dave, honey, I know you think the girls are happy without you, but have you thought they might be even happier with you in their lives?'

Dave didn't say anything.

'I don't know why Bec hasn't been in contact with you— I'm sure she could have found you quite easily—but you're their dad and you shouldn't ever stop trying to connect with them. Don't ever think you'll make their lives poorer by being part of it. You're the older adult so it might be you who needs to make the effort again. Let's not forget there's every chance they've been told you don't want to have anything to do with them.'

CHAPTER 22

Sassi pushed the wheelchair into the lounge room and left it next to her grandfather's chair. He could walk without the chair, but Rasha had suggested they hire one from the hospital so she could take him out for longer walks along the street.

'It is much nicer out in the sun,' she said.

'Such a good idea,' Sassi agreed.

Pa had liked the first walk he'd had outside when Rasha had taken him the day before, but he hadn't been able to go too far as his legs weren't strong enough.

Rasha was kind and gentle with him, linking her arm through his to support him, sharing little smiles and laughs when she pointed out something new to him. A little flower growing in a crack in the cement or a bird in the trees that lined the street.

Sassi knew Rasha was the right person for this job.

Now, Pa held the side of the chair and got to his feet, shuffling around to get himself settled and ready to go.

'Jarrah, get out of the way,' Sassi told the dog, who was sleeping at the foot of the chair. A heavy thump of the tail and then Jarrah gave Pa's hand a lick and stood in the doorway, an expectant look on her face.

'Don't get your hopes up, Jarrah,' Sassi said. 'I've got work to do. I'm trying to buy a new ute.'

Amber walked down the hallway towards the front door and Sassi glanced over, hoping to catch her eye. Since Sassi had asked to have a conversation about her father, Amber had avoided her and it appeared that she had no intention of changing her behaviour today. Casting a disapproving eye over Jarrah, Amber disappeared through the front door, letting it bang behind her.

Sighing, Sassi waited until Pa was comfortable and then pushed him to the back door, where Abe had installed a ramp the previous day. The wheelchair slipped easily down the incline and onto the lawn.

'Here we are, Rasha. Ready when you are,' Sassi said, squinting against the bright sunlight. 'Pa, do you want sunglasses?'

The old man nodded and held his hand up to stop the glare.

'Hat, too.' Rasha patted the top of her head, pausing as she hung a towel on the clothesline.

Inside, Sassi found the required items next to Pa's chair and grabbed them. Then stopped. The silence in the house was unnerving. Amber always made some type of noise. The distinct clicking of her tongue when she was annoyed was the most obvious. But now the house was still. Maybe she'd gone to the shops, since she'd left through the front door.

'Mum?'

There wasn't any answer.

As she headed to go back outside, Sassi glanced through the kitchen entrance and saw her mother's notepad on the kitchen table. She ducked in to check and see if her mother had left a note to say where she'd gone.

Nothing but a shopping list.

In the passageway, Sassi stood quietly next to her mother's bedroom door and heard nothing.

Outside, Sassi put Pa's hat on while he arranged his sunglasses.

'Where would you like to walk today?' Sassi asked.

'Emtry.'

That was a new word. Emtry?

Pa touched his left hand. His wedding band.

'Oh, cemetery?' Sassi asked.

He nodded.

Rasha took the washing basket back inside, while Sassi squatted down.

'I'm not ready to go to the cemetery yet, Pa. I think Rasha should take you. Is that okay?'

Another nod and Sassi pointed the way to Rasha when she returned. 'It's not far. Just down this street and follow the signs.'

'I will.'

Pa pointed at Jarrah, who was sitting straight up, ears pointed skywards and eyes alert.

'Do you really want to take her?'

Pa nodded and held out a shaking hand for the lead. Getting it from the outside table, Sassi clipped it on and Jarrah danced around, twisting the cord around Sassi's legs.

'Stop it,' she told the pup. 'Sit.'

It took a few moments before Jarrah did as she was asked, and Sassi could untangle herself. Jarrah's whole body was quivering with excitement. Finally Sassi handed the lead to Rasha. 'Good luck!' she said.

Pa gave her a salute, then he was lifting his face to the sky, drinking in the sun and the gentle breeze that was blowing.

She wondered if her pa felt like he was seeing and feeling everything for the first time again, by his look of pure pleasure. Sassi watched them go and then went back inside. She wanted to get out her laptop. The ute that Abe had found for her was just what she wanted and the payout from the insurance company had hit her account yesterday.

She could have a set of wheels by the end of today if she was lucky. The front door slammed and the footsteps on the wooden floorboards in the hallway told Sassi Amber was back home.

Her hands hovered over the keyboard while she thought. There was no one other than the two of them in the house. Maybe now was the perfect time.

Stuff it.

Amber wasn't in the kitchen so Sassi knocked on the spare bedroom door.

'Yes?'

'Can I come in?'

There was a silence, then a couple of thuds as if her mother was putting things in her suitcase and tidying up quickly. The door opened and Amber held up her hand. 'I do not want to have this conversation with you, Sassi.'

Sassi's nostrils flared as she drew in a deep, angry breath. She hadn't even said what she wanted, although Amber was right that she wanted to speak about her father.

'You know what?' Sassi replied calmly, ignoring her mother's crossed-arm stance. 'I'd rather not have the conversation either, because it should have happened when I was born. I had the right to know from that moment. I shouldn't be twenty-eight and still having to ask and getting the "talk to the hand" look you give, but the fact is I'm entitled to know who my father is. And if you're not going to tell me, I'll be doing my best to find out any other way I can.'

'I don't know how you're going to do that,' Amber snapped. Then she stopped and ran her fingers through her hair, as her face softened. 'I'm sorry, Sassi. I don't have many nice memories from back then and it's something I really don't like to talk about. Could you try to understand? Please?' Amber moved around the room, straightening the bedspread and shifting books from one shelf to another.

Turning her back on her daughter as she'd always done. But her moves were sharp and nervous, and for once she looked small and vulnerable.

Amber had never allowed any of her family to get close to her. Didn't allow them in her life. She barely had a relationship with Abe and her nephews' reactions to her recently told their own story.

No one in the family had even met Zola.

'Tell me about Zola,' Sassi said, changing the subject as she slipped down the wall and rested against it.

'What about him?' Amber glanced over at her before she smoothed the wrinkles out of the bedspread, now avoiding Sassi's eyes.

'What's he like? I've never even seen a photo of him.' Sassi considered adding, *Does he even exist?* but thought better of teasing Amber the way she would have done with Abe.

'He's lovely. Kind and thoughtful. A good farmer.'

Sassi assessed the answer. The words gave her nothing. 'Where did you meet him?'

'Ha, where does anyone meet someone in Australia? The pub of course.'

'Here? In Barker?'

Amber rolled her eyes. 'You're not serious, are you?'

'Well, where?'

Pursing her lips, Amber shook her head. The answer was dragged out of her, rather than given. 'Adelaide.'

'Did you ever think about having any more kids?'

Amber reeled, her face ashen. 'Why would you ask that?'

'I don't know. Maybe Zola wanted kids with you? You've never talked about having any more, but still . . .' Her question faded.

'No. We didn't have any children.' Amber drew herself up and looked down at Sassi, sitting against the wall. 'Now, if you wouldn't mind?' She indicated to the door. 'I have things I need to attend to.'

Only then did Sassi notice a laptop computer open on the bedside table.

'Do you do the farm books for Zola?'

Nodding, Amber looked over at the laptop. 'Yes, and I pay the servants and farm workers. It's pay day today, so I need to make sure everyone has their money. There are young girls who work for me, not even sixteen yet. No one can do without their wages,'

Sassi lifted herself from the floor and leant against the doorway as she thought about what it was like to be sixteen. The age her mother had been when she had given birth to her.

To be interested in boys, and sex, was a whole new world that needed exploring. What if someone took advantage of that?

Sassi had to choose her next words carefully. This could be why her mother pushed her aside, why she didn't seem to love her. Why she could leave her daughter with her parents and run away to another country.

Because that's what Amber had done her whole life. Run away.

'Mum . . .'

This time Amber whirled around and pointed her finger at Sassi. 'Enough!' she snapped. 'I will not discuss this with you. I refuse to have the subject of your father mentioned in my presence. If you really want to know, go and do some detective work yourself. You said you were going to. Now get out of my room and leave me to my work.' She almost jumped towards the door and slammed it shut, causing Sassi to stumble backwards into the hall.

Not moving for a moment, Sassi's mind continued to turn somersaults and connect dots. Her breaths were short and sharp and then she shook her head as if trying to ward off what she somehow knew. 'Oh no. Oh my god,' Sassi staggered blindly towards her own bedroom.

Had her mother been raped? Is that how she was conceived?

Thoughts were colliding like fireworks. The distance, the lack of love. Why would her mother love a daughter who had been born out of violence? If this indeed was the case.

The house was too small, the walls were closing in on her. She had to get out. Reefing open the front door, Sassi stumbled down the steps and out into the front yard. Blood pounded in her head. Everything she had ever thought she'd known had just been turned upside-down. Never once had the possibility of rape entered her mind before today. She had just assumed her mother had slept with a boy, maybe her boyfriend, and become pregnant. How naive she'd been.

Out the front gate and onto the street, she walked and jogged and then walked again, not going anywhere but not able to stay still.

Her mother had gone through hell, then had to give birth at sixteen. Sassi had never really done the sums before, but now she realised that her mother would have been fifteen when she'd fallen pregnant. Even if her mother hadn't been raped, she was still under the legal age. And that was statutory rape, even if it was consensual.

But Sassi was growing more and more sure that Amber had been raped.

They should find whoever did this to her mother and charge them. They could still do that, couldn't they? Hadn't there been some historic charges laid against men in parliament recently? Putting a perpetrator in jail would help her mother heal, Sassi was sure.

But who could help her?

'Mia,' Sassi said aloud.

She pulled out her phone and found Mia's phone number. 'Please answer,' she said as it rang and rang.

'Sassi, hi,' Mia said, just as Sassi had given up hope of speaking to her immediately.

'Mia, are you around? Can I come and see you?'

'Sure. Are you okay?'

'Not really. I'd like to talk to you about . . .' Her words failed. 'I just need to talk to you.'

'Okay. At the station? Or somewhere else?'

'I'm nearly at the footy oval. Can you meet me there?' Sassi looked around to get her bearings.

'Give me ten minutes.'

Sassi stood at the oval and put her hands on the steel fence. It was hot to touch but right now she barely felt the heat. Where could it have happened? Who would do something . . .

She jumped over the fence and onto the grass. She began walking around the edge, the white line indicating the boundary under her eye. One foot in front of the other. Step, step, step.

The next time around, Mia fell in alongside her. 'Are you okay? You look like you've had a bit of a shock.'

Sassi stopped and turned her face to Mia. 'Can you charge someone with rape twenty-nine years after the fact?' she asked directly.

Mia opened her mouth in surprise, then her face changed, and she ran her eyes all over Sassi. 'Has someone done something to you?'

'Mum. I think Mum was ra-raped. That's why I was born.' She brushed at her cheeks now. Tears had found their way to her eyes and spilled over.

'Oh, Sassi.' Mia put her arms around her and patted her back.

'How do I find out who did it? We need to charge him. Put him in jail so Mum can have some type of closure.' Sassi groaned at the word 'closure'. 'I guess she's not going to get any of that every time she looks at me, is she? No wonder she's spent so much of her life away from here. From me. God, what memories I must bring up for her.'

'Okay, hold on, you said, you *think* she was raped. What's made you come to this conclusion?'

Sassi let Mia lead her over to a bench, while she asked the question calmly. They sat down, Mia gripping Sassi's hands, which was good, because they were shaking and Sassi couldn't keep them still.

'It's the only thing that makes sense. There's always been so much secrecy around who my father is. His name isn't on my birth certificate.' She shrugged. 'That isn't unusual, but Granny wouldn't talk about it when I asked. Mum just told me moments ago that back then was a pretty awful time and she refused—she actually said the word *refused*—to talk to me about it.

'I stopped asking when I was younger because I never got anywhere, and Granny loved me so much that it didn't matter that Mum wasn't around and neither was my father.'

Mia's face was full of sympathy. 'Sassi, I hate to be the one who tells you this, but there is absolutely nothing to go on with what you've just told me. Your mother hasn't confirmed anything and it's not even hearsay. This is an idea you've had.'

'But what else could it be?' The words exploded from her. Why else would her mum have run away as far as she had?

'This is going to sound horrible, but maybe it's as simple as she didn't want anyone to know. Maybe he was married, or someone in authority like a teacher. There's plenty of other reasons she may not have wanted to tell you.

'And I'm not surprised she said it was a tough time in her life. Who would want to be looking after a baby when she wasn't more than a child herself?'

Sassi swallowed a few times, taking in Mia's words, then shook her head. 'No, I'm sure she was raped. You didn't see the look on her face, or how fragile and vulnerable she seemed. Mum isn't either of those things. Her personality is businesslike and arm's length. That's the way she's always been, and yet Abe is the exact opposite and he was brought up the same way as Mum was. Something had to happen to make her like that. It seems so obvious. I don't know why I didn't think of it before now.'

'Okay, okay, let's just calm down. Take some deep breaths while I go over a few things for you.' Mia breathed slowly herself, encouraging Sassi to copy her. 'Let's say that what you've told me is correct. From a police point of view, we need a few things here. First, your mother would have to come to us and file a complaint. We need some type of evidence. Proof that what she's told us is true. That would enable us to press charges. There would need to be some type of historical evidence, too. Maybe she confided in a friend or made notes in a diary. Even a report from the doctor if she went to one.

'Twenty-nine years later, she's probably got rid of the clothes she was wearing, so there wouldn't be any likelihood of collecting DNA.' Mia let go of Sassi's hands and turned her own up as if helpless. 'It would be incredibly hard to prove rape. Her word against someone else's. How can we be sure, twenty-nine years later, that the act wasn't consensual and only now is she telling people it was rape?'

Sassi was incredulous. 'Why would she do that all this time down the track, if it wasn't true?'

Mia held up her hands in a calming gesture. 'In saying that, if she told us who it was, we could collect DNA and you could get a DNA test done, but all that is going to prove is the person is your father. Not that he raped your mother. Proving rape is incredibly difficult if it happened two hours ago, let alone twenty-nine years ago.'

CHAPTER 23

The ute that Abe had lent Sassi was parked out the front of Pa's house and she threw her bag on the passenger's seat. She'd not managed to buy her new ute today—her mind had been full of these other, more pressing thoughts. All she wanted to do now was get to the farm, where she was safe and wouldn't have to see Amber.

'I'll only be gone a few days,' Sassi said quietly to Rasha. She hadn't seen her mother since their conversation earlier that day. 'I'm just going to stay with Abe and help him get ready for seeding. You'll be okay?'

'Of course.' The woman's beautiful honey-rich tone washed over Sassi. She felt she could fall into Rasha's arms and be hugged tightly into her breast. This woman was homely and motherly. Everything Amber wasn't, and every-thing Sassi was craving right now.

Swallowing the lump in her throat, Sassi gave a wan smile then jumped into the driver's seat and turned the key.

She hardly noticed the drive to the farm. The bitumen road was smooth and straight and her brain kept repeating what she thought she knew.

Abe had to know something about this. He had lived in the house when this had happened. Surely there would have been crying and fury. Maybe even secrecy. He must have noticed something different about the atmosphere of the house. About Amber.

But what if Amber hadn't told her parents about the rape?

Jarrah hung out the back of the tray, her ears pushed back in the wind, tongue hanging out. Sassi wanted to curl up with her, just wrap herself around her dog's warm body and sleep. She was so tired. And she missed her granny.

If she slept, she wouldn't have to feel all these things. How nice that would be.

Still, there would be no chance of sleep with the twins around.

At the thought of those two little boys, she gave a small smile. It hadn't been that long ago she'd decided that all grieving families should have four-year-old twins, because they couldn't let anyone be sad for long. Maybe that's why she was heading out to the farm again.

The mailbox was up ahead, the marker to turn into the driveway.

Sassi came out of her trance and realised where she was. She checked her mirrors and put on the indicator.

The gravel driveway was smoother than it had been when she'd been out a few days ago. Looked like Abe had gone over it with the grader.

Galahs swooped and soared through the tips of the gum trees and flew in front of her as she navigated the driveway's twists and turns before pulling up alongside the house.

Renee stood on the verandah, a cup of tea in her hand, looking out across the lawn and wild bougainvillea that grew along the fence. Creek gravel stretched from the house yard to the sheds. One shed held machinery, and the other was the shearing shed. Behind the shearing shed was a set of yards and a loading ramp then, beyond that, the paddocks where Abe and Sassi had roamed freely during their childhood.

'Want one?' Renee called out, holding up her cup, as Sassi pulled up.

'Have you got anything stronger?' Sassi opened the door and let Jarrah off the chain.

Renee glanced at her watch. 'It's four in the afternoon.' There wasn't any reproach in her voice, she was merely commenting.

'And seven o'clock somewhere,' Sassi said, grabbing her bag and climbing up the steps.

'Beer, wine or whiskey?'

'That could be a country song title! Beer, please. Where are the twins?'

'Beer's there.' Renee pointed at the outdoor fridge next to the geranium pots. 'They're up in the woolshed. Abe sent them to sweep it out.'

'Are you shearing?' Sassi opened the fridge and pulled out a stubby.

'No, he did it just so that I could have a break.' Her hand found her stomach and she cupped it protectively. 'Abe said he told you about the baby?'

'He did. Congratulations. How do you feel?'

'I'm so tired. And I feel sick all the time. But I'm not vomiting. Not sure if that's a good thing or a bad thing.'

Sassi heard the satisfying fizz as she twisted the cap off. She took a long swallow of her beer.

'I'm told ginger helps,' she told Renee, 'but I guess you've tried everything already?'

Renee nodded. 'Plus more. Look, here's Abe.' Renee's gaze swept towards her husband, who had come out of the machinery shed and was now headed towards the house.

'I really need to talk to him, Renee. Could I steal him for an hour or so?'

Renee looked surprised. 'Sure. I'll walk up to the shed and check on the boys.'

Sassi felt her heart swell with gratitude. Renee hadn't asked questions or pried. If she had, Sassi still hadn't reached an answer she would have been happy to share. Giving her a hug, Sassi thanked her.

Abe waved and Sassi collected three beers from the fridge, plus her open one, and went over to meet him. Holding out the beer, she said, 'You're going to need this.'

⁓

'I can't believe it,' Abe said as he rubbed his hand over his hair. 'Are you sure?'

They were sitting on the lawn, underneath a large gum tree and little pieces of bark kept falling on them as the galahs and white cockatoos chewed and pecked at it.

Loud cawing from further down the creek came from the crows.

'I was so young when Amber got pregnant—there's eleven years between us, remember.'

'I know, but I thought you might remember if there was a heap of yelling or crying or something. I don't even know how Granny and Pa would have reacted. Do you think she would have told them the truth?'

'Your guess is as good as mine, but if she had, they would have taken her to the doctor and got the police involved, of that I'm certain. That's what any parent would do.' Abe glanced over at her and then handed her another beer.

'Ta.'

'You know, Sassi, if my daughter came to me and said she'd been raped, I would hunt down the bastard who did it and cut his balls off. When you have kids, you realise that there is no greater love. As a parent you would do anything to keep your kids safe.'

'But they didn't,' Sassi said.

'Maybe they did and never spoke about it. We've got no idea. Maybe the bloke is already in jail. Just because Amber isn't giving you a name doesn't mean he got away unpunished.'

Sassi paused, she hadn't considered that option. 'How do we find out any of this?'

'What about your mate down at the police station? Can she put something into a computer and ask?'

'I'd reckon there'd be a privacy issue.'

Abe let out an abrupt whoop. 'What about newspapers? If there was a trial or something the court case would have to be listed there.'

Sassi sat up straight. 'You're right. Does the library have archives of old newspapers.'

Abe raised his shoulders. 'Dunno, but it wouldn't be hard to find out.' He stopped for a moment. 'There are some old diaries in the shed that Dad used to write in. Renee and I packed them up in plastic containers, so they didn't get damaged. There might be something in those, although the pages I glanced through were more records of what was happening on the farm rather than anything personal.' He took another sip of his beer. 'Still, that doesn't mean anything. Let's have a bo-peep.'

'We know what dates we're working with,' Sassi said. 'It's not like we're going to have to read through every year.'

'Come on, grab another couple of beers and we'll go take a squiz.' Abe got up and dusted the leaf litter from his shoulders. He looked up at the tree. 'Bloody galahs,' he muttered. 'Those mongrels chewed the two-way aerial in my truck last harvest. I had to leave it parked at the silos because they closed before I could get the grain sampled. Came back the next morning and couldn't work out why the girls in the sample hut weren't answering me when I called 'em up.'

'Their screech always reminds me of the farm,' Sassi said, following him out the gate. 'This is always home. The hills, the creeks, the gums. The galahs. This is what I love.'

They walked in step together towards the shed, their boots kicking up dust. Jarrah puffed alongside them as Abe's two dogs ran in a wide arc in front.

'There's been something I've been thinking about and I wasn't sure whether to broach the subject with you,' Abe said hesitantly. 'To be honest, I'm not sure now is the right moment either, but I'm running out of time.'

Sassi stopped and looked at her uncle. 'What's wrong?'

'Nothing's wrong, just more of a proposal for you.'

Sassi relaxed slightly and continued walking, but she was listening.

'You know how hard it is to get staff at the moment and then, when you do, they're not always trained the way you'd like them to be. Not enough experience or don't work sheep the same way I do. It's frustrating! Anyhow, I haven't been able to find an employee who I've been happy with and I was wondering if you'd like to . . .'

Sassi stopped and stared at him. 'What, work for you?'

Abe shook his head. 'No, you need to be able to get some part of the profit. We're family and I can't in fairness just pay you a wage and not expect that you won't want more.

'See, the farm down the road is for sale, and if we bought it, there'd be enough for everyone. And in time, we could keep buying more land. Make sure there's enough for my kids and your kids if you have any. Partners.'

'Are you serious? Have you talked to Renee about this?'

'Yeah. We think it's the perfect solution to our labour problems. And we'd have you home.' He gave her a cheeky grin. 'A built-in babysitter.'

Sassi snorted. 'For whom? The twins or Pa?'

'Both!'

Abe slid open the door to the shed, the screeching startling the birds and sending them into the air, flapping with annoyance.

The light inside the shed was dim with ribbons of sunlight streaming in through the holes in the tin. Dust particles rose and danced through the air as Abe's and Sassi's movement disturbed them.

Sassi was quiet, thinking through what Abe had suggested. She had to be logical with this decision, not just jump up and down shouting *Yes!* Which was what she wanted to do. There were plenty of family farm businesses that went wrong because of problems between members and she didn't want that happening to the Stapletons.

'Abe, what's the set-up with the farm now? Do you own it or is it in Pa's name? How is it run?'

'It's still in Pa's name, but it comes to me on his death. At the moment I pay a discounted lease rate to them . . . Well, just Dad now. That's always given them more than enough to live on and be comfortable. If they wanted something bigger, like a new car or a holiday, the farm paid for it. The farm will pay for Rasha and her care, and if he does have to move to a home, then the farm will pay for that, too. We'll pay for whatever he needs.'

'Surely Mum needs to make a contribution?'

'No. The discounted lease is so the farm would look after them in their old age.'

'Ah. Well, we'd have to make sure that was what was going to happen. What if he changed his mind?'

Abe pulled down some boxes from a shelf in the shed and started flicking through the books inside. 'Here, you look in that one,' he said. 'I've got a copy of his will. Both Mum and Dad updated theirs just before Dad's stroke. Nothing has altered since then. The family lawyer would get in contact with me if anything had changed. At this time in his life, everything has already been decided. He's not coming back to farming, if you hadn't noticed.'

Despite Sassi's stomach still being in knots, and her fear of what her mother must think every time Sassi came into her view, excitement was growing within her. She'd love to come back to her home. To work the land alongside Abe. That's all she'd ever wanted to do. And soon there would be a new baby to cuddle.

At the thought of another little human, Sassi remembered she hadn't answered Ewin's texts yet. Last night she'd typed out a response to him: *Nothing to apologise for. Hope you're well.* Then deleted it. The words had felt too impersonal after everything they'd shared over six years.

Her common sense had nudged her: *The way he left you was pretty impersonal, so the answer is fine. Send it.*

But she hadn't. Maybe today.

She turned her attention to the box of diaries. 'The year 1995 is what we're looking for.'

'Let's look back into ninety-four, too,' Abe said. 'Just in case.'

'Here's eighty-four, eighty-five . . .' Sassi flicked through, checking each gold-embossed year on the black leather covers. 'Remember how Granny used to give these diaries as Christmas presents. I'm sure she got a bulk discount wherever she bought them. Pa and all of his family used to get one, didn't they?'

'Yeah, and I used to want one, because it meant you were a man with a business. She gave me my first one the year I left school and was coming home to work on the farm.' He smiled. 'I really thought I'd made it.'

'Interesting, isn't it, because she never gave me one.'

'You're a girl,' Abe said in a scornful tone. 'These were only for the men of the family.'

'Ah, not people who worked and needed to keep their life in order then. Only men?'

They both laughed, then Abe's laughter cut off.

Sassi looked up from the box and saw him holding up a book. He held it out to her.

'Here's 1995,' he said.

Sassi didn't reach for the diary immediately, but slowly her hand came out and she sank onto the floor, the book resting on her lap. Her hair fell in front of her face as she opened the cover.

Her grandfather's familiar neat cursive, before he'd been unable to hold a pen, made her throat constrict. She put the diary down.

'Do you ever feel like we've grown old and we shouldn't have? You know, we're not grown-up enough to handle what life gives us and we still need our parents? Or grandparents, in my case.'

'All the time,' Abe said.

'Me too.' She flicked the page to the first of January, ignoring the notes Pa had made about the chemicals and drenches he'd used on the stock and in the cropping program.

There were notes on what dates the rams had gone in and when the opening rains had come. Seeding rates for every paddock and a happy birthday written on the dates of the two kids—Amber and Abe.

There was a note on 16 July that Abe had come down with chicken pox, and then on 23 November, a workman, Craig Hander, had cut his wrist badly enough for Cora to take him to the hospital.

The only mention of Amber was on her birthday.

CHAPTER 24

Mia raised her hand to knock on the door but let it drop a little. Then before she could change her mind, she rapped loudly. A police officer's knock.

A knock that she and Chris had practised when they were in the academy, after they'd had a few beers. They'd sit at the bar and bang on the wood, until one of them decided it had sounded like a true knock that a police officer would use.

'Mia.' Kim gave a large smile and opened the door further. 'Come in. Are you looking for Dave? He's on the verandah.'

'Yeah, if you don't mind. What are you cooking? Smells yummy, as usual!' Following Kim into the kitchen she nodded yes to the coffee when Kim pointed at the kettle.

'Cakes today. Cakes for all my oldies for their morning and afternoon teas. They all still love stopping at nine thirty in the morning then three in the afternoon. I think they've got the right idea, taking a real break for half an hour and then getting back to work. We seem to have forgotten how to do that.' Pulling the tea towel that was hung over the oven rail aside, she checked the tray inside. Mia could see the cake was golden on the top.

'That's true. Nan used to put the closed sign up in the shop for an hour at lunch and sneak away to sit under a tree to eat the sandwiches she'd brought from home and have a cup of tea out of the thermos.

'Do you know, I think tea tastes sort of exotic out of a thermos. Probably because we don't do it much anymore.'

Kim laughed. 'I know what you mean. Anyhow, go through. You know where to find him.'

Mia took the cup that Kim offered her and went into the lounge room, stopping briefly to look at the photos on the wall. There was a new one in a silver frame. Two girls smiling widely, dressed in jeans and jumpers. They looked like feminine versions of Dave. Maybe these were his daughters about whom he spoke so rarely.

Her stomach twisted a bit as she heard Dave cough, and she opened the door to go outside. She wasn't quite sure how to start the conversation. There were two things she needed to talk to him about, and she hoped that he wasn't still angry with her.

The patio was warm with the late afternoon sun, shadows of gum leaves swishing across the table and across the man sitting there, while a sprinkler lazily watered not only the lawn but the magpies and willie wagtails, which were bathing themselves beneath the heavy drops.

'Hi,' she said quietly. 'Are you busy?'

Dave turned at the sound of her voice and she saw that he had a notepad and pen in front of him and a beer next to his hand.

'Hi, not at all. Come on out.' He pushed a chair away from the table with his foot and indicated for her to sit. He turned the pad over, but not before Mia had read the blank heavy strokes.

Dear Bec and Alice.

'How'd you go with the speed checks?'

'Yeah, no problems.' Mia put the cup on the table and brushed the leaves off the cushion of the chair before she sat. 'I didn't pull anyone up. All very well behaved. Few caravaners, but more cars than anything.'

'Not surprised at the caravans. That time of year. Still,' he mused, 'every month of the year seems to be tourist season these days. And that's a good result with the radar. Word must've got out we're patrolling.'

'I flipped the two-way onto channel forty and there were a few people who called up letting other cars know I was in the area. That might've helped.'

Dave nodded. 'Bush telegraph.'

'Um . . .' Mia looked at her hands and then over at Dave. 'I didn't spend as much time out there as you wanted, though.' She rolled the edge of her shirt between her fingers.

Dave regarded her and she was relieved to see his eyes weren't cold this time. The blue was normal, calm. Waiting for her to tell him what had happened.

She breathed a sigh of relief. Dave was fine.

'I got a call from Sassi asking to speak with me. She sounded pretty shaken, so I turned around and came back.'

'What's the problem?' He linked his fingers together and leaned forward.

'I don't know if we can do anything, Dave, but I thought you might know, local knowledge and all. The Stapletons are a local family, aren't they? They've been here for ages?'

Dave nodded. 'They're farmers, but I'm not sure how many generations back they go.'

'This is way out of left field, but Sassi seems to think her mother was raped and that's how she was conceived. She's in a pretty bad way. Do you know anything about . . .' Her voice trailed off as Dave shook his head.

'That would've been before I was transferred here. I know you think I know everything about Barker, but I don't. Kim's the one you need to talk to if you're looking for information that far back. Obviously she won't know about any police records or the like.' He got up and went to the door. 'Are you free, honey?' he called. Turning back to Mia, his face was troubled. 'What makes Sassi think that's the case?'

Mia explained what Sassi had told her. 'And, look, I said there could be any number of reasons that Amber didn't want her to know who her father was. Not just because she didn't want to remember anything nasty.'

'And that's true,' Dave agreed. 'Does she have any evidence?'

'Not that I'm aware of. Her mother didn't admit anything to her this morning, only hinted that it might be the case. I'm not sure she even went that far. It seemed she just refused to have the conversation with Sassi, but Sassi has taken that to mean what she's come up with is gospel.'

'That'll be pretty hard for her.'

'Yeah. Anyhow, Sassi's decided to go stay with Abe for a few nights. Told me she didn't want to be near her mother, only because she didn't want to add to her distress any more than she had for the last twenty-eight years.'

Dave screwed up his nose. 'Ah.'

'What's up, love?' Kim asked, standing in the doorway. Her face was red from the heat of the oven.

Dave repeated the story and asked if she knew anything.

'Oh, god, that sounds terrible. Poor Sassi. Poor Amber.' Kim came over to the table and sat down, the expression on her face troubled. 'Let me think, how long ago?'

'Twenty-nine years, or thereabouts.'

'Okay, so I would have been . . . yeah, and Mum and Dad had already passed so I was in the roadhouse.' She looked over at Mia apologetically. 'Just trying to trace it through to where I would have been then.'

A magpie waddled away from his shower and threw his head back, warbling up into the setting sun.

'You know, I can't remember anything like that happening. And don't quote me on this, but nothing rings a bell. There's certainly been some horrible things happen in Barker, tragic deaths and so on, but I'm not remembering a rape. Of course, if someone had wanted to sweep it under the carpet . . .' She huffed a little. 'What I know about country towns is that anything is possible.'

'Can you tell me much about Amber and the Stapletons?' Mia asked.

'Hmm, not that much because they seemed normal. If there is such a thing. Church every Sunday—Mr Stapleton was a staunch Catholic, but he was also a member of council for a while, too. Yeah, that's right, I'd forgotten about that.' She nodded to herself. 'Mrs Stapleton, always quick with a smile and chat. Always seemed busy. Buzzing around like a bee.

'And the kids, well, Abe loved footy and farming, and Amber, she was quiet. No, quiet isn't the right word. She observed everyone. I do recall feeling like she watched me from a distance when I was making her milkshakes.' Kim grinned and held up a finger. 'Now, I remember what food and drink almost every person in this town likes, and that's because I care about food and patronage. It doesn't mean I always remember details about their lives.'

Mia wanted to laugh, but she was too strung out. Too worried that Dave hadn't said anything more. She shot him a glance. He was sitting back, listening to Kim.

Still, she told herself, that was Dave. He was quiet, thoughtful and proactive, rather than reactive. Exactly how he was asking her to be.

'As I mentioned to Dave, I know that Amber went to boarding school in Year Eight and then was asked to leave when she got pregnant.'

'Whatever happened, consensual or not, it may not have been here in Barker. It could have happened while she was in Adelaide,' Mia said.

'Fair chance, I'd say,' Kim agreed.

'See, this is why I think there is something to what Sassi has told me. Amber has treated Sassi almost as if she doesn't exist. Like it's too painful to be around her.'

'I can understand where you're going here, Mia,' Kim said, nodding her agreement. 'But maybe she just didn't want her. As cruel and harsh as that sounds, it happens. Girls get pregnant and they never want their child. Women get postnatal depression and don't want their baby. Even a child that's been conceived "through love", as it were.' Her fingers made quotation marks. 'Just because a woman gets pregnant does not mean she's going to love her baby.'

Mia stared at her, horrified. 'Don't mothers fall in love with babies when they're born, even though they think they don't want them for the whole pregnancy?'

'In an ideal world,' Kim said. 'But it doesn't always happen.'

Mia didn't answer for a moment, trying to comprehend what Kim had just told her. Again, she realised how naive she was. There was still so much to learn. 'Okay, so there's nothing we can do to find out. Could we see if there was a report?'

Dave shook his head. 'We need to have a reason to go looking, and until Amber comes to us, we don't. Unless

Sassi can give us some type of evidence. The trouble is we have to wait for Amber to want to press charges.'

'Shit. That's awful,' Mia said. 'There must be something we can do?'

Kim got up. 'I just need to check my cakes.'

Mia waited until Kim had left before she turned back to Dave, speaking quickly. 'I wanted to apologise. I've taken on board what you said and I realise you're right.' She gave a half smile. 'I thought you were being unfair. But the more I went back over what you said, I could see what you were saying. I hope I've not only listened, but I've heard you this time.'

'I'm glad, Mia. Because you're a good copper. Only you end up letting your heart rule your head sometimes and you can't do that.' He paused and swallowed hard. 'And I have an apology for you. The way I spoke to you wasn't right and I certainly could have done better. I'm not going back on anything I said to you—all of that still stands— but, for the delivery part, I'm sorry, too.'

'Apologies all round,' Mia said, not really sure what more to say. Thanking him didn't seem appropriate.

'Now look, Mia, I'm sure you think all I'm doing at the moment is lecturing you, but this thing with Sassi, it's the perfect opportunity to bring another side of small-town policing up.'

Mia felt like sagging, but reminded herself that she was lucky to be able to learn from Dave.

'Okay.'

'When we live in these towns where we know everyone and people know us, we have to fit into the community. Like you're doing, playing tennis and so on. We end up making friends. It's hard when our friends come to us for help and there is nothing we can do. You might find that Hopper blows numbers when you breath-test him on the way home in two weeks' time and he leans on you to forget the charge. Or Hamish might get caught speeding and he could ask you not to give him a ticket. When these sorts of incidents come up, separation from you as the friend to you as a police officer is imperative.'

Mia took a sip of her coffee and listened. She knew this but there must be a reason why Dave was bringing it up now.

'We've got lots of records at our fingertips. Like you mentioned before, historical reports and charges. The ability to find out if people we've put away are still in the clink.' Dave paused and looked out to the sunset before raising his beer to his mouth. 'We can't access them without reason. If Sassi comes to you again, remember you are a police officer first and a friend second.'

Mia nodded. She knew, but she hadn't been put in a situation like Dave had mentioned because she'd only been stationed in Barker for less than a year.

'It's bloody hard what we do, Mia.' Dave stared out across the land to the paddocks beyond. 'Bloody hard.'

CHAPTER 25

The land stretched out before Sassi and Abe.

The soil was red and rich and the plains were devoid of any trees, save for the small scrubby bushes that lined the fences and driveway. This was cropping country. Not station and sheep country.

'What do you think?' Abe asked, as he kicked the soil with his boot, digging down beyond the surface.

'I think we'd grow some good crops, although it is just on the northern side of Goyder's Line. And I know you keep telling me it's okay to crop north, but Goyder knew something when he surveyed this area way back when.' Sassi bent down and dug in the ground with her hand, letting the lumpy dirt run through her fingers.

Abe nodded. 'I agree, but if we buy this place, the next one might be closer to Broad River, which is south of the line. Then we're spreading our risk across a few different rainfalls and soils. Depends on what farms come on the market and if we can make our figures work, doesn't it?'

'What a goal to have, though,' Sassi said, her skin tingling with excitement. Never in her wildest dreams had she imagined that she might end up farming back in Barker.

'So we'll make the offer?'

Sassi glanced back over at the real estate agent who was leaning against his car, waiting for them to make a decision.

'Do we need to talk to Pa first?' she asked. 'I know he doesn't speak very well, but he's still totally switched on in every other aspect.'

'We don't need his permission. The security for the bank would be this farm itself. The budget that we did last night shows it's going to hold its own, so we can do this in our own capacity. But if it would make you more comfortable to speak to him first, we can do that.'

She gripped the fence, thinking hard. Was she brave enough? Her life had been in New South Wales for so long now, to up-end everything and come home was certainly a dream come true, but she'd be leaving behind a life she'd built: friends, work colleagues, a really good job. The only thing she had in Barker was . . . family.

And all for the uncertainty of seasons, interest rates and grain prices.

She tried to find her voice of reason as she looked out over the open plains. They were wide and fertile, surrounded by a ring of hills. What an opportunity!

'What's the average grain yield through here?' Sassi asked.

'Two tonne. Higher than it is at home, but we're a good thirty kays further north from here and, as we all know, the higher up we go, the less rainfall. Average of about two fifty to three hundred mil rainfall. That's enough to grow a good crop, if the rain falls within the growing season. And if it doesn't, we've got contingency plans. Buy sheep and turn them in on the crop, then sell them. If we don't get finishing rains, we can make hay. You know we have to be flexible and look outside the square to make a go of farming up here. It's not called marginal country without reason.'

Sassi dug out the budget they'd done last night and gave it another once-over, trying to think if there was anything they'd forgotten to put in.

The budget had been a quick one, on the back of an envelope. Pa had always said if the figures worked there, they would work in a monthly budget program. 'We'd have to upgrade some of the machinery. Or at least have a tractor and an air seeder down here. We can't be running the machinery up and down the road. It's not time effective.'

Abe leaned forward and tapped a couple of figures. 'I know we're not one hundred per cent sure about interest rates, but if we can pick up something at a clearing sale within this price, we can have a tractor and air seeder here. Not every piece of machinery needs to be new, does it? We can work up to that. That's what Dad did. I know there're plenty of farmers around here who have massive machines, but they've been on the land for generations. We've only been here two and there's still work to be done to grow the business.'

'I totally agree.' Sassi put her hands in her pockets and rocked on her heels. To her left was a fenced-off stone memorial structure, a plaque telling of a train wreck in the early 1900s. She pointed to it. 'Did you have to learn about that train crash at school? The story has always freaked me out.'

Abe grinned. 'We were coming back from Broad River a while back and there was a full moon. The twins were just about asleep but not quite, and I had to slow for a couple of emus. Anyhow, Jimmy looked out of the window and asked if I could see the man running across the paddock.'

Sassi turned to look at him, horror on her face.

'Yeah, I couldn't see anything, but he swore black and blue there was a man running towards us, waving his arms for help.'

'Must've been his imagination. He's only four. He couldn't have seen anything like that.' She paused. 'Could he?'

Abe turned to her, his eyes serious. 'That's my point. He's only four so why would he make up something like that? Two firemen were killed in that head-on train crash. And a heap of cattle.'

'I know. I can remember Mrs Hempton standing in front of the blackboard telling us exactly what happened. Not something you can forget once you've heard the details.' She slid another glance towards Abe. 'You don't really think Jimmy saw anything, do you?'

It was pretty hard to believe that ghosts existed out here in the midday sun, when the temperature was pushing thirty degrees and the sky was such a vivid blue it made you want to stare at it all day.

'I don't know. I'd give him the benefit of the doubt, because I've never told him the history of the train crash.'

Sassi shook her head as if to clear it. There were always old wives' tales about people who had died out here in the bush. A bloke roamed the hills looking for his dog that had been killed by a dingo. A child held a lantern and walked the road, calling for her mother, who'd died after being bitten by a snake.

Everyone loved a good ghost story, and when the land felt as ancient as time itself, there were many tall tales to tell.

'Not sure you're making me feel like I want to live down here by myself,' she said with a half smile.

Abe clapped her on the shoulder. 'Not to worry. Barker's not that far away. You'll be able to slip back into town if you get scared.'

Sassi gave him a friendly push. 'Right-oh, if we're going to put this offer in, we'd better do it, hadn't we?'

Agreeing on the price, they began walking back to the real estate agent.

⌒

Sassi felt a little sick with nerves, but more excited than she had in many, many years. She had just changed her life. Well, not to get too far in front of herself. The owners had to accept the offer, but if all went according to plan, she was coming home.

'I think,' Abe said, tapping the steering wheel as they drove towards Broad River, 'that the first year we should grow wheat. I know canola is a higher paying crop, but it's also higher input. Not only in terms of money, but work. Needs to be sprayed all the time.'

'Would canola be okay to grow out here on the plains? Isn't it too dry?'

'There were about three blokes who had a crack last year. Came off for them. Of course, the year has to go with you. I often don't make a final decision about what I'm going to grow until the death knock. I keep enough seed to be able to go in with wheat or barley. If the break is late, or we get a heap of rain, I make the call just as I'm about to seed.'

'That must play havoc with your budget.'

'I talk to the bank manager monthly. She knows what's happening on my farm before Renee does sometimes. It's a good financial decision to have an excellent relationship with your bank manager and accountant. He or she will be your closest friend for a long time.'

'My boss told me something similar once, too. The year that we had all that rain and had to buy in grain to feed the cattle, we would've been to Greg—he was the bank manager then—six or seven times that year. Because I did all the feed budgets, he wanted to catch up with me as well. The boss had to approve them, but Greg would ask me to explain the details.' Sassi pondered her words. 'You know the funny thing about that is he didn't need to. As a bank manager he knows how to read budgets, find holes or problems with them. He did it so he could get to know me. I also know he has three kids who are four, eight and ten. A wife who plays tennis on Wednesdays and he likes his steak medium rare!'

Abe laughed. 'He sounds like a great bank manager.' He tapped his fingers on the steering wheel again. 'Are you going to hand your notice in?'

'I don't think I can until we know if they've accepted the offer, can I?'

'Well,' Abe said, changing down a gear as he slowed for a truck in front of them, 'the job on our farm is still there. If we don't get this place, we'll just keep turning up at farms that are for sale until we manage to buy one.'

Another sick feeling in her stomach, but this time it was hard to tell if it was nerves or excitement.

'What do you say, Sass? Going to come and work with Uncle Abe?' He flashed her his cheeky smile.

'Yes,' she said without thinking any harder than she already had. 'Yep, I'll come and work with you, Abe. Let this be the start of a great partnership.' She held up the water bottle she had in her hand and clinked it to his travel mug. 'Oh my god, did we really just make an offer?' she asked in wonder.

'Yeah, we really did. Here's to many long years working together.' Abe turned to smile at her again. 'It's good to have you home, Sassi.'

In that moment Sassi felt as if her life had slipped back onto the axis it should have always been on. She grinned back at him.

'Now on to business. I'll make an appointment with my bank manager this afternoon. See when she can fit us in. We'd better get moving on getting the finance approved,' Abe said.

Sassi wanted to clench her fists and jump around with glee.

'And we'd better find Dad's original will when we go and see the bank manager,' Abe said coming to a stop in front of the car dealership in Broad River. 'I think the bank will need to see it to know the farm is coming to me, when we go to get the loan. They usually want you to show them your soul before they'll give you anything.'

'Do you know where it is?'

'Filed in the office somewhere. Both the lawyer and I have a copy, but Dad has the original.'

'Shouldn't be too hard to find. I haven't been in the office, except to turn the lights off. But from the doorway it looks like everything is pretty neat and tidy.'

'Good. Right-oh, I'll see you at Dad's in a while. I'll go and tell him what we're up to.'

Sassi waved goodbye and took a breath. In the display area of the car dealership was her new second-hand ute. Bright red with a black trim, spotlights, lift kit and basically all the bling she could have ever wanted.

She was going to feel like a million bucks with a brand-new farm and new second-hand ute.

CHAPTER 26

'So that's what we're hoping to do, Pa,' Sassi said, her eyes shining. 'What do you think?'

Pa raised his fist in a 'you beauty' manner and shook it slightly before giving them a crooked smile. ''Inkie.' Dinkie!

'Oh, Pa. What have you done there?' Sassi leaned forward and touched a deep purple bruise on the top of his arm.

Her grandfather jerked his arm back and made a brushing motion as if to say, *Don't worry about it.*

'Is it sore? It looks it. What do you think, Abe?' She turned to her uncle.

'Looks like he's given himself a bump, doesn't it? What did you run into, Dad?'

Again, the brushing motion. *Don't worry about it.*

'Okay, okay.' Abe held up his hands to pacify the old man. 'So, what do you think of our news?' he asked, sitting down on the lounge. 'I seem to remember you spent a bit of time on that farm we'd like to buy when you were younger, didn't you? Shearing or something?'

A sharp nod. Yes. 'S'goo.' It's good.

Almost bouncing with pleasure, Sassi smiled. 'I can't wait to get my teeth stuck in,' she told them. 'I want to re-fence a couple of paddocks, make them a little bigger than what's there now. The machinery shed also needs reroofing.' She turned to Abe. 'We'll have to make sure that goes in the budget with the bank. If the tin comes loose any more than it is, and there's a big wind, we might lose the whole roof.'

'Hold on, hold on,' Abe said with a grin. 'Let's not get too far in front of ourselves here. We haven't heard back from the real estate agent yet.'

'I know, but I've got a really good feeling about this.'

'It might be that you're about to get the shits,' Abe said.

Pa gave a cackle and pointed to his cup.

'More tea?'

The elderly man nodded.

Sassi got up to put the kettle on as the front door slammed and Amber came in carrying a shopping bag.

All Sassi's happiness disappeared as soon as she saw her mother. She tried to smile and say hello, but Amber only nodded and turned into the lounge room where Pa and Abe were.

In the kitchen Sassi switched on the kettle and put two heaped spoonfuls of tea leaves into the pot. There had been nothing in the diaries about Amber. Nothing even about the pregnancy. On the day Sassi had been born, Pa had made a note saying his first grandchild had arrived; a screaming bundle of arms and legs with a shock of black hair.

The note of black hair didn't help much in her quest to find out who her father was. The whole family had black hair.

Realising the kettle was squealing, she turned off the jug and splashed hot water into the pot, wondering if she should go back and sit in the lounge room with everyone or just take everything in and leave. She could say she was going to ring her boss to excuse herself.

Abe came into the kitchen. 'Have you seen Rasha?'

'I think she's out at the clothesline again. I heard noise from the laundry and Mum came in from the front.'

'I want to tell her what a bloody good job she's doing. Have you noticed how clean the house is and how happy Dad is? He's smiling whenever she's around.'

'Do you know, when I walked in today, I thought I'd come into the wrong house,' Sassi said. 'I reckon she's even taken the curtains down in the sitting room and washed them. Granny wouldn't have been able to do that for ages.'

'Yeah, thank goodness she decided to come and live in Barker. We'd be hard-pressed to find anyone else to do all this. Although, I'm not sure how she's finding the time to care for Dad and clean as much as she is.'

'Here, you want to take this into Pa? I'll have a quick look in the office and see if I can find the paperwork you wanted. Is there anything else you need? Oh, and did you tell him we were going to take the will?'

'Yep, all sorted. Maybe just bring everything you think might be important. How did the ute go?'

'Like a dream. It's the flashiest car I've ever driven! I'm going to go to the library on the way home today and ask about archived newspapers, since we didn't have any luck with the diaries.'

'Right-oh.' Abe picked up the cup and teapot. 'I'll just let Amber know what we're up to as well. Then I'll go and see Rasha.'

As Sassi passed the lounge room door on the way to the office, she looked in. Amber was sitting next to Pa, her arm on his chair. She was leaning in talking to him quietly and Abe was pouring the tea. Pa was leaning back in his chair, eyes shut. The room looked peaceful and contented, and Sassi felt her heart squeeze with love for them all. And sympathy for Amber. Then her mother's voice came to her, loud and clear.

'You're doing what?'

'It's a great opportunity for everyone,' Abe told her.

There was silence and it was hard to tell if Amber's comment had been made in surprise or anger.

In the office, Sassi stood in front of the desk and assessed the room. Where to start?

On the desk was the silver envelope opener Pa had always used to open his mail. Next to it was the desk calendar and fountain pen he favoured. Sassi picked the pen up and ran her fingers over the tip. It left a blue stain on her fingers.

The top drawer held biros, rubber bands, liquid paper— nothing of interest.

Second drawer: a telephone book from 2005. She doubted

there'd been another one printed since then. Everyone just used Google to find phone numbers these days.

The third drawer held the diaries Pa had kept since he'd moved into town. She didn't touch them. She already felt as if she was in a space she shouldn't be.

Lever arch folders were in the bookshelf above the desk, so she leaned over to take one out. Invoices from the last five years.

The next one held bank statements. Granny must have done the filing because Pa wouldn't have been able to with his shaking hands.

Her phone buzzed and she grabbed at it, hoping it was the real estate agent.

Ewin. She took in a sharp breath.

Can we please talk?

Putting the phone back on the desk, she ignored his message. He didn't have a right to demand anything from her. He gave that up when he walked out on her without an explanation.

Still, there was a part of her that wanted to snatch up the phone and dial his number. To tell him what she and Abe had planned. How he wasn't included.

Sassi put her hands on the desk and leaned forward, taking a few deep breaths.

Her phone was still in front of her, open at Ewin's messages.

She had closure, didn't she?

Maybe not enough.

Hi Ewin, thanks for getting in contact. I'm pretty busy at the moment, so I'll get back to you when I have some time. Sassi.

When had they drifted apart? she wondered after turning her phone to silent and putting it back in her pocket. How do couples become strangers? was a more important question.

When they first moved in together, they'd laughed and talked and loved as if there were no tomorrow. Ewin had liked pulling her to him, snuggling on the couch, asking about every aspect of her day, not wanting to miss a thing.

She'd loved hearing his voice and feeling his arms around her as he told her what they'd sprayed or seeded or maintained.

So how do couples become strangers?

The back door slammed bringing Sassi out of her reverie.

'In my opinion you're both taking a huge risk,' Amber's voice floated down the hall. 'Why would you put everything on the line when the business is profitable as is?'

Abe's low voice spoke earnestly, although Sassi couldn't hear what he said. She'd leave him to smooth everything over with her mother. Not that it was any of Amber's business.

The next lever arch folder she pulled out was marked *IMPORTANT.* All the files were inserted into plastic pockets and the one on the top was Pa's birth certificate. Her grandparents' marriage certificate. She flipped through. Title for the farm. Bank loan documents for years before. Bank notice to say the farm had been paid off.

Three plastic pockets in, she found her grandfather's will.

She decided to take the whole folder. There seemed to be lots of official documents that might be needed, and it would be better to take too much than too little. The quicker they could get the loan approved, the better.

She turned to leave and jumped when she saw Rasha in the doorway. She hadn't heard her and the woman was standing almost right behind her.

'Shit, you gave me a fright.'

'Sorry.' Rasha's eyes went to the folder Sassi was holding then back to her face.

'No bother,' Sassi said. 'Just didn't hear you there. I was going to come and find you. You're doing such a great job with Pa. Are you enjoying being here?'

'Yes, Sassi. It is good.'

Sassi loved her smile, so bright and happy.

'Have you taken Pa out today?'

'Not today. He is tired. Needs to sleep.'

'Did he have a bad night?' Sassi looked at Rasha with concern.

'No, I think not. Just—' she searched for the word '—age.'

Sassi nodded. Older people were the same as old dogs. They liked to sit in the sun and doze.

'We play—ah, no, I'm *teaching* Pa to play cards. That's what we did today.'

'Did you? I didn't even know there was a pack of playing cards here. What game?'

'Poker. My friend taught me when I arrived in Australia. It is fun.'

'Did you know that's a gambling game, Rasha?' Sassi laughed. 'People play to win money! I hope you didn't let Pa diddle you out of any cash.'

A frown creased Rasha's smooth forehead. 'Diddle? I don't know . . .'

'Sorry, diddle is an odd word. It means to cheat, or to take your money unfairly.' Sassi waved it away. 'Doesn't matter, I was trying to be funny. I'm headed off now. Is there anything you need?'

'I need cleaning fluid. This one.' She held out a bottle of disinfectant.

'No worries, I'll bring you some back tomorrow when I come. See you then.' Sassi felt Rasha's eyes on her back as she left the house, and for some reason she felt a twinge of unease.

The library was a cool reprieve from the sun when Sassi walked in. The desk was straight inside and a lady with glasses on the end of her nose looked up, offering a smile.

'Can I help you?'

'I hope so,' Sassi said, letting the door close gently behind her. 'Do you have any archived local newspapers here? From thirty-odd years ago?'

The woman shook her head. 'No, we don't have anything like that, but the council might. They've got a small museum in one of their rooms and I know they've got a large cellar where they store lots of records. They might be able to help you.'

'Great, thanks.'

'If you don't mind me asking, what are you looking for? I've lived here my whole life and I might know something about what you need.'

Sassi opened her mouth to tell her but then shut it again. She wasn't sure she was ready to tell anyone else about what she suspected. Instead, she said, 'Birth notices. From when I was born.'

'Oh, you were born here? Lovely. What's your name?'

'Sassi Stapleton.'

'Ah yes, Sassi, I was so sorry to hear about your grandmother. A lot of our oldies seem to be passing on recently. So sad.'

Sassi nodded. 'Well, thanks anyway. I'll have a go at the council.'

'There is a births, deaths and marriages register at the Catholic church, love. The priest there used to record everyone who passed through his church.' Then she stopped as she fiddled with the mouse on her computer, to bring it to life. 'I'll just check and see what the hours are. Hmm, I think the priest is actually away in Adelaide this week. You might have to wait until . . .' Then, as if a thought struck her, her gaze slid from the screen to Sassi. 'Um, although, you may not have been christened there. Yes, actually I think the council is your best shot, love.'

'Thanks,' Sassi said brightly, but wanting to put her fist through the computer. As if she needed any reminding of her illegitimate status. Or her fatherless one.

Leaving the building as quickly as she could, Sassi got into her ute and took a few deep breaths, before thumping the steering wheel. She wished she'd never clued herself on to what might have happened to her mother.

Not *might have*.

Did.

Did happen to her mother.

She was sure of it.

CHAPTER 27

'Honey, I have some news.' Kim met Dave at the door and handed him a beer.

That always meant she had something serious to talk to him about.

'Okay.' He accepted the beer and gave her a kiss, then followed her down the hall. 'What's up?'

'I had a phone call today. From your mum.'

'Really.' Dave put down his beer and unbuttoned part of his shirt, running a hand around the neck to make sure he was able to breathe. He shouldn't be surprised. His mother had always been tenacious. 'How is she?'

'Good. She's moved into a smaller unit from when we were there last. The garden got too much for her. She's enjoying the smaller place. Easy to look after.'

'Did you get an address?'

'Of course.' She gave him a quizzical look as if asking whether he thought she was an imbecile.

'Sorry, of course you did. Is she well otherwise?'

'Yeah, she is and so is your brother. Dean's managing well, considering his arm was caught in an auger a while ago. He's almost got full movement back, even though the doctors didn't think he'd ever use it again.'

'That's great to hear.' Dave thought of the family farm which had been leased out while Dean went through his rehab. Maybe his brother would go back to it, start farming again. Dave was about to ask Kim, then realised that would give her the perfect lead-in to what he knew was coming, so he shut his mouth and waited.

'Anyhow, she'd like you to call her. She did ask three or four times if her letter had arrived. I told her three or four times that it had.' Kim gave him her generous smile. 'But I'm not one hundred per cent sure she believed me when I told her you would ring her.'

'Okay, I'll do that tomorrow. How about we go and have tea at the pub tonight? Save you cooking? You've been doing that all day.'

'Nice deflection, Dave Burrows, but that's not going to work. There's also the little matter of the message Dean left on your mobile phone that you didn't answer.' This time she crossed her arms like an irritated schoolteacher. 'Yes, your mum told me about that.'

If Dave hadn't been annoyed at the mention of his brother's message, he would've pulled her to him and told her how beautiful she looked when she was exasperated with him. He really wanted to kiss her right now.

Dave thought it might have been three weeks ago that Dean had called.

'Mate, it's been months,' his brother had said. 'Any reason you've dropped off the face of the earth? I thought we'd sorted everything through, and you were going to stay in contact? Anyway, I wanted you to know that I'm a bit keen to find Adam. I know our younger brother really went off the rails but that's no reason not to see where he is. Give us a ring back, yeah?'

Dave had been distracted at the time and had not called. Then the letter from his mother had arrived and he'd decided it was easier to be an ostrich than face all of his unresolved feelings.

'I haven't called him back,' Dave said. He turned and grabbed his beer, taking a few swallows before he moved to the bedroom to get undressed.

Kim followed as he knew she would. 'Dave . . .'

But he wasn't having it. 'Can you let me deal with this in my own way?'

'Your mother and your brother have nothing to do with your girls,' Kim said. 'I know you had a shit time when you were kicked off the farm and you've decided to continue on with those feelings all through your life. I really love knowing I've married a man who doesn't hold grudges.

'Didn't we just have a conversation about what might happen if internal affairs come looking at you? Maybe the only way you'll get to see your mother is if she comes and visits you in jail.'

Kim stalked out of the room, leaving Dave to his thoughts.

'And yeah, let's go to the pub tonight for dinner,' Kim called over her shoulder.

Sighing, Dave got into the shower and let the hot water run over his face. He scrubbed at his skin, wanting to wash away the prickly feelings he was having.

When he'd decided to move to South Australia to be with Kim, he hadn't given his family one thought. In fact, he'd not had any contact with them for years at that stage. They didn't come to his and Kim's wedding because he didn't invite them.

Actually, he didn't even tell them about it.

Ah. Now, that was a thought. Maybe there was some like father, like daughter in Bec. Not that he was going to admit that to anyone.

Still, he'd managed to do just fine without his family, thank you very much and . . . But then it hit him. He remembered the night he'd sat outside and stared at the engagement photo of Bec and Justin. He remembered the angry crack of knuckles on jaw when he'd slammed his fist into Nathan Woodbridge's face.

And he remembered why he'd done it.

Because he missed his daughters. Because he was hurt and sad, and those emotions often manifested as anger. The pain he'd felt seeing Bec's face had been physical.

Shame rushed through him.

His mum, Carlene, had always loved and supported him. She wasn't the one who had sent him on his way from the farm. She hadn't even known his father's plans. Carlene had been just as shocked and sad and outraged as Dave had been. But a wife's place was with her husband. That was the way it was for his mother's generation.

What would I do if I wasn't a wife? she'd asked Dave in a letter. *Yes, leaving your father would be an option, to make him see sense, but just in case he didn't come round, and I had to stick to my guns, what would I do if I wasn't a wife?*

He'd wanted to ask what she would do if she wasn't a mother, but that had seemed unfair at the time.

None of the fallout had been Carlene's fault, as it hadn't been Dean's or Adam's either, yet Dave was still punishing them all as if they were his father.

He got out of the shower and rubbed himself dry. If he dried himself vigorously perhaps the itching on his skin would stop. The scratching of knowing he'd done something wrong. Something he didn't want to fix, yet he must.

His mobile phone was lying on the bed and he picked it up, bringing up his mother's mobile number. For a long while he stared at her name. Finally, sitting down on the bed, towel around his waist, Dave typed out a message with one finger.

Hi Mum, got your message. Will ring soon.

Were the words enough? Should he add more? Tell her he finally understood what she must be feeling?

That was a bit heavy to put in a text message. He hit send and brought up his brother's number.

Sorry been flat out. Will ring tomorrow.

He put the phone down, refusing to look at it when he heard a ding come back straightaway.

The family issues could wait until tomorrow. Or later.

⁓

'Can we just drop in to Mr Stapleton's house before we go to the pub?' Kim asked. 'I want to give him this freshly made trifle for dessert.'

Dave sighed. 'You're worse than me, never having a night off. I thought we'd go to the pub and ignore the world for a few hours.'

'Seems to me that you often ignore the world of family,' Kim said. Then she made a face. 'Oops, did I say that out loud?' She half-smiled because her tone was light and, despite what'd she said before about grudges, neither of them was ever angry with the other for long.

'Yeah, you did, and you know it. Look, I'll ring Mum tomorrow, okay? I mean it.'

Kim held out her little finger. 'Pinky promise.'

Dave rolled his eyes but did as he was asked. 'I sent both her and Dean a text message a little while ago.'

'Ah, well done, you,' said Kim. 'Let's go.' She winked. 'Via Mr Stapleton's house.'

Dave pulled her into a hug. 'Thanks for putting up with me,' he said, bending down to kiss her.

'Yeah, well, sometimes you're not that easy to deal with!' She smacked her lips together indicating she wanted another kiss and he obliged. 'Did I tell you I saw Rasha down the street today?' she asked after Dave had let her go. 'She had the two littlies with her. Fatima is gorgeous. She told me today that her teacher has asked her to teach the class some Sudanese words. Isn't that great? And Kamal, he's still a little shy, so he didn't say much, just held his mum's hand and looked at me with those beautiful big eyes of his.'

Dave opened the car door for her and took the bowl of trifle, putting it on the back seat. 'Considering the prejudices small country towns are known for, I think Barker is above others in that respect. If we ignore the minority of the old busybodies who seem to have their noses out of joint.'

'Pfft,' Kim said with a wave of her hand. 'They don't matter. Rasha said she's loving working over at the Stapletons'. You deserve eleven out of ten for setting that up.'

'Joan had a fair bit to do with it all,' Dave said, glancing in the rear-view mirror as he reversed the car. 'She was the one who told me Rasha would excel at this kind of employment. They go to the same church, apparently.'

'Well, Rasha is happy so everything is working out. Oh, look, there's Mia.'

Dave slowed the car next to his constable, who was walking along the footpath. 'Hi, you off to the pub, too?'

'Thought I'd head down for one. Clear my head.' Mia was fresh from the shower, her hair still wet.

'Good plan. See you there.' He put the car in gear, while Kim gave a little wave.

A few minutes later they parked in front of Mr Stapleton's house. 'Want me to come in?' he asked.

'If you like.' Kim opened the door and reached in for the dessert, before pushing open the gate.

She tapped gently on the front door and waited, while Dave stood behind her.

No one answered, so Dave rapped, then tried the door handle. 'Hello?'

Amber rushed from the kitchen. 'Sorry, sorry, I didn't hear you. Can I help? Oh, you've brought more food. Gosh, we have so much already!'

'I was making trifle and I know that's one of his favourite desserts so I thought we'd pop in to drop it off and say hello to Mr Stapleton.'

'Down here,' Amber pointed and went through.

Kim stopped and looked at a photo that was hanging in the hallway. Mr and Mrs Stapleton, Amber and Abe, when they were children. The one next to it was missing Amber, but Sassi was included, a roly-poly toddler with a quick smile and sparkling eyes. Kim thought she looked just like Amber.

She felt Dave push her gently towards the kitchen and refocused. A few steps and she was there.

'Hi there, Mr Stapleton,' Kim said as she waved the plate around. 'I've brought you your favourite sweet. The trifle!'

Mr Stapleton looked at her blankly, not smiling, then his eyes slid back to his plate. Half-eaten lamb stew, with beans, peas and mashed potato was in front of him. A little gravy was dribbling from the side of his mouth so Kim picked up a napkin and wiped it away gently.

'Have you had a nice day?' she asked. 'I saw Rasha took you for a walk yesterday. Must've been lovely to get out of the house.'

'Don't think he's having a good night, somehow,' Amber said. 'Not talking very much.'

Mr Stapleton focused on Kim, then Dave, and suddenly he smiled. As if he understood what Kim was bringing him.

His shirt sleeves slid up as he reached out to take the plate. Kim saw how thin his skin was and winced. A couple of little scabs were showing and a purply coloured bruise. One, two and a third one. All on his upper arm.

'Mr Stapleton, have you had a fall?'

He didn't answer, only took the plate, and reached for a spoon.

'Oh, can you see those bruises?' Amber leaned over to look. 'They look nasty, don't they? I wish I knew how they got there.' She picked up the half-eaten lamb stew and scraped the leftovers into the bin. 'He must have knocked himself when he was getting in and out of bed, I think.' She shook her head. 'He won't let me help him with that.'

'They're a bit awful looking, aren't they?' Kim agreed. She turned her attention to the elderly man. 'Do they hurt, Mr Stapleton? Do you need to see a doctor?'

Ignoring her, he started eating the trifle.

'It's a well-known fact older people bruise very easily,' Dave said, looking at Mr Stapleton's arms. He ran his eye over the old man for any other damage. 'Sometimes they look like they've been hit with a sledgehammer and all they've done is bumped into the corner of their bed.'

Kim nudged Dave. 'Mr Stapleton can hear every word you're saying, can't you, love? Let's talk to him, rather than about him, okay?'

Mr Stapleton shovelled in another mouthful of trifle and chewed with his mouth open. Kim noticed that Amber looked away.

'Okay, well, we'd better get along,' Kim said. 'You enjoy that trifle, Mr Stapleton. I made it especially for you. And please try not to hurt yourself again.'

''ank.' Thanks.

Kim patted his shoulder and smiled. 'See you later. And you, too, Amber. How much longer do you have here in Barker?'

'Not long. I'll probably go in the next couple of days. There are problems back home that I need to help with.' She put the plate in the dishwasher and stood up, stretching her back. 'Life moves on, doesn't it? We can't stop working because we've had a family tragedy.'

'That's true,' Kim agreed. 'Okay, enjoy your evening.'

Back in the car, Kim put her arm around Dave's shoulders as he drove. 'When I get old, will you bring me my favourite food and care for me?' she asked.

'I'd do anything for you,' Dave told her. 'You know that.'

'Trouble is, I don't want to get old. Let's make sure we die together. Right at the same time. Coz I don't want to live a single day without you.'

Dave reached for her hand and turned it over, kissing her palm. 'I don't suppose we'll get any say in that, but I'd prefer it like that, too.'

'My aunty used to say it takes courage to be old. I think she was right.'

CHAPTER 28

Sassi rubbed her hands over her tired eyes and took another sip of water. 'Okay, let's go through this again.' She put her finger on the Excel spreadsheet on the computer screen and pointed to the seeding costs column. 'We've got chemical, fertiliser, fuel, R and M.'

'Insurance and seed cleaning costs.' Abe spoke around the pen that was in his mouth. 'Good. And here, this is the bottom line of expenses. Across here, yep.' Now he pointed. 'This will be what we're able to repay each year.' He leaned back in his chair. 'Let's print this out so I can see it on one page in front of me. I'll want to go through the budget again tomorrow after I've had some sleep. I reckon you can always pick up mistakes when you've been away from it for a little while. On the surface, it's a really strong budget. Tess, the bank manager, will be happy with it, I'm sure. And our equity is strong. That'll help.'

'When's our appointment to see her?' Sassi asked.

'Tomorrow morning. Now, where's that paperwork you brought back from Dad's?'

'Here.' Sassi reached down alongside her chair and grabbed the lever arch folder. She handed it to Abe, who flicked through and found the title to the farm.

'Oh, brilliant. I was wondering where that was. And the copy of the will. That's great,' he slid it out from the plastic pocket and glanced over the first page.

On the desk, next to the keyboard, Abe's phone lit up. They both looked at the name on the screen.

Real Estate Agent.

'Here we go,' he said and crossed his fingers before he pushed the button to answer. 'G'day, mate. How're you getting on?'

Sassi leaned in to see if she could hear what the man was saying, but the words were muffled.

'Daddy, Daddy?' Jimmy came running in holding a Tonka truck, and Abe shot to his feet and put his finger in his ear, turning away from the little boy.

Sassi got up, too, and ushered her nephew out into the hallway. 'Shh, Jimmy, Dad's on the phone. Can you go back to Mum?'

'Mummy can't fix this; it needs Dad's stick thingy. With the sparks.'

'The welder? I'm not sure a welder is going to work on plastic, but we'll get it fixed in a little while. Where's your brother?'

'Asleep on the couch,' he answered scornfully, as if sleeping in the middle of the day was the biggest sin for a four-year-old when there were Tonka trucks to be pushed and dirt to move around.

'Can you just give Dad and me a moment? We won't be long.' She gently pushed the little boy away and went back into the office, closing the door firmly on his protests.

Abe was putting the phone down on the desk. He looked grim.

Sassi stood there, waiting. Unsure of what to read into his response. Then a grin broke out over his face, and he punched the air.

'They've accepted our offer.'

'Oh my god.' Sassi's hands flew to her cheeks and her heart thumped in her chest. She stared at Abe, not moving. 'We did it?'

'Well, there's still a bit more work to do. We've got to finalise everything with the bank tomorrow, but yeah, looks like we're going into business together. All subject to finance of course.'

Renee opened the door, wiping her hands on a tea towel. 'What happened? You've heard something?'

'We got it,' Abe said to her. He pulled her into a tight hug and Renee leaned against him, cupping the back of his head with her hand.

'Your dreams, sweetheart, they're coming true.' Then she reached out her hand for Sassi's. 'Welcome home. Welcome home and here's to being business partners.'

Jimmy came running in now, missing his pants. Harry, who was rubbing his eyes as if someone had woken him, was just behind and he, too, was missing his pants.

Sassi felt an hysterical giggle erupt out of her as she realised she was going to be here all the time to watch these boys grow up. Not just quick visits here and there.

'Oh my god, boys! Why have you taken your shorts off?' Renee looked as if she was ready to throw them both outside.

'What's going on?' Harry asked. 'Why are you all—'

'Where are your clothes?' Renee asked again, pulling away from Abe now. 'Come on, let's get them on. You can't run around the house without at least jocks. No one wants to see anything else.'

Abe dropped down onto his knee and gathered the boys into a hug. 'We've just had some good news. And we'll be able to tell you about it in a while, but right now, it's a secret. When we can, we'll tell you, but just know it's very good news and you boys are going to love what we've done!'

'I can keep a secret!' Jimmy yelled. 'Tell me!'

'Pants, Jimmy!'

'Me too!' screamed Harry.

Without thinking, Sassi snatched up Harry and raced out into the kitchen. On the lounge were two pairs of shorts and jocks. Dropping him down and then tickling him under his arms, she put the pants on his chest. 'Put 'em on quick. Before Jimmy gets here and Mum gets cross.'

Harry, giggling wildly, stuffed his stumpy legs into one leg, then the other. 'Ta-da!' he crowed, with his arms out as if he was a showman. Then he spun around, showing off.

'Perfect,' Sassi told him.

Jimmy came running in behind and threw his arms around Sassi's legs.

'Quick sticks, yours are here,' she told him, unpicking herself from him.

'Why do we have to be quick?' Jimmy wanted to know, his little face curious as he hopped on one leg, trying to get them on without falling over.

'I don't know,' Sassi said with a grin, 'but look at you both. You're dressed now!'

Harry glanced down at his legs and then Jimmy did the same. The looks on their faces were comical when they realised they'd been duped into getting dressed when they hadn't wanted to.

'Right, twins, at the table please,' Renee said. 'Lunchtime.'

Abe came into the kitchen with his briefcase. 'Sassi and I are going to have to go and see Dad, love. Will you be okay here?'

Renee gave him a kiss and smiled. 'Course.'

Abe nodded to Sassi and, dropping a kiss on each boy's head, she followed him out to the ute.

'I might take my ute, too,' she told him. 'The lady at the library said I could try the council offices for newspapers, so once we've been to see Pa, I might check that out.'

'We should go to the bank, Sassi. I know our appointment's tomorrow, but we need to tell Tess what's going on. Give her the heads-up. You're going to have a lot of other time to research this now you're going to be home for good.'

Sassi nodded. 'Sure. I can do it later. But I'll still take my ute. I can ring my boss on the way in and stay after we've been to the bank.'

Abe nodded. 'No worries. See you in there.'

The excitement made her want to jump up and down still, but she tried to keep it out of her voice as her boss answered her call.

'Sassi, good to hear from you. How are you feeling? Over the accident?'

'Hey, boss, I'm not too bad. Much better than I was. Still got a bit of bruising but that'll go in time.'

'How's your grandfather?'

Sassi quickly filled him in, then asked, 'Is everything running okay back there? How are the cattle looking?'

'Had a truck this morning and the last lot of results were tickety-boo. I'm happy, but I'd rather you were back here overseeing everything.'

Sassi heard the question in his voice, instead he asked something else.

'Got your new wheels yet?'

'Sure have, she's a sweet piece of machinery, let me tell you. It's red and black to begin with.'

He laughed. 'There's a statement.'

There was a slight pause then Sassi said, 'Anyway, boss, I'm ringing with some other news.'

'Ah, I thought you might be.' His tone was knowing. 'Hit me with it.'

'I've been offered an opportunity to go into business with my uncle back here at home.' Sassi kept her eyes on the road as she spoke. 'This morning, an offer we put in on a farm was accepted. I'm really sorry, but I won't be coming back.'

The silence stretched out so long, Sassi thought they'd lost the connection.

'Well, Sassi,' her boss finally said, 'I can't say I'm surprised, and I can't say I'm not disappointed to see you go. You were a real asset to this business.'

'I didn't know this was coming, boss. I really didn't.'

'You're moving on to bigger and better things, I can't be upset with that, Sassi. Congratulations, you've done very well for yourself. Tell me about the farm.'

'It's five thousand acres on the plains south of Barker. It's a good cropping block.'

'No cattle though?'

'Country isn't really suited to them, but some people do run cattle up this way. We'll just see how the seasons turn out and if I can bring any in. I'd like to because, as you know, cattle are my first love, but I'll be content just to be farming back here.'

'I'm glad for you. Truly.'

'Would it be okay to leave my gear there for another week? I know you'll need the house for the next person you employ, but I should be able to get away by then, come back and pack up. See you all and say goodbye.'

'No worries. We'll see you in a week. And, Sassi, congratulations again.'

'Thanks, boss,' she said quietly and hung up.

A few moments later, she parked behind Abe's ute in the driveway at Pa's. Abe was on the phone, so she got out and started up the steps, only to stop in surprise.

'How dare you do something so despicable!' Amber's voice was so high, she was almost screeching.

Sassi rapped on the door of Abe's ute and then took off at a run towards the house, taking the steps two at a time.

Amber's voice was coming from the kitchen. Another few steps and Sassi was looking at a scene she couldn't quite comprehend.

Rasha was cowering in a corner, her eyes frightened and pleading, arms crossed over her chest. Her head was shaking back and forth. 'No, no, no.'

'Why are you hurting him?' Amber spat at Rasha. 'What do you want from my father?'

Amber was standing over the other woman, her face red with anger.

'Let's see how much you like it when the boot is on the other foot!' She brought her fist down fast towards Rasha, striking the woman on the arm. Then another blow and another.

Rasha brought her arms up to protect her head.

Sassi couldn't move, only watch She was so shocked. She couldn't believe her mother was capable of such violence against another human.

'Hey, hey! What the hell is going on here?'

Amber didn't even turn her head as Abe rushed into the kitchen. Her entire focus was on the woman in front of her and she was staring at her with pure hatred.

Rasha yelped and tried to move, but Amber pinned her in the corner. 'You can stay there, bitch! I'll show you what it's like to hurt an old man.' Lowering her voice, she added,

'And then I'm going to call the police and have you charged. You've picked the wrong family to try to steal from.'

'Amber! What the fuck?' Abe grabbed his sister and pushed her away from Rasha, while Sassi swooped in front of Rasha and helped her to her feet.

'It's okay,' she told the shaking woman. 'It's okay.' Her eyes went from Rasha to Amber to Abe, willing someone to tell her what to do. Never, ever in her life had she seen anything remotely like this. Such anger and fury.

Stumbling over the bin and falling onto her arse, Amber shot straight up again. 'I'm not the one you should be stopping, here!' she yelled. 'It's her!'

Sassi felt Rasha shaking. 'None of us are going to hurt you, Rasha, while Abe and I are here, I promise.'

'Amber, tell me what the bloody hell is going on here,' demanded Abe. 'What do you think Rasha's done?'

'It's her,' Amber yelled. 'Of course it's her. Who else would it be?'

'Doing what?' Abe yelled back at his sister.

Amber's face was flushed red and her eyes were glinting with fury. 'This!' she spat and stalked out of the kitchen and into Pa's bedroom.

Sassi followed, still holding Rasha's hand, pulling her along gently.

Pa was sitting up in bed, but he didn't look like the Pa Sassi knew. She glanced over at Rasha in disbelief, but the woman's eyes were cast to the floor and Sassi couldn't read her face.

Pa was propped up against his pillows, eyes closed, his chest moving with shallow breaths. A deep purple bruise covered one cheek and the arm resting on the bedspread was red and angry looking. Another bruise waiting to come out.

Sassi let go of Rasha. 'No,' she whispered, hesitantly. Too many thoughts crowded in. Rasha wouldn't do this. And if for some crazy reason, she did, why?

'Wha—' Sassi wanted to run to Pa, hold him, smooth away the pain. 'No.' She took a step away from Rasha now. 'Did you?'

The woman said nothing. Sassi couldn't believe that Rasha would hurt another person, but she couldn't ignore the fact the woman wasn't defending herself. Unease swept over her.

'Jesus, what's happened here?' Abe pushed past Sassi. 'Call an ambulance. Has he fallen or what?' He raced to hold his dad's hand, but Amber pushed him back.

'Leave him, he's okay. I've checked him out. She's done this. I told you when you hired her you can't trust servants with anything. She's probably been stealing, too. Have you noticed anything missing?'

Sassi pulled out her phone and dialled Hamish's number. He'd given it to her when she'd left the hospital in case she became ill in the middle of the night.

'Hamish, I'm sorry to bother you. Have you got time to come over to Pa's house, please?' Her voice was trembling.

'Sassi, what is it? Are you okay?'

'I am, Pa isn't. Could you come?'

'I'm on my way.'

Sassi let the phone drop back into her pocket and stood taking shallow breaths.

'Get out of the way, Amber. I need to check out Dad.' Abe towered over Amber but she didn't move. 'I can help him.'

Amber crossed her arms. 'You need to get the cops here and make sure they see Dad just as he is now. How dare she do this to a defenceless old man!' she hissed. 'Go on, Abe. You're the one who lives in Barker. Call the police and get this woman arrested.'

'Hamish is coming,' Sassi told them.

Abe took his phone from his shirt pocket. 'Rasha,' he said, now looking at the woman, 'please tell me you didn't hurt Dad.'

Instead of answering, she turned her head away.

Amber's face curled into a mean smile as Abe dialled the police station. 'This will be on your head, brother. On your head.'

CHAPTER 29

'Did he fall?' Mia asked Hamish in a low voice as they wheeled the trolley out to the ambulance.

'I don't think so. To me it looks like he's been hit with a clenched hand to the head multiple times. The swelling and bruising on his arm reminds me of the Chinese burns the mean kids would hand out at school. His injury is probably consistent with his skin being twisted in opposite directions.'

Dave came out holding Rasha by the arm and helped her into the police car. Slamming the door closed, he called out, 'Abe is going to bring Amber down to the station. How long do you think you'll be?'

Mia looked at Hamish for direction.

'Half an hour max,' he answered. 'I only need Mia to help me unload at the other end then she can head back to you. Doc is en route from Broad River and I can stabilise Mr Stapleton with the help of another nurse.'

'Right, see you back at the station as soon as you can, Mia. We'll have to interview everyone. Can you also ring Kim and get her to pick up Rasha's kids from school? Ask her to take them home and look after them until we know what's going on here.'

Mia started. 'Is she allowed to do that?'

'Kim is able to be a foster carer,' Dave told her.

'No worries.' Mia nodded then helped lift the stretcher into the ambulance and lock it into place.

As she walked to the driver's seat, Sassi, Abe and Amber came out the front door. Abe and Sassi looked as if they'd been beaten themselves, the shock settling across their faces. Amber, on the other hand, looked triumphant.

'Can you drop my briefcase off at the bank?' Mia heard Abe ask Sassi. 'Then you go to the hospital to be with Dad. When I've spoken to Dave, we'll swap places so Dave can talk to you. Okay?'

Mia didn't hear Sassi's answer, but she saw her get the briefcase out of Abe's ute and put it in her own. She looked as if she was trying to walk through wet sand.

'I'll be two secs,' Mia said to Hamish. She jogged across to Sassi and put her hand on her arm. 'Dave and I'll get to the bottom of this, I promise you.'

Sassi turned to her, a flood of tears starting now. 'I have no idea what just happened, Mia. Look, I'm not close to Mum, haven't been for many years as you know, but that behaviour? Well, none of my family would ever do anything so out of character without a really good reason.' She swiped at the tears. 'And I can't believe that Rasha would do what

Mum is accusing her of. She's fitted into our family too well. She must love Pa because of all the amazing things she's done with him.' She looked hopefully towards Mia. 'Unless Pa fell and Mum's got the wrong end of the stick?'

Her hopeful glance made Mia want to run away. She already knew that this man had been hurt deliberately.

'Don't worry. We'll sort through it.' She squeezed Sassi's arm again, and ran back to the ambulance thinking about Dave's lecture about separating yourself from the people who were your friends in a small country town.

The ambulance was quiet as Hamish hooked up the machines and checked Mr Stapleton's blood pressure and vitals.

'Mr Stapleton, you're going to be just fine,' Hamish said. 'Your heart is strong, blood pressure a little raised, but not enough to concern me. I'll get your face cleaned up at the hospital. That's where we're taking you, okay? To the hospital.'

There was no answer.

'You'll be safe there.'

Mia dialled Kim as she drove and told her what had happened. 'Are you able to pick up the kids from school so they're not coming home to an empty house?'

'God, that's terrible,' Kim said. 'Of course I will.' She paused. 'Is Mr Stapleton going to be all right?'

'Well, he's old, but there aren't any visible serious injuries, only bruising and swelling. Anyway, I'd better go. Guess we'll know after the doctor has looked at him.'

'Tell Rasha not to worry about her kids at all. I'll make sure they're cared for until she comes and gets them. Good luck.'

'Same to you.' Mia hung up and glanced over her shoulder at Hamish. 'Okay?'

Hamish nodded as he held Mr Stapleton's hand.

It took only ten minutes for Mia to finish at the hospital and another ten to walk back to the station.

Joan was behind the desk, looking shaken but still professional.

'Dave is speaking with Rasha in the interview room. He said for you to go in. The others are waiting in separate rooms at the back.'

'Thanks, Joan,' Mia said, nodding her head.

Knocking firmly, she waited until she heard Dave invite her in.

'Constable Mia Worth entered the room at two forty-five pm. Now, Rasha, back to the job. You were telling me you'd been hired to help care for Mr Stapleton. How steady was he on his feet?'

'Could walk, not far but, yes, sometimes a bit, ah . . .' She shook her hands.

'Unstable?'

'Yes.'

'To your knowledge has he ever fallen?'

'No. Not when I've been there.' She shook her head to emphasise her words.

Rasha was speaking quietly and without emotion, her hands folded in front of her on the table but she wasn't looking Dave in the eye. Instead her gaze was firmly fastened on the worn tabletop. Now Mia was feeling the same uncertainty that she was sure Sassi would have felt when she'd heard Amber's accusations.

An innocent person would be holding eye contact, making sure the person doing the interviewing was convinced they were telling the truth.

'Is part of your job to wash and dress Mr Stapleton?' Dave continued.

'I shower him. Help dress him. Clean the house. Those jobs.'

'Have you seen any injuries before? On his body.' Dave used his hands to indicate up and down his own body.

Rasha didn't move for a moment, then slowly shook her head.

'Can you give an answer for the recording, please?'

'I have not seen injuries.'

Mia didn't believe her answer. Dave mustn't have either because he asked, 'Are you certain, Rasha? I need you to know I'm here to find out the truth, and if you haven't had anything to do with Mr Stapleton's injuries, then you have no reason to be frightened.'

Rasha didn't answer at first, then whispered, 'Yes.'

Dave shifted in his seat and seemed to be thinking of another question, while Mia jotted down a few notes. Her mind was racing. Why was Rasha being so submissive? Did she think that if she answered every question she'd get out faster and back to her kids?

'Do you know how Mr Stapleton came to get his injuries today?'

'No.'

'Kim has your children, Rasha,' Mia leaned forward and told her. 'They'll be looked after until you get them. You don't need to worry about them, okay?'

Again, Rasha was very still as she composed an answer. 'Thank you.'

Her posture didn't change and Mia felt frustrated by the woman's demeanour.

'Can I get you a coffee or tea?' Dave asked Rasha.

'No.'

'Is there anything you'd like to tell me?' Dave asked quietly.

'No,' she replied.

Letting out a deep sigh through his nose, Dave sat back and tapped the table. Mia knew his hands were tied until he got some answers to his questions.

'Okay, Rasha, I have some other things I have to do now. You'll have to stay here until I've finished my inquiries.' He paused, and Mia knew it was to give Rasha time to say something, to defend herself, but the room was silent.

'Do you understand what I just told you?'

'Yes.' Rasha gave one nod and stayed still.

Dave got up and indicated for Mia to follow him outside.

'Right, we need to check with Hamish as to the nature of Mr Stapleton's injuries and how they were acquired.'

'I already did. He thinks the one on his arm is a Chinese burn kind of injury and the one on his face is from being punched.' Mia moved from foot to foot, waiting to see what he'd say next.

Dave ran his hand over his face, then shook his head. 'Is that something he'll attest to in court? We'll have to get a statement from him and the doc.'

'Do you want me to ask him to come in for a formal interview? And the doc before he heads back to Broad River?'

'Let's deal with the others first. Hamish and the doc aren't going anywhere, but I'm not convinced Rasha and Amber won't do a runner if we let them go.' Dave paused in the doorway. 'Well, not a runner, but Amber's made it clear she's not staying in town for long as it is.'

He led the way into the next room and sat down.

'Why do I have to be here when I haven't done anything wrong?' Amber snapped as soon as they entered the room. 'I want a lawyer.'

'Sure, we can get you one,' Dave said as he pulled out a chair. 'It'll take a few hours for someone to get over from Port Augusta, when all we're doing is having a chat. But no problems.'

Amber reared back. 'I don't want one of those lawyers, I want one from Adelaide. A decent one.'

'Well, that will take longer. But, Amber, if you haven't done anything wrong, why would you bother to wait that long when all you have to do is answer my questions and you can be on your way? I haven't charged you with anything, although Rasha may ask us to press assault charges on you.' He paused for effect. 'You did assault Rasha, Amber.

I had to ask Hamish to assess her injuries to see if they were bad enough to go to the hospital to be seen by a doctor.'

'I'd like to see her try.'

Amber's face was red, her neck blotchy as she dragged in a breath.

'Are you okay?' Dave asked. 'Would you like some water?'

'What I'd like is for you to charge that woman with abuse of an elderly citizen and let me leave. I really don't see why I have to answer any questions when I haven't done anything wrong.'

'I understand you're worried about your father,' Dave said. 'So let's get through these routine questions as quickly as we can. Now, do you want that lawyer?'

'Just ask your questions,' Amber said, slumping towards the table, her chin in her hand, 'so I can leave. I have to be back in Adelaide tomorrow because I've got flights booked for the afternoon.'

Mia made a note and privately thought Amber wouldn't be going anywhere. There was more than one afternoon's worth of questions here.

'Let's start at the beginning,' Dave said kindly, but still with a no-nonsense air.

Mia listened as Dave slowly and methodically worked his way through the questions, as he had with Rasha, trying to find differences in their answers.

'You employed Rasha to help care for your father?'

'We all were there for the interview—Abe, Sassi and me. Dad was there, too. Look, I have to say I had some concerns about hiring her. She has young children and

I wasn't sure she would be able to be on hand as much as I knew we were going to need her. But the short answer is yes, she was employed to care for Dad.'

'Did you know Rasha before she came to the house for the interview?'

Amber frowned as if it was a trick question. 'No,' she answered. 'How would I? This is the first time I've been back to Barker in many years.'

'Right. Did you have any other concerns that Rasha might not be able to do the job she is employed for?'

Amber paused, fiddling with the sleeve of her jumper. 'Like I said, her children were a problem for me, and, look, I just didn't trust her. There's no reason for this, other than a gut feeling.'

'I see and do you get these feelings often?'

Mia wondered where Dave was going with his questioning because he'd always told her to trust her instincts.

Amber leaned forward and spoke as if Dave had no idea what he was talking about. 'Yes, I do, and normally I always follow them.' She wiped away an invisible piece of lint from her jeans. 'One other time I ignored the feeling that something was wrong and didn't do anything about it. I've forever regretted that decision.'

Mia watched Dave nod and also lean forward as he scratched his cheek. 'Do you employee people on your farm overseas?'

Straightening now, Amber shook out her hair. 'What does this have to do with what that woman did to my father?'

Dave sighed. 'Look, Amber, I'm not the enemy here. I'm the bloke who is going to try to find out what happened to your father, and why, so can you cut me a bit of slack here and answer the question?'

Mia had to work hard to stop her eyebrows shooting up so high they would have left her face. Dave had just flicked from bad to good cop in a sentence. She leaned forward, wondering where he'd take the questioning next.

'Yes, I employ people on my farm.'

'Thank you. Okay, so moving on. Your mum died recently, had she ever spoken to you about your father being unsteady on his feet?'

'Not that I can remember.'

'And while you've been in Barker, has he had a fall?'

'He had one that I know of recently, but from my understanding there weren't any injuries from it.'

'And how has your father been at walking?'

Amber groaned and her head fell forward. 'Dave, you know all of this. You've been in the house enough times to know he is a frail old man. His wife has just died, and he is sad and lonely and feeble.'

'I'm sorry to bore you with these questions, but I have to gather as much information as I can. It's all routine, so don't be concerned. Now, one more. Have you noticed unexplained injuries anywhere on your father's body before today?'

Frowning, Amber wrapped a strand of hair around her finger and didn't answer for a moment. When she did, her words were slow and thoughtful.

'Not really. There was the occasional bruise and red mark, but I put that down to being old. But Dad had red marks, chaff marks I suppose, between his legs. I noticed them the one time I dried him after a shower and I never said anything to anyone, because,' she shrugged, 'I don't know what's normal for an old man and what isn't. Maybe his jocks had chaffed, but I remember thinking it looked like a nappy rash. Sassi used to get them when she was a bub.'

'When did you notice this?'

'Well, it would have had to have been on a weekend, because Rasha has been doing most of that type of work. I feel uncomfortable, um—' She broke off.

'It must be very hard seeing your dad incapacitated.'

'Confronting.' Amber looked down and picked at a piece of loose skin around her fingernail.

Dave turned to Mia. 'Do you have any questions, Constable?'

Taken by surprise, Mia shook her head, then changed her mind. 'Actually, I do. Where have you been staying since you've been here?'

'At Dad's.' Amber seemed as if she had run out of energy as she answered.

'And what are Rasha's hours of work?' Mia held her pen ready to write the answer down, even though the interview was being recorded.

'She starts once her children have gone to school and then goes home when school is finished. After dinner she comes back to help put Dad to bed.'

'I see, so you have quite a bit of time alone with your father?'

Mia could see Dave's eyes bulge at the audacity of the question. She hadn't exactly worked up to it.

Amber eyed Mia, her face hard. 'Is that an accusation, *Constable*?' Her implication by the way she said constable was clear.

'No, not at all,' Mia said. 'I'm trying to establish time-frames. Again, these are routine questions.' She fell back onto Dave's well-rehearsed line. Out of the corner of her eye, she thought Dave ducked his head to hide a smile.

The steeliness on Amber's face vanished and she took a tissue from her pocket. 'I apologise. My comment was uncalled for. I know you're only trying to help us.'

'Yes, we are and we can understand your shock,' Dave told her. 'And we want to get to the bottom of what has happened as much as you do. Do you need a break, or a drink of anything? We can get you a coffee or something similar?'

Amber shook her head. 'Let's keep going.'

'Do you get along well with your father?'

'Of course, he's my dad. We're not super close. We haven't argued badly since I was a teenager. I guess we grew out of the volatile relationship we had.'

'Can you give any details about your father's injuries today?'

'Well, not how he got them. I was out last night so Rasha put him to bed by herself, and by the time I came back, the lounge room was empty. I didn't look in on him because

Rasha was just leaving and said he was fine. Sometimes he has a tablet to make him sleep a bit better. Older people seem to have trouble sleeping, don't they? Rasha said he'd had his medication and was already asleep. I didn't see him until this morning after Rasha had checked on him. As for his injuries, well, there was bruising on his face and arms, but that's all I can tell you.'

'Right and what time did you discover your father had been hurt?'

'Not long before Abe and Sassi came in. I had work to do for the farm so I slipped out very early and got a coffee and then went back to reconciling bank accounts before Rasha arrived.'

'To clarify,' Dave broke in, 'this is your farm in South Africa, not Abe and your father's farm?'

'That's right.'

'How did you know Rasha had arrived?' Mia asked.

'I heard her moving around the house.'

'And Rasha didn't come to you to ask for help or request a doctor? She didn't knock on your door, looking for help?'

'She did not.' Amber shifted her head defiantly as if making a point. 'But, to be fair, Dad's door was shut and we did have an agreement that if Dad was having a bad day and wanted to sleep for longer, we kept the door closed. She may have thought he was still in bed.'

'Do you think it's possible that your father fell out of bed during the night? Did you hear a bang or noise of any type?'

'No. I didn't hear anything.'

'And where were you last night? You said you went out.'

Amber looked down at her hands. 'Yes, I did.' She didn't continue.

'Amber?'

'Look, I know you need to know where I was, but you'll have to make do when I tell you that where I was has nothing to do with anything.'

Mia's head shot up from the notes she was taking. Her gaze slid across to Dave.

'Amber, come on, you know that we have to ask and you have to give an answer,' Dave said.

'Well, I'm not going to tell you.'

Mia leaned back in her chair, just as Dave had done many times, and searched the woman's face for a tell. For something that would indicate she had a secret, and a big one at that.

Amber's face was deadpan.

Dave regarded Amber coolly now. Gone was the friendly bloke appealing for answers. 'I will be circling back to this question if I have to, Amber, you can be assured of that.'

CHAPTER 30

Sassi walked in the front door of the police station and looked around. An older lady wearing sensible pants and shirt was standing behind the front counter, on the phone. She held up one finger indicating for Sassi to wait.

A door opened at the back of the office and Mia walked out. She stopped when she saw Sassi. 'I thought you were going to be at the hospital with your grandfather. Is everything okay?'

Sassi nodded. 'Pa is going to be fine. It's all superficial. Seems to be our family's new buzz word. "Superficial".' She used her fingers to make quotation marks.

'Did you ask him anything?' Mia said as the woman behind the counter hung up the phone and wrote something on a pad.

'No, I didn't want to upset him, and he didn't tell me anything either. In fact he didn't speak at all. Kept his eyes closed the whole time.'

'Was he conscious?'

'Hamish said he was, but he wasn't talking to him either.'

Dave and Abe emerged from the back office. 'Thanks for helping us out,' Abe said, shaking Dave's hand. 'What do we do now?'

'Thanks for answering my questions. I'd like to brief both you and Sassi at some point, but if we can talk to your father that would be helpful. What do you think? Would he be able to cope?'

'I don't know. Hamish will tell you.'

'I've just come from the hospital,' Sassi said.

'Ah, Sassi,' Dave said, seeing her for the first time. 'And how was your grandfather?'

'He's conscious, and the nurses were looking after him, but he wasn't interacting with anyone. I agree with Abe. Could you talk to Hamish first? We don't want Pa to be any more upset than he's already been.'

'Of course, we'll check first,' Dave said. 'Look, now that you're both here do you want to have a chat about what we know? I have a small amount of info to pass on.'

'Yeah,' Sassi answered without hesitation. 'Yes, please.'

Abe nodded. 'That'd be great because I can't understand what's happening. Neither Amber nor Rasha could have done this. There has to be another explanation.'

Mia went to the door that divided the front of the station from Joan's desk and unlocked it, letting Sassi through.

'Come and sit.' Dave indicated the vinyl chairs that lined the wall. 'Do either of you want coffee?'

'Just tell us what you know,' Abe said.

'Look, someone has hurt your father. It's impossible that he's sustained the sorts of injuries he has from a fall. Hamish and the doctor have confirmed this via text message to me. And because I've been talking to Rasha, Amber and you, Abe, I haven't had a chance to text him back.'

Sassi turned to Abe but the look of shock on his face only mirrored her own.

'No. That can't be right.' Sassi stuttered as the ramifications of the truth began to circulate through her.

'Well, let's start with the arm. It's swollen and red. There's bruising beginning to come out and there's a little tear to the skin here.' Dave handed Abe his phone and showed him a photo. Pinching his fingers together, Dave enlarged the area where the split was. Abe blanched and handed it on to Sassi, who took the phone with shaking hands. 'As people get older their skin gets thinner and it doesn't take much for an injury to look horrid.'

Tears filled Sassi's eyes when she saw the red welt marks and deep bruising on her grandfather's arm in such close detail. 'Oh, Pa. Granny would be horrified.'

'This is what a Chinese burn looks like. Another person has done this to your father. He hasn't fallen out of bed or bumped into something. This injury has been inflicted by another person.'

Dave was repeating himself, but Sassi thought he was doing that to make sure they understood.

She understood perfectly. Someone had hurt her grandfather.

Sassi saw Abe swallow and shake his head.

'Well, who was it?' Sassi asked. 'We all know that neither Mum nor Rasha would do this.'

'Abe, we've established where most people were last night, but I haven't asked about Renee. Was she at home?'

Abe's face and neck went red at the question, and Sassi thought he was going to punch Dave, so she quickly answered for him.

'We were all at the farm last night. Me, Renee, Abe and the twins.' She paused. 'But I guess that doesn't really give you the alibi you're looking for, does it? Family being each other's alibi. Can you check our mobile phones or something?'

Dave smiled. 'I'm dotting i's and crossing t's. That's all. If I need to dig deeper, I will. Has there ever been any indication that either Amber or Rasha would hurt Mr Stapleton?'

'Sassi just told you,' Abe said. 'It can't be either of them. Could someone have tried to burgle the house?'

'I agree with Abe! Rasha's been a godsend,' Sassi told them. 'She's taken Pa out for walks, the house has never been so clean and she was teaching him to play poker last time I talked to her.' Sassi faltered as she spoke. Taking a breath, she said, 'Look there were a couple of times recently I've felt that Rasha had too much ownership over Pa, but it wasn't enough to concern me. My assumption was that she loved her work and she was grateful for the job. She never said as much, but her attitude and actions told us that.'

'Ownership?' Dave asked.

'It's hard to explain. Like she questioned why I was there. When I was in the office recently, Rasha gave me a bit of a fright because I didn't hear her come into the room and I felt she was giving me the once-over as to what I was doing there. I didn't think anything of it at the time, just an uncomfortable feeling, you know?'

'Okay. Is there someone else who might have wanted to hurt Mr Stapleton?' Mia asked.

'No, look, Mum can be a bit standoffish and cold, but she wouldn't hurt her own father.'

'Let's go back to the burglary proposition. Is there anything from the house missing?' Mia asked. 'Money, items that are valuable? Could this be a reason that Mr Stapleton was hurt?'

'Oh,' the word popped out of Sassi before she'd realised it was coming. 'I noticed a few days ago the silver tea set that Granny used to have on the sideboard had gone, but I just assumed that it had been shifted or put in a cupboard. I didn't even mention it to anyone and I haven't looked for it.'

'But that was a few days ago and these injuries were caused last night,' Mia said.

Dave leaned forward, nodding. 'Perhaps Mr Stapleton interrupted them this time. Can you and Abe go through the house, checking to see what else is not there?'

'Yep, we can do that,' Abe said, standing up. He was like a cat on a hot tin roof, needing to move but not sure where to go next.

326

'I'll go and speak to your father,' Dave said, 'unless you've got any objections?'

'One of us should be there to help interpret for you,' Sassi said. 'He finds it hard to talk.'

'Okay, which one of you would be better to do that?'

'I should check the house,' Abe said. 'Sassi only comes and goes, whereas I'm here all the time.'

'That's settled. Mia you're with Abe. Sassi, you can come with me.'

He ushered them outside and Mia took one patrol car and Dave pointed at another. 'Here we are, Sassi. Let's see what we can work out here.'

They drove to the hospital in silence, Sassi's head still spinning from the revelations. As they parked, she turned to Dave. 'Why do people hurt older people? Is there a common reason?'

'Money. Money is the root of all evils,' Dave told her as he got out. 'When you see elder abuse, someone is usually skimming money from bank accounts or selling goods from the houses. If we don't get anywhere here today, I'll probably have to ask for access to your grandfather's bank statements. See what we find there. But look, burglary could also be an option, depending on what Abe and Mia find. I don't want to jump to conclusions just yet. A case like this needs to be handled with kid gloves.'

Sassi nodded her head. 'We'll give you whatever you need, Dave. Abe has power of attorney and access to everything.

'As for Mum, well, she's not in need of any money. Granny told me a couple of months ago that Mum and

Zola had come into some money from his family. Quite a lot, apparently. I guess Rasha hasn't got too much because she's working two jobs. She's still stacking the shelves at the supermarket, you know.'

'Yeah, Kim told me that.' Dave turned his attention to the nurse at the desk. 'Can we see Mr Stapleton, please?'

'Room twelve.' She smiled. 'I think Hamish is still in there.'

Sassi took a deep breath as she followed Dave down the corridor. She wanted Pa to talk, but at the same time, she didn't, because what would he tell them?

'G'day, Hamish,' Dave said from the door. The nurse looked up from his wristwatch, where he was taking Pa's pulse, and nodded. 'Can we come in?'

'Yeah, Mr Stapleton's awake, aren't you, mate? Just a bit sore and sorry for himself.'

Sassi watched as Pa's eyes flicked towards her and then to Dave. He pushed himself back in the bed a little, fear registering on his face.

'Oh, Pa!' Distressed, she ran forward and grabbed the arm that hadn't been hurt. 'It's okay, Pa. Dave and I are here to help. We want to find out who did this to you.'

Pa turned his head towards Hamish and wouldn't look at her.

Sassi tried again. 'Pa, honest, we only want to help.'

Dave stood at the foot of the bed now. 'Mr Stapleton, you've been badly hurt through no fault of your own. Please let me help you. Anything you say to me is confidential.'

'Oooh.' No.

'Does your face hurt, Pa?' Sassi tried changing the subject but he still didn't look at her.

Hamish indicated for them both to stand outside for a minute. 'Let me have a go. He trusts me.'

Sassi wanted to fly at him. 'He trusts me, too,' she told him.

'I'm not sure he trusts anyone right now,' Hamish said bluntly. 'I reckon the injuries show why, don't you?'

Sassi reared back at his words. 'You don't think I had anything to do with this?'

'I know fear when I see it,' Hamish said.

'Oh my god.' Sassi couldn't think of another thing to say. She could only watch as Hamish went and sat back alongside her grandfather and spoke quietly and gently to him. She watched Pa's body relax and a calmness come over his face. Tears ran down her cheeks. Why wasn't he trusting her? She'd never done anything to Pa.

Her mobile phone rang and she looked at the screen. Clearing her throat and wiping her tears away, she walked away from her grandfather's room. 'Abe?'

'Were you given Mum's engagement and eternity rings?' he asked without saying hello.

'No. They were never for me. They were always going to Mum.'

'They've gone along with Dad's good watch. Can you let Dave know?'

Sassi beckoned to Dave. 'Abe's found some jewellery missing from the house.'

'Do you have photos of the items?'

Sassi repeated the question to Abe.

'Probably. I'll have to look. I'll ring you if I find anything else.'

She put the phone back in her pocket and jumped when Hamish came out into the corridor.

'He won't talk,' he said. 'You might as well leave because he's not going to be saying anything and I don't want him any more upset than he already is. His blood pressure started to go up when you both arrived.'

Sassi wrinkled her brow and swallowed hard. 'But why won't he talk? This doesn't make any sense. He could just tell us and he'd be safe.'

'I guess it's his prerogative to do what he wants, Sassi. Maybe that makes him feel safe now.'

Dave nodded at Hamish's words. 'Thanks for trying, mate. I'll be back in touch.'

Sassi had to run to keep up with his long strides. 'Why won't he talk to us?'

'Because someone has threatened him, would be my guess, Sassi. Someone has got something on him and he's too frightened to speak. I would be, too, if I was elderly and reliant on people to help me. Especially if my face ended up looking like that. Wouldn't you?'

Dave's mobile rang. 'Mia?' he answered.

Sassi's head shot around. Why was she calling? She was with Abe. What had they found now?

'Right, we're on our way.' He got into the car and started the engine. 'We're going to your grandfather's house.'

~

'Tell me again,' Dave instructed, as he stood rigid in the kitchen.

Sassi couldn't believe what she'd just heard. She put her hands over her mouth to stop herself from crying.

Abe held up his hands. 'I don't know. Tess, my bank manager, just called. Sassi dropped some paperwork in there this morning. We've put an offer in on a farm and I wanted Tess to start looking at our borrowing capacity as soon as she could.

'Dad always planned to leave the farm to me. I've got copies of his will that say that. His lawyers have the same copies. But the original was always kept at Mum and Dad's. Now Tess has just rung to say the will doesn't reflect what I've told her. Apparently, the farm is being left to Amber.'

'How interesting,' Dave said.

'I picked it up from the bank so I could show you.' Abe leaned forward and went to take the will out of the plastic sleeve.

'Don't touch it,' Dave said and moved forward to push the contents away. He turned to Mia. 'We need to get this to Adelaide and have it fingerprinted. You'd better drive it down. I'll pull in some favours in forensics and get it processed ASAP.'

'What are you going to do about Amber?' Abe asked, getting to his feet. 'She wouldn't have hurt Dad, that bit

I know, but I'm damn sure she's capable of getting a will changed.'

'Yeah, this could just be a coincidence,' Sassi said.

'It could be. But I need to ask you: can you be sure she wouldn't have caused those injuries?'

'He's her father!'

'I saw her in the office,' Sassi said, suddenly remembering. 'Twice. I never took any notice. I came back to the house unexpectedly each time and she'd been in there. The lights were still on. The second time I saw her walk out of the room.' Her sentences were short and fast, just like her breathing was.

'Right-oh, we're going to lock this house up and put crime scene tape across the door,' Dave said. 'Then, Mia, you're off to Adelaide and I'm going to have another chat with Amber. Sassi, Abe, you head home. Just don't go too far in case we need you.'

'Hang on,' Abe said. 'Hang on. It was Amber who attacked Rasha. Why would she accuse Rasha if she did it herself? It can't be Amber, it just can't be.'

'Have you never heard of hiding in plain sight?' Dave asked. 'Some criminals often turn up to help with an investigation or try to blame someone else. It's a clever thing to do because they're not suspected at first.' He paused. 'But they usually get found out.'

CHAPTER 31

'Amber, what do you do in South Africa?' Dave asked, crossing his ankle over his knee.

'We're farmers.'

'Do you like it over there?'

'It comes with its challenges. Life can be dangerous but, yes, I do like it.'

'Your farm, is it profitable?'

Amber bristled. 'I can't see how that is any of your business, but I'll humour you for now. Yes, it is. We make a very comfortable living from it.'

Dave smiled. 'Now, according to Sassi, you were to inherit your mother's wedding and engagement rings. Is this correct?'

Amber's eyebrows shot up in surprise. 'I didn't think anything had been put in writing but, yes, that had been discussed. A long time ago. I'd forgotten about that until now. I wonder where they are.'

'Well, it appears there're a few valuable items missing from your parents' house. These pieces of jewellery are part of what's missing.'

'Rasha must've stolen them,' Amber said in a flat voice. 'I've met people like her before. They lure you in and make you trust them, then they rip everything out from under you.'

Dave nodded. 'Had you noticed anything missing from the house?'

'That's hard to tell. I'd say no, but it's been a while since I've visited so things get moved or changed around.'

'Tell me about your farm.'

'What's to tell? We grow macadamias and green maize.' Amber cocked her head to one side, a questioning look on her face.

'Do you have employees?'

'Yes, you've asked that question before. You know I'm still curious as to why you need to request this information when we should be talking about Dad. And,' she pushed up her sleeve to check her watch, 'I need to leave for Adelaide soon.'

'Yeah, I'm aware of your flight details. Just a few more things to clear up.' Dave stopped and tapped on the table as if thinking of a question. In reality, he knew exactly what to ask, but like all good performers, he needed to set the scene. 'Amber, I'm wondering if you've lost anything to "these types of people" as you call them. People who have lured you in and made you trust them?'

'What?' Amber stared at him, confusion crossing her face.

'Have you lost anything to people who have made you trust them, then shown themselves to be different from who you believed them to be?'

Amber pressed her lips together but didn't answer.

Dave stood and paced the room. 'See, I'm having trouble trying to work out why you'd want to hurt your father, Amber, and then try to blame it on someone else. A woman who is helping your dad and making him happy.'

'You don't know what you're talking about.'

'Don't I?' Dave raised his eyebrows.

'Not a clue.'

'So nothing's happened in your life, here or in South Africa, that has made you hold a grudge against another person?'

'Absolutely not.'

Dave pulled a newspaper clipping from his pocket and looked at it for a long time before handing it to her.

'See, Amber, I did a bit of digging before I came back in to talk to you. Google is a wonderful invention for getting information quickly. Especially if what I was looking for had made the news. And if I'm right, this is your farm?'

Amber looked at the clipping and pushed it away. 'No, no, it isn't.'

'Your name is right there. So is Zola's. Zola was your husband?'

Amber stared down at the paper.

'Now this news article is dated twelve months ago. You haven't had a farm in that long. Zola died that long ago, too.' Dave tried to make his words gentle as he sat back down and leaned forward. He stared at Amber earnestly.

Her mouth had puckered and now there were tears on her cheeks.

'Amber, what you've been through is tragic. Awful. And I can see why you would want to hurt whoever murdered your husband. But Rasha isn't that person.'

Amber looked up now, a strange look in her eyes. 'They executed Zola in cold blood and took our land.'

'Who did, Amber?'

'People we trusted. They worked for us, like Rasha. Working on the farms, in our house, caring for our animals. They saw that we had money and they wanted what we had.

'I'll admit, I wanted to punish Rasha. Unreasonably, perhaps.' Her voice held no emotion. 'It was a woman like her who betrayed Zola and me. She worked for us and then her family came in and burned our farm to the ground, forced us off our land. Land that we had bought legitimately.' She spoke simply. 'No, it wasn't Rasha's family, but she reminded me of that woman and I hate her. I hate all of them more than you could know. But I hate my father the same amount.'

Amber continued to speak as if she was unloading a burden which had been tearing at her all of her life. She talked and talked, and when she'd finished, Dave walked out of the interview room, reeling.

In his office, Dave stood staring blankly at the wall, his mind racing, working out what he should do now. How much of this did he have to tell Mr Stapleton's family? How much could he get away with leaving out? None of what he'd just heard would benefit anyone.

When he'd first started in policing, Spencer Brown, his mentor and partner from his first posting at Barrabine, had told him about a case which hadn't been in the public interest to pursue.

The man who was guilty of the crime was dying. There were no witnesses to confirm the knowledge that the police had come into. It was the victim's word against a dying man and, although Spencer had wanted to charge him, he'd been told that the cost to the public purse was too high.

'Dave?'

'Mm?' he turned at the sound of Joan's voice.

'Kim just phoned to ask what the update on Rasha was.'

'I'm about to cut her loose. Tell Kim to bring the kids to the station, and then she can take them all home and make sure they're okay. Actually, I wouldn't mind Rasha going to the hospital and Hamish checking out her arm. When I looked in on her a while ago it was beginning to swell. I should have had her checked out first.'

'Okay.' Joan paused. 'You all right?'

Dave looked at her and blew out a breath. 'I actually don't know,' he said. He turned and went into the room where Rasha was. She didn't look as if she had moved since he had last checked on her a few hours ago.

He smiled. 'Ah, Rasha, what a horrible thing to happen to you as you're starting your new life here in Barker. I'm sorry you've been through this.

'You can go home to your family now. Kim is bringing your children and she's going to take you to the hospital to get your arm checked.'

'I can go?' Rasha's eyes were hopeful and she took her hands from the desk.

'Yes, and you won't need to come back in here again. I know you didn't hurt Mr Stapleton. But I have one more question. Why didn't you tell us Amber had hit her father? What made you lie for her?'

Rasha was quiet and she seemed to be weighing something up. 'Amber is not going to come after me?'

'Not a chance,' Dave said.

'My visa, and my children's visas. She threatened to have them taken away from me so I wouldn't be able to work. She told me that she would report me and have me deported.' Rasha took a deep breath.

'I left my country, my family, everyone I ever knew for a country where my children could grow up with opportunity. I was not going to risk having that taken away from them. Not by a woman who was so unhappy and angry within herself.'

Dave nodded. He'd suspected as much.

There was nothing left to say, so he held the door open for her, while Joan handed back her handbag. Together they watched from the doorway as Kim pulled up, and two children tumbled out of the back seat of her car, their arms outstretched.

Rasha dropped to the ground and gathered her kids into her arms, hugging them as if she hadn't seen them for a year.

'That Amber is a piece of work,' Joan muttered. 'She should be jailed for what she's done to that woman.'

Dave raised an eyebrow.

'Well, it's obvious, Dave. You've let Rasha out and Amber is still in the interview room. Clearly, you're happy that Rasha is innocent.' Joan turned on her heel and went back to the counter.

Acknowledging the sense in Joan's words, Dave rocked on his heels and returned the little wave Kim gave him as she herded the family back into her car to drive them to the hospital, then home.

His mobile phone buzzed and he took it from his shirt pocket and looked at the screen.

His mother.

Dave closed his eyes while the phone vibrated in his hand, then put it back into his pocket. He didn't have the energy to deal with his mum right now.

In his office, he rewound the recording of the interview with Amber and put his headphones on. He wanted to hear what she had told him again, before he made a decision.

⌒

'Shearing at our place was always good fun. As kids, we were allowed to work in the yards and sweep the board in the shed if we didn't get in the way.' Amber's voice was hard and brittle. Dave could see her face as she'd told him this, only an hour beforehand—tight, angry, hurt.

'This particular year, when I was fifteen, Dad told me I shouldn't go into the shed anymore. Apparently, I wore shorts that were too short and tops that were too revealing.' Amber rolled her eyes. 'He never went as far as to say that I'd be tempting the shearers, but he may as well have.'

'But you went into the shed anyway?' Dave asked. He had a feeling he knew where this story was going.

'Not at first, but on the last day, the shearers' cook asked me to take smoko into the shed for everyone. Of course I did as I was asked, because that's how we were raised.' Amber's fingers were linked together so tightly her skin was pulled white. 'And until then I had done exactly as Dad had asked. We were obedient kids.

'That afternoon, I was the only one in the yards. Abe and Dad had taken a mob of sheep back to the paddock, and I was backlining the last ones. You know, to stop any lice that might have been there.' She took a shuddering breath, then seemed to call on all the anger she'd held inside herself for twenty-nine years. Amber straightened her back and spoke clearly, without emotion. 'There was a tiny shed that we kept all the sheep husbandry products in, attached to the back of the shearing shed. I had to go and fill up my backpack, and while I was there, a shearer came in. Told me he'd been watching me for the whole two weeks. That I was just his type.' She stopped.

Dave said nothing and the silence spun out over the tape, hissing until Amber spoke again.

'He raped me in the shed. Pushed me to the ground and fell on top of me, grunting and moving. I . . . I . . . Ah. I tried to scream but he had his towel over my mouth. You know how shearers always get around with a towel over their shoulder? I thought I was going to suffocate.'

'Do you know his name?' Dave asked.

There was another silence. He imagined her shaking her head as she had done in the interview room. Her hair swinging around her face, hiding her set features.

'I need to hear it for the tape, Amber,' Dave had said quietly.

'No. He was a transient bloke. We'd never seen him in the shearing team before and he never came back. But Dad,' now her voice was trembling, 'Dad came in just as he was pulling his pants up. It was so clear what had just happened. I was crying and bleeding, and all the shearer did was give Dad a wink and go back out to the shed.'

Dave was silent, unable to find any words. If an animal like this man had hurt Bec or Alice, Dave would have found the man and made them front up to the full force of the law.

After he'd handed out his own punishment.

'What did your father do?'

A jarring laugh. 'Nothing. He stared at me, then said, "What did you do?" like it was my fault.' A hiccup now, as if getting the words out had released all her pent-up feelings.

'Did your father know who he was?'

'If he did, he never told me. I've been searching for the shearing payment records while I've been home. Thought maybe they'd be in the office and they'd list the names of the people who'd been paid. But the invoices are from a contractor and they only list how many sheep were shorn, not the name of the shearer.' She gave a quivering sigh, and Dave imagined her tracing the scratches on the table in front of her. 'I went to Adelaide to research where the shearing contractor was now, but he's been dead for years and no one has any of his records anymore. I've got no way of finding out who that bastard was.'

Twenty-nine years ago an unnamed man raped an underage child and got her pregnant. The shearing contractor was dead, Mr Stapleton was almost that way. Spencer Brown came to mind and he dropped his head.

Not in the public interest to continue.

'What happened once the shearers left?'

'Nothing. Dad assumed I'd asked for it. He blamed me, and when I tried to tell Mum, she shook her head as if I was telling her a fairy story.' Her voice hardened again. 'It wasn't a fairy story when I found out I was pregnant. But it was still my fault.'

Dave couldn't see how anything good was going to come out of what he'd just heard. Sassi would be devastated and there was no one he could charge. He could only hope that confirmation of what Sassi already suspected would help, but he knew it wouldn't.

Amber could be charged with assault, but what was the point in that? Rasha would be happy if Amber just went back to South Africa. She didn't want anything to upset the life she was creating for her children.

He also assumed that Amber wouldn't come back to Barker any time soon. There was nothing here for her now.

⌒

Dave left the station, collected three beers from Hopper and then walked to the edge of the creek on the other side of town.

Twisting off the cap from the first beer, he threw it hard and fast, down in among the stones. He was littering, but right now, he didn't care.

What to do?

Amber hated her father with good reason. She hated people who she'd trusted and who had hurt her, with good reason. He didn't think she hated her own daughter, but found it difficult to be around her. Perhaps with good reason.

His phone rang. Mia.

'Amber's fingerprints are on the will,' she said. 'You can charge her with trying to defraud her father and with his assault.'

'Circumstantial,' he told Mia. 'She could have been finding the will for Mr Stapleton.'

'What about all the other items that she took?'

'I haven't found them in her possession and neither have I found money in her bank accounts.' This wasn't strictly true, he hadn't looked. But it didn't matter to Dave. All he could see was a hurt and frightened little girl, who had been let down so badly by her family. He felt he needed to protect her now.

'We haven't got enough. I think I'll cut her loose tonight and do a bit more investigating.'

'Really?' Mia's voice rose.

'Yeah.'

'She's a flight risk surely?'

'I don't think so,' Dave said, knowing the opposite was true. If Amber got out of the country on the flight she had already booked, he would let her go.

Dave hung up the phone and stared at the setting sun.

Who was he to play God? Was this the right decision? He didn't have the answers.

The phone rang again and this time he didn't recognise the number.

'Detective Burrows,' he answered as a flock of white cockatoos flew overhead.

Silence.

'Hello? Anyone there?' He took the phone away from his ear to check the call was still connected. 'Hello?'

'Um, Dad?' The voice was tentative and Dave felt his body grow still and goosebumps cover his arms.

'Hello?' His voice was croaky now.

'Dad?' Her voice was stronger this time. 'It's me, Bec.'

EPILOGUE

Sassi grabbed the gate and swung it closed and then ran to grab the second one, swinging it hard, too, before the first one opened again.

The front gates of Dinkie Downs were difficult to shut, because they both swung back on themselves every time she had to close them.

'I'll help!' Jimmy ran from the ute and grabbed one side, with his grubby little hand while Sassi held the other.

'Thanks, Jimmy. We'll have to fix these so they don't do it anymore.'

'The ones in Shepherd's Hut paddock do the same thing. Dad swears at them when he thinks we're not listening. Mum would tell him off if she heard.'

'I bet she would. Right-oh, let's go and meet Mum and Dad, shall we?'

'And Ruby,' Jimmy said with awe in his tone.

'Yes and Ruby. She's very beautiful, isn't she?'

'I dunno. She's a baby and doesn't say much.'

Sassi giggled. 'I don't suppose she does.'

Abe and Sassi had split caring for the twins between them after Ruby had been born, two days ago. Hamish had insisted that Renee have a few more days in hospital than normal because, as he said, 'Once you get home you'll be run off your feet with those two in the house.'

The twins seemed to run on energiser batteries. Never going flat. Still, on the thirty-minute drive back to Barker, Jimmy fell asleep.

So Sassi made a phone call. 'Hey, how's it going?'

'Nearly finished, what about you?'

'Just left so I won't be long.'

'I've got a table booked at the pub.'

'See you soon.'

Sassi smiled as she pushed the disconnect button and focused on the warm feeling that was spreading through her chest. She couldn't wait.

As the white lines flew by the driver's side window, she leaned her elbow on the door and thought about the last six months. Never had she believed such contentment existed.

Abe and she had formed a strong working partnership. They had disagreements, but nothing they hadn't been able to work through.

The new farm had flourished under her care; an updated fertiliser regimen after some soil tests and a good rain had brought the land to life. Sassi was now the shepherd for one thousand ewes and two thousand hectares of crop.

She worked hard and was exhausted every night, but she loved it.

Mia had become one of her closest friends, and they spent many Friday nights on the verandah of each other's houses, winding down from the week.

Last week, Sassi had given Mia a sketch of her driving a police car, and Mia had let out a peal of laughter and poked fun at her own serious expression.

They'd also spent many hours talking about Amber and the situation around Sassi's birth.

Amber had just disappeared. The night that Dave let her leave the station without charge, she went back to the house where her parents had lived, cut through the crime scene tape and taken a few more items of value.

But Sassi had overlooked all of that, because what she had also taken was a photo of Sassi herself. The one that Granny had displayed with such pride on the bookshelf.

When she'd realised it had gone, Sassi had known that even though her mother couldn't stay, she still needed part of her daughter with her. That made Sassi happy and sad at the same time.

No one knew where Amber was because she hadn't returned to South Africa.

As for Ewin, Mia had suggested that Sassi didn't return his text messages and, eventually, he stopped trying to contact her. Some nights, Sassi felt a twinge of regret that she didn't know what he wanted, but for the most part, it didn't bother her. Keeping her heart and emotions in check were too important.

Thinking back to the awful days when Pa was still in hospital, Sassi wasn't sure how she would've kept going without Mia's and Hamish's friendship. Pa had been frightened of not only her, but of Abe and Renee as well. He hadn't been sure who was hurting him, as it had come to light that the sleeping tablets he had been taking in the evenings had also been put in his cups of tea every morning.

Sassi still couldn't reconcile her mother could do that, but the evidence had been clear. Pa had been confused and terrified, until Dave had stepped him through the happenings and Amber's disappearance.

Now, Sassi flicked on the blinker and pulled into a park in front of the pub. She saw Mia's car there and smiled again. She couldn't wait to see the look on everyone's faces.

Opening the ute door, she reached over and gave Jimmy a little shake. 'Wake up, sleepyhead! We've got a surprise for you.'

He groaned and yawned, peering out the window. 'I thought we were going to see Ruby.'

'She's coming to us,' Sassi told him.

'Sassi!'

She turned at the sound of her friend's voice and waved at both Kim and Dave as they walked hand in hand towards the pub.

'What's going on?' Kim asked. 'We got the message to meet you here.'

'Yeah, what's the surprise?' Jimmy asked, appearing at her side.

Laughing happily, Sassi shook her head. 'Uh-uh. You're going to have to wait. Come on, let's get a drink. Do you want a fire engine, Jimmy?'

'Cor, can I? Mum says—'

'If you use your manners,' Sassi said.

'Please,' Jimmy answered straightaway.

'Come on then.'

Inside, Sassi waved at Mia, who was sitting at a large table, set for twelve people. *Mia worked quickly*, she thought.

'Hi, Hopper,' she said, holding out her phone. 'We're very much in need of two fire engines—' She broke off as the door opened and Renee backed in, pulling a pram, Harry behind her.

'Why do we want two fire engines?' Jimmy asked.

'Look, your brother and sister are here,' Sassi told him and went to hold the door for Renee. She kissed her aunt's cheek and reached down to touch Ruby's cherub-like face.

'Abe's just getting Pa into the wheelchair,' Renee said.

'Excellent.' Sassi stayed holding the door, giving Pa and Abe a kiss as they came in.

'We're over there,' she told them, pointing to the table. 'Let's get everyone sitting down as quickly as we can. I'll go and get the others.' She winked at Abe, then glanced over at Mia.

They caught each other's eye and nodded. Mia got up and went to Sassi.

'Ready?'

'Sure am.'

Mia disappeared outside for a few moments, then appeared again, leading a blindfolded Rasha and her two children, while Sassi opened the door.

'Okay, now there's a step here,' Mia said, holding the children's hands tightly and passing Rasha's over to Sassi.

'Another few steps,' Sassi told Rasha. 'Okay, stand here.'

'What are you doing?' Rasha asked.

'You'll see. Are you ready?' She pulled off the blindfold and Mia held up a sign as everyone started to clap.

You can't choose your family but the friends you choose can be your family.

'You've been saying that you didn't have a family here, Rasha,' Sassi said over the top of the cheering. 'We want you to know you do and it's all of us.' She turned and spoke to everyone at the table. 'Everyone here tonight has been so important and helped us through this horrible time. We wanted to thank you all.' Her eye caught Hamish's as he slipped in the door and sat down quietly. She gave him a wink. 'Even you, Hamish.'

'Well, of course.' He stood, and gave a theatrical bow.

'So tonight, we just wanted to publicly thank you all, especially you, Rasha. And Pa has got something he wants to say.'

Abe, who was sitting next to Pa, helped him stand and took a piece of paper from his pocket. Pa reached out for Rasha's hand and smiled, giving it a few pumps up and down.

Clearing his throat, Abe started to speak. 'Rasha, Dad has told me what he wants to say and I'll read it to you, but first I want to let you know all of this has been done in consultation with the family and we're really happy with his decision.'

Rasha sank into a chair and pulled her children to her.

'Rasha, I want to offer you the use of my house rent free until you either decide to leave Barker or buy your own home. It's time for me to get more care and I know you will look after our house very well.'

Pa pumped Rasha's hand again and then let it go as she snatched it away to cover her mouth and let out a sob. 'You can't be serious?'

'We're very serious,' Sassi said, slipping her arm around Rasha's shoulders. 'We want you to have a home for you and your kids.'

'I don't even . . .'

'You don't have to say anything,' Abe said and clapped his hands. 'Right first round of drinks is on me. Who wants what?'

Kim leaned forward and rubbed Rasha's shoulder, speaking to her quietly as Sassi sat down in between Hamish and Mia.

'That's pretty bloody special,' Hamish said, running his hands through his hair.

'Thanks for helping me organise this, Mia.' Sassi gave her friend a hug. 'Renee going into labour early put us all in a bit of a tricky situation.'

'Easy as. It was good fun.' Mia raised her glass and all three friends clinked together.

Kim changed seats and came to sit next to them. 'That was a beautiful thing to do.'

Sassi looked to where Rasha and her two children were gathered around Pa. Dave was talking to Abe, and Renee had hoisted Ruby onto her lap, while Jimmy and Harry touched her head gently.

'It was Pa's idea, and I think it's a great one.'

'We all do, too,' Kim said.

'Rasha is part of our community now. Meeting you all—' Sassi felt her throat close over and she swallowed hard. 'Well, I didn't think coming back to Barker would have as many benefits as it has.'

'Sassi!' Dave came over now, holding a schooner of beer. 'Tell me, you were deciding what you were going to call your new farm last time I saw you. What did you settle on?'

'Ah well,' Sassi sat forward, her eyes shining, 'there's a story behind the name. When I told Pa that I was moving there, he said—well, in his own language—"That's just dinkie." Remember how in the old days dinkie used to mean great or grand?'

'I thought it meant to give someone a ride on a bike,' Mia said.

'Yep, that too. Anyway I thought dinkie was pretty cool, so I named it Dinkie Downs.'

Dave let out a laugh and held his glass high. 'Well, that's just dinkie,' he said.

ACKNOWLEDGEMENTS

Firstly, a massive thanks to Anna Hill. You're incredible despite what you make me do! #wwammd

To all you readers, thank you. Again, if you didn't read, then I wouldn't write.

To everyone at Allen & Unwin, with special mentions to Robert, Annette, Christa, Matt, Andrew, Sarah.

Gaby—agent, friend and confidante. Thank you for carefully holding and crafting my career over the last fourteen years. Here's to a few more yet!

Booksellers, librarians, you all are an author's biggest asset. Thank you.

Rochelle and Hayden.

DB. Simply the best!

Oh, actually, Cal and Aaron, you're both simply the best, too!

To our wonderful friendship group; it's so wonderful to be among you.

Jack the Kelpie. With each passing book you're getting older and I'm not sure any wiser. It's a very good thing I love you, you strange, but gorgeous animal.

'There is no friend as loyal as a book,' Ernest Hemingway. Well, Mr Hemingway, I have to beg to differ. Detective Dave Burrows is just as loyal inside the pages of these books, so any reader gets double loyalty right there. To wherever that idea of creating Dave came from, I'm grateful. He really has changed my life. #everyoneneedsadave

With love,

Fleur x